D0482052

ALWAYS OCTOBER

BRUCE COVILLE

ALWAYS OCTOBER

HARPER
An Imprint of HarperCollinsPublishers

Always October

Text copyright © 2012 by Bruce Coville

Title page art © 2012 by Andrea Femerstrand

All rights reserved. Printed in the United States of America.

No part of this book may be used or reproduced in any manner whatsoever without written permission except in the case of brief quotations embodied in critical articles and reviews. For information address HarperCollins Children's Books, a division of HarperCollins Publishers, 10 East 53rd Street, New York, NY 10022.

www.harpercollinschildrens.com

Library of Congress Cataloging-in-Publication Data

Coville, Bruce.

    Always October / Bruce Coville. — 1st ed.

        p.   cm.

    Summary: Best friends Jake and "Weird Lily" enter the monster-filled land of Always October, made famous in Jake's grandfather's books, to save a foundling, who becomes a monster during the full moon.

    ISBN 978-0-06-089095-7 (trade bdg.)

    [1. Adventure and adventurers—Fiction. 2. Supernatural—Fiction. 3. Monsters—Fiction. 4. Best friends—Fiction. 5. Friendship—Fiction. 6. Foundlings—Fiction.] I. Title.

PZ7.C8344Alw 2012   2011044622

[Fic]—dc23   CIP

                                                  AC

Typography by Carla Weise

12 13 14 15 16 CG/RRDH 10 9 8 7 6 5 4 3 2 1

First Edition

FOR MY PALS AT TOG,

with thanks for the support,
the suggestions, and the laughter!

SPECIAL THANKS

*to two wonderful weavers: Kristin Rowley,
in whose house I first saw and fell in love
with a Loom Room; and Sarah Saulson,
my weaver neighbor, who graciously let me
visit her studio exactly the moment I most
needed to see a weaver at work.*

CONTENTS

ALWAYS OCTOBER

1

(Lily)

◇ ◇ ◇

HOW IT ALL STARTED

We've only got two weeks before Jake has to turn into a monster for the first time. Gramps, Mrs. McSweeney, and I are pretty sure we've got everything set to deal with it. Even so, I've decided Jake and I should write down our adventures now, *before* the big night. After all, if things don't go the way we hope, his mother will need to know what happened.

The police, too, probably.

I'm going to start because I know Jake will never begin on his own. Once I get the story rolling, I think I can push him to fill in his parts.

So, first things first. I'm Lily Carker, mostly known

as "Weird Lily." I got my nickname when I made the mistake of singing my new song, "How the Wolf Ate Gramma," for show and tell. It was something I'd just written for my collection *Ballads of Death and Destruction*, and I was very proud of it. I suppose the fact that I was in second grade at the time didn't help.

I haven't made that mistake again.

Even so, the name stuck.

I live with my grandfather, Gnarly, who runs the cemetery.

"Jake" is Jacob Doolittle. Jake lives with his mom on the other side of the cemetery from me and Gramps. Their house is as big and fancy as ours is small and simple. It even has a tower. Awesome!

On the other hand, both houses are pretty run-down.

Jake is the cutest boy in class. Jake himself is kind of clueless about this, but he's a boy, so that's to be expected. (It's probably going to make him mad that I wrote that, but it's the truth, so there.)

I made a big mistake because of his cuteness when I moved to Needham's Elbow, back in second grade: I told him I was going to marry him someday.

Actually I told the whole class, since I said it during show and tell.

You'd think I'd learn.

Jacob wouldn't talk to me for a long time after that. I can't say that I blame him.

Here's how we finally got to be friends: Toward the end of fourth grade I was picking flowers in the old section of the cemetery when I heard someone crying. It's not unusual for people to cry in the cemetery, of course, but usually it's over someone who has just died. Since this crying came from the far side of a tombstone dated 1863, I wondered if it might be a ghost. So I peeked around the tombstone.

It wasn't a ghost—it was Jacob. (He wasn't "Jake" to me yet.)

It was easy to guess why he was crying. Everyone in our class knew that something had happened a few weeks earlier so that Jacob's dad wasn't around anymore. What that something was no one seemed to know, though there were a lot of guesses, some of them pretty nasty.

The thing was, I understood better than most how Jacob felt, since something similar had happened to me just before I finished first grade. At least I knew my parents were still alive, even if they didn't want me. In Jacob's case no one seemed to know whether his dad was dead or had simply taken off.

Until his dad disappeared, Jacob had been pretty normal, and pretty popular. After it happened, he started acting strange. (And trust me, I know about strange!) It took me a while to notice, because it was little things . . . touching his desk three times before he sat down, or making sure his books were properly organized before we went to the cafeteria. If Mrs. Gorton made him get in line before he was ready, I could tell he felt nervous and unhappy. Sometimes I would catch him tapping his fingers against his thumb . . . little finger, ring finger, middle finger, pointer finger, over and over. After a while I worked out that the faster his fingers were moving, the more upset he was.

Anyway, that day in the cemetery I figured I knew why Jacob was upset. I also figured he didn't want to talk about it. But I also knew a third thing . . . sometimes it feels good just to have someone with you when you feel that way.

So I sat down beside him.

Jake lifted his head, glanced at me, then put his head back down. He continued crying, only a bit softer. Finally he stopped, sat up straight, wiped his face, and whispered, "Thanks."

That was all he said before he got up and walked away.

Even so, things were different after that, and we both knew it.

It started slowly. Jake and I walk to school and

the fastest route for both of us is the dirt road through the center of the cemetery. Afternoons I started waiting for him at the cemetery gate. He didn't seem to mind, and pretty soon we started walking home together directly from school. We got teased, of course . . . the usual "Oooh, Jacob loves Lily!" kind of crap, but it wasn't too bad.

After we had been doing this for about a week, Jacob said out of the blue, "Why does your grandfather hate me?"

"He doesn't hate you!"

"Then how come he yells at me whenever he sees me in the cemetery?"

I frowned. "Okay, I guess he does *act* like he hates you. I don't know why." To change the subject, I turned to something I had been wanting to get off my chest. "Um . . . about that 'marry you' thing in second grade. That must have been pretty embarrassing. I'm sorry."

Jake smiled. "Yeh, I got teased about it a lot. Now I get teased about other stuff, by everyone *but* you. So I guess we're even."

Relief!

After that things were easier between us, especially when we discovered that we both like monster movies and horror stories. We started to swap books.

One day he made my head explode by handing me a stack of novels by Arthur Doolittle.

"He's my favorite writer!" I cried. "I've always thought it was cool that you had the same last name."

"Of course I have the same last name. He was my grandfather!"

I went a little spazzo then, but Jake shrugged like it was no big deal.

"What happened to him, anyway?" I asked. "I've never been able to find out why he wrote so many great books and then just stopped."

Jake frowned. "Neither has anyone else. Arthur disappeared—"

"You call him Arthur?"

Jake's face hardened. "He just took off on the family about twenty-five years before I was born. I never met him, and I sure don't think of him as 'Grampa'— not after he abandoned my dad that way."

"What happened?" I asked.

He shrugged again. "Family legend says he had been acting crazy for a few years. Then one day he was just . . . gone. Supposedly he left a note, but I've never seen it."

After a while we started a book club and made a hideout in one of the mausoleums, which are these cool stone buildings in the rich people's part of the cemetery. They store the bodies above ground (in coffins, of course) instead of burying them.

We cleaned up inside, then made a library, both of us donating books and comics. The real gems came from Jacob, because his grandfather not only wrote horror stories and novels, he also collected them. Jacob didn't bring any hardcovers, but he contributed several paperbacks, including my all-time favorite Arthur Doolittle book, *A World Made of Midnight.* This was the story where he first described the monster world that he called Always October. It was also the book that made him famous. Most of the books he wrote afterward featured Always October in some way, but *Midnight* was always my favorite. I had read it about a dozen times.

Because the air in mausoleums tends to be damp, we kept the books sealed in plastic bags to protect them. Also, Jacob created a file card system to make sure that we knew exactly what we had.

When I asked him why he was so organized, he blushed and said, "Makes me feel safer."

I thought about it, and figured I understood.

After that day we talked about more personal stuff. We're almost through sixth grade now, and pretty much best friends.

The day Little Dumpling arrived, Jake and I were in the mausoleum-clubhouse talking about the biggest problems in our lives. At that moment it was Jacob's third-quarter report card.

"You got an *F* in math?" I asked, staring at the horrible grade in amazement. "How did you manage that? You're brilliant at math!"

He shrugged. "Brilliant at math, not so brilliant at homework."

I knew that the real problem was he spent so much time trying to get his papers perfect that he rarely managed to finish them.

I looked at him sternly. "This is serious, Jacob. I don't want to have to do seventh grade without you!"

"Ouch!"

"Sorry, but that's where things are heading. I would take it as a personal favor if you would at least *try* to pass."

"I *am* trying! I just . . ."

His words trailed off, and his eyes grew wide.

I didn't have to ask why. I had heard it too.

2

(Jacob)

THE THUMP ON THE PORCH

Lily is such a brat! She knew if she stopped there, I wouldn't be able to resist picking up the story. But she's right. We really should get this written down before my first transformation.

So—what we heard just then was something scratching at the back wall of the mausoleum. Lily's eyes bugged when she caught the sound. I suppose mine did too, because it was super weird. To begin with, that wall is thick. Even if someone *was* scratching on it from the outside, we shouldn't have been able to hear it inside. Secondly, though we weren't hurting anything, we knew we weren't supposed to be in there. So the idea of getting caught was scary.

My fingers were counting off against my thumb, but I decided I should do the guy thing of being brave. So I shrugged and said, "Probably just a branch moving in the wind."

"There *aren't* any branches back there," Lily pointed out. "No trees or bushes at all. It's just lawn."

Still trying to be brave, I said, "Should I go see what's doing it?"

She thought for a minute. I knew she was thinking because she was chewing the end of her right braid. Lily has long black hair that she keeps in two braids. The right one is her thinking braid. She saves the left one for when she's angry. When she starts chewing *that* one, I get nervous. Finally she said, "We'd better hide. It could be my grandfather. It would *not* be good for him to find us here."

I nodded, and we scooted into the retreats we had worked out when we'd first made the place our clubhouse: a pair of spots on opposite sides of the building, each behind a low platform that held a coffin. When we had chosen the hidey-holes, they had been dusty and filled with cobwebs, and I had kind of freaked about how filthy they were. But after we cleaned them out, they weren't too bad.

Lily told me once that when she was in her hiding spot she would lie on her back, fold her arms over her chest, and pretend she was a corpse. I suppose when your best friend is the gravedigger's granddaughter and her nickname is "Weird Lily," you have to expect such things.

As for me, I preferred to crouch in a position that would let me leap up and run. The problem with this was that my knees would begin to hurt after a few minutes. Fortunately, the scratching stopped before my legs got too sore.

Lifting my head so I could see over the coffin, I called softly, "I think it's okay."

Lily popped up on her side of the room and glanced toward the back wall. Her eyes grew wide. Without saying a thing, she pointed.

I saw it at once: a circle on the wall, about a foot wide, that seemed to be glowing. It was dim, and you had to look twice to be sure it was really there. Even so, it was pretty freaky.

"Maybe just a shiny spot on the stone that we never noticed before?" I ventured, trying to keep the quaver out of my voice.

"I don't think so," said Lily. She stepped from behind the coffin, went to the wall, and pressed her hand against it. Without turning, she motioned for me to join her. "Does this feel warm?" she whispered.

I touched the spot. It didn't feel that warm to me, but to be sure I walked to the east wall and pressed my hand against that one. Definitely cooler! I returned to the back wall and tried again. Lily shook her head. "It's gone now."

"Are you playing with my mind?" I demanded.

I still hadn't forgotten the time she had convinced me that some nights she slept in the mausoleum.

"No mind games!" she said, pulling the ends of her braids so that they crossed over her heart—her way of saying she is being totally honest. "I'm just trying to figure out what's going on. Let's go look from the other side."

Lily went first, in case it *had* been her grandfather. After she had checked, she gave the all-clear signal and I followed her to the back of the mausoleum. The outside wall was blank and unmarked.

I knelt to study the grass. "No sign of it being stepped on," I said.

Lily shook her head. "Okay, that was really strange."

"Which probably means you liked it!"

She grinned. "Of course!" Then her face grew solemn again. "Even so, I want to know what was doing it."

My reply was interrupted by a rumble of thunder. I glanced up. The sky had gotten dark. "I'd better get going. The storm is going to hit soon, and Mom will be mad if I come in wet."

"The real storm is going to be over that report card," said Lily.

I shuddered. The thought of showing my mom that *F* was far more frightening than hanging out in a mausoleum with Weird Lily Carker and hearing mysterious scratchings on the back wall.

As it turned out, Mom didn't get angry. That would have been unpleasant, but better than what actually happened, which was that she started to cry. Not wailing sobs or anything. She just sat and stared at the report card until tears rolled down her cheeks.

I really, *really* wished she would just yell at me and get it over with.

Finally she put the card on the table—we were in the kitchen—and left the room. I sat where I was, feeling like a steaming pile of dog poo. Or, more precisely, what a steaming pile of dog poo would feel like if it also felt miserable and frightened.

After a while I sighed and started up the back stairs. Front or back, going upstairs takes some time, since I have to touch three important spots along the wall to do it. I can't explain why this is. It's just that ever since Dad went off on a caving expedition and never came back, I have to do certain things. If I skip them, my gut gets tight and I feel sick and scared. The only way to make the feeling go away is to go back and start over again.

The upstairs hall is lined with portraits of my ancestors, including a painting of Tia LaMontagne, my sort-of grandmother. Tia had been married to Arthur Doolittle for a few years, then mysteriously disappeared. That's why I call her my sort-of grandmother: though she was married to my grandfather, she's not my father's mother.

Tia was a painter, and the second floor of the tower used to be her studio. It's a guest room now, though we haven't had any guests since Dad disappeared. A door in that room leads to the third level of the tower, which is where my grandfather had his writing office. I'd never been up there. It's locked, and according to my father, his mother threw away the key after Arthur abandoned them.

Tia was far and away the most beautiful of my relatives, but in such an odd way that the picture gave me the creeps. Even so, sometimes I would stop and stare at it. Unlike the other portraits, this was set outdoors. Dressed in a black gown, Tia sits in front of a large tree, her legs folded to the side. The ground is covered with brilliantly colored leaves, hidden in places by strands of mist. Tia's hair, redder than the most scarlet of the leaves, tumbles over her shoulders like a river of flame, reaching nearly to her waist. Her right hand, lifted to shoulder level, points toward the enormous full moon that floats over her right shoulder. Her left hand rests in her lap, thumb and little finger folded under.

Three details make the picture particularly strange. First, it's set in the cemetery; behind her are tombstones and a mausoleum.

Second, on the moon are the hands of a clock. It is five minutes to midnight.

Third, despite her smile, a tear is trickling down her cheek.

Dad used to stare at the painting too. If I came up beside him while he was doing so, he would put his hand on my shoulder and say, "My father used to say there was a long story behind that picture, and the key to the family mystery. When I begged him to explain, he would only say, 'I'll tell you more on your eleventh birthday.'"

That was all Dad ever said about it. He didn't need to say more. I knew that by the time he had turned eleven, his father was gone.

Like father, like son . . .

In my room I lined up my pencils by length, then took out the picture I was working on, an attempt to copy the cover of one of my grandfather's books. It was cool: two horrifying monsters wrestling in a swamp while behind them a beautiful woman without many clothes presses herself against a big old tree, screaming.

I love drawing. It's about the only time I can shut out the world and not think about stuff like how many times I have to touch the door before it's safe to open it. I got so lost in the picture, I almost forgot about the trouble with my mother.

Then I smelled the hamburgers.

Mom knows I can't resist hamburgers, so she cooks them whenever she feels she might be even partly in the wrong. It's her way of apologizing without actually having to say "I'm sorry."

Mom isn't a big talker.

I tried to resist but the smell was too good. Before long I was downstairs, setting the table—my role when Mom cooks apology burgers. Later, as we were clearing the dishes, she said, "I have to work on that tapestry I'm making for the new hotel over in Winchester. Want to join me in the Loom Room while you do your homework?"

Mom's a weaver. She does most of her work on a big loom Dad built for her back when I was a baby. Later he made a much smaller version for me. Mom had been using it to teach me to weave. I liked it; the rhythm was relaxing. I don't use it anymore, though. I stopped when Dad disappeared.

Mom's big weavings hang in art galleries. One is even in a museum. After Dad disappeared, her weavings changed. Some, filled with dark, jagged designs, were downright disturbing. That was why I was glad when she got the hotel commission: it forced her to create a design more like her work used to be.

It had been a long time since she'd had a new commission. Fortunately, she has a part-time job teaching weaving at the community college. Otherwise, we'd really be in trouble.

"Well?" asked Mom, interrupting my thoughts. "Do you want to join me or not?"

I shrugged. "I guess so."

"All right, get your books."

Even though I was pretending it was no big deal, I loved being in the Loom Room. It's at the front of the house, in the base of the tower. The racks of yarn make it look as if someone has spilled a rainbow on the wall. Behind the bench where Mom sits is a picture of Penelope, weaving as she waits for Odysseus. To Mom's right is a painting of Arachne, who was turned into a spider for boasting that she could weave better than Athena. Above my own loom, which—with the help of a piece of plywood— I now use as a desk, is a picture of the three fates weaving the destiny of all mankind.

The storm had broken and rain was pounding

against the windows. Mom worked on her tapestry. I pretended to work on my math. Everything was very cozy.

Actually, I didn't *plan* to pretend about the math. I really did want to get the work done. But my mind kept wandering, distracted partly by the pleasure of watching my mother's slim, quick fingers manipulate the bright strands of yarn, partly by the howling of the wind. I was trying to force my attention back to my own work when a rumble of thunder shook the house.

As it tapered off, we heard a loud thump from the porch.

Mom looked up. "Go see if the wind blew something over, would you, Jake?"

I sighed, but mostly for effect, stepped into the front parlor, and turned on the light. (With money so tight, we don't leave on lights we aren't using.) Even *with* the light the room was gloomy, since it's covered with dark-brown wallpaper. Every time I saw that paper, I felt a twinge. Dad had always said he was going to take it down someday. Now every time I saw it I wondered if "someday" would ever come—if he was dead, or had simply gone missing like his own father. If so, might he improve on his father and actually come back to us?

At the front door I was touching the knob for

the third time when another bolt of lightning split the sky, this one so close I could hear the crackle of the electricity. The thunder followed almost immediately, shaking the house.

I waited for it to fade, then pulled the door open.

A small cry at my feet caused me to look down.

I let out a yelp of surprise.

3

(Lily)

◇ ◇ ◇

OUT OF THE BLUE

Most of what happened that first night went down at Jake's house. Even so, I need to put in something about what I did, since it turned out to be really important.

So . . . after supper and homework I decided to go back out to the cemetery. I *love* being there when the rain is pounding down and the sky is exploding with lightning.

Grampa was napping on the couch, which made things easy. I slipped on my raincoat and boots, grabbed a big umbrella, and headed for the door. The wind was strong, and I had to be careful not to let it blow the umbrella inside out. I headed for our library. It's incredibly cool to sit inside that mausoleum and read scary stories while a huge storm is shaking the world.

As I got close to the building, someone— someone really big—came running out. I ducked behind the Crawford family tombstone so I wouldn't be spotted, but I was madder than the Phantom of the Opera listening to a bad soprano. Who else would be in the cemetery at this time of night? More important, what was he—I assumed it was a he, because of the size—doing inside our mausoleum?

The books! I thought suddenly. *Someone is trying to steal our books!*

That might sound silly, but even though they were only paperbacks, I knew some of the books Jake had brought were collector's items. I also knew they meant a lot to him. I was so upset at the thought of losing them that it didn't occur to me it was unlikely anyone else even knew they were there.

Once the intruder was out of sight, I ran to the door. It was wide open. Well, that wasn't so strange. The thief probably didn't care about closing up after himself.

What *was* strange was the blue light coming from inside.

Cautiously, I peered around the door frame.

The entire back wall of the mausoleum, the one where Jake and I had heard scratching earlier that day, was glowing.

Irresistible.

I walked toward it.

It wasn't so strong that it hurt my eyes, and I couldn't feel any heat coming from it, so I reached out to touch it. The instant I made contact, the beautiful glow died. Everything went black.

From the other side of the wall came a howl of rage.

I turned and ran.

4

(Jacob)

LITTLE DUMPLING

The reason I yelped was that directly at my feet lay a basket woven from coarse black twigs.

Actually, the real reason for the yelp was what was inside the basket: a baby, bundled in a black blanket.

It cried out again, then stared up at me as if it expected me to do something. So I did. Lugging the basket into the house, I bellowed, "Mom, you'd better get out here!"

She shot out of the Loom Room. "What is it, Jake? Is anything—" She stopped in her tracks when she saw the basket. Eyes wide, she came to kneel beside it. "Poor little fellow," she murmured, stroking the baby's cheek.

"What makes you think it's a boy?"

"Mothers know these things," she answered, chucking the baby under the chin.

The kid gurgled with delight.

While Mom fussed over the baby, I took a closer look at the basket, which was wet from the storm. That black blanket bothered me. I mean, who wraps a baby in a *black* blanket? Then I spotted a piece of coarse paper tucked next to the baby. I pulled it out and unfolded it. The edges were slightly soggy, but the center was dry and the ink had not run. I'm going to copy it over, so anyone who reads this can see how bizarre it was:

> To the Family in This House,
>
> Please take care of my baby. I am in a desperate situation and must leave little Dum Pling behind. Please, please protect him! This is more important than you can imagine.
>
> Thank you.
> M.A.

"Better look at this," I said, handing the note to my mother, who by this time had picked up the baby and put him over her shoulder.

Outside, the rain continued to hammer at the windows, lightning flashed ever more frequently, and thunder rattled the roof with increasing force.

Mom read the note, wiped away a tear, then handed the paper back to me. Cuddling the baby close, she whispered, "I'm so sorry, sweetie. But your momma brought you to the right place. We'll take good care of you."

The kid burped, then puked on her shoulder.

Mom sighed. "Get the paper towels, would you, Jake?"

I scooted off to the kitchen, flicking on lights as I went. More important, I made sure to touch all the right spots on the wall.

"How do you know the note came from the baby's mother?" I asked when I came back. "Couldn't it have been the father?"

"Mothers know these things," she repeated, taking the paper towels.

I rolled my eyes. She had been using that phrase a lot since Dad disappeared.

"So what are we going to do about, um, *it*?" I asked.

"He's not an 'it,' Jacob, he's a little dumpling, just like the note says. In fact, I think that's what we should call him." She patted his cheek. "Don't you agree, Little Dumpling?"

"That doesn't answer my question. What are we going to do about, er—Little Dumpling?"

"For now, not a thing."

"Are you kidding? We have to do *something*!"

"Jacob, nothing we can do tonight can't wait till morning—and there's no point in going out in that storm."

As if to prove her point, a huge bolt of lightning hissed down from the sky.

Rocking from side to side, she patted the baby's back. "The little darling is in no danger here. And it's possible his mother might change her mind and come back for him. Just look at that note."

"I know! It must have been written by a crazy person!"

"Jacob! You have no idea what kind of stress this baby's mother might have been under. I don't want him gone if she returns."

"Why should we give the baby back to someone who left him on our doorstep? She can't love him very much!"

Mom's eyes flashed. "Jacob Doolittle! Have some compassion. We don't know what drove that poor woman—"

"Or man!"

"—that poor *woman* to do this. If she does come back, perhaps we can help her."

We can barely help ourselves, I thought. *What are we going to do for her?* Fortunately, I was smart enough not to say this out loud.

Another enormous crack of thunder made us both jump. To our surprise, the baby laughed.

"What a good Little Dumpling," cooed Mom.

I made a face. "What kind of baby laughs at sudden noises?"

"A brave one, of course."

The baby grinned at me over Mom's shoulder. It had chubby cheeks and huge green eyes. The smile was so adorable that, almost against my will, I put out a finger.

The baby grabbed on and began gumming.

It was soggy but funny.

"Oh, dear," said Mom. "I bet he's hungry. I wonder if he's on solid food yet. Come on, Little Dumpling, let's rustle up some grub."

In the kitchen Mom made me hold the baby while she worked the blender. Soon she had a bowl of vegetable glop that looked like something from a swamp. The baby actually seemed to like the stuff. At least it liked the first few spoonfuls. Then it started blowing out whenever she put some in its mouth. Soon goo was flying in all directions. When the baby landed some in my eye, I said, "I think Little Dumpling has had enough!"

The fact that the kid had managed to get me in the eye was fairly impressive, since I was holding it with its back to me.

"You're probably right."

Mom's face and blouse were dotted with blobs of green. Even so, she looked really happy. She fetched a washcloth and wiped off my face, then the baby's. "Hold him for a bit longer while I get clean clothes," she said when she was done.

I scowled, but I didn't really mind. It was kind of fun to have a baby around. I bounced Little Dumpling on my knee and sang one of Lily's bizarre songs. The baby laughed, a gurgling sound deep in its throat. I would have been almost sorry when Mom returned if it hadn't been for another sound I heard just before she got there—and the smell that followed.

"I think Little Dumpling has some, er, *dumplings*," I said, holding the baby out to her.

Mom rolled her eyes. "I'm pretty sure there's a half box of paper diapers in Junk Room B. Go get them, would you?"

Yes, we have *two* junk rooms. That's because my father had been such a pack rat that it took two rooms to hold all his stuff. Actually, it's not fair to blame Dad for *all* the mess; it had been building up for at least four generations.

Given my other problems, I sincerely hope I haven't inherited the overwhelming-need-to-save-useless-crap gene that seems to run so deep in our family.

As I started to go, Mom added, "After you get those, scoot up to the attic and bring down the old rocker."

I sighed but went to do as she asked.

The gentle creak as Mom rocked back and forth while crooning to the baby made the house feel warmer, despite the howling wind. I realized that since she had changed the diaper, she would know one thing for sure. "What's the verdict?" I asked. "Boy or girl?"

"Boy," she replied. "Definitely."

I was a little annoyed that she had been right.

After a few minutes of rocking she looked at me and said, "Better get back to that homework, son."

I refrained from saying, "Better get back to your weaving, Mom," and went to the Loom Room to fetch my math book.

She was still rocking when I returned to kiss her good night.

"Sleep tight, don't let the bed bugs bite," she said.

I know that's supposed to be a little blessing of

some kind. Personally, I find it pretty creepy.

"I'm going to wait up, in case Little Dumpling's mother comes back," she added as I left the room.

I should have seen what was coming right then.

5

(Lily)

◇ ◇ ◇

OUTLAWS

When I met Jake in the cemetery the next afternoon, I said, "You're not gonna believe what happened last night!"

He said exactly the same thing at exactly the same time.

We sounded a little like Sploot Fah, though we hadn't met him yet, of course.

I could tell Jacob was afraid I was going to punch him in the arm and shout, "Jinx! You owe me a Coke!"

He *could* have done the same thing to me, of course, except he gets so freaky about it that I knew he wouldn't. Which was why I didn't do it either. The first time I jinxed him, he wouldn't say a word until he actually went back to his house and got me a soda.

He can be so weird.

Finally Jake said, "You go first."

I figured this bit of courtesy was because he assumed whatever news I had, his would be even cooler. But after I told him about seeing the person running out of the mausoleum the night before, and the glowing blue wall that blinked out when I touched it, he looked both amazed and a little deflated, as if he wasn't going to top my news after all.

Even so, his news was plenty weird. When he was done telling me, I cried, "OMG! What are you gonna do?"

Jake shrugged. "Mom probably took him to the police, or social services, or something like that while we were in school today."

Only it turned out she hadn't, which Jacob told me on the way home the following afternoon.

"Why didn't she?" I asked, fascinated.

"She's still hoping the real mother will come back."

"I sincerely doubt that will happen."

I based this statement on personal experience.

Jacob nodded. "Me, too. Also, she's asked me not to tell anyone, which I think means we could get in trouble for this."

"You told me."

"You don't count."

"Thanks a lot!"

"Come on, Lily, you know what I mean. Anyway, she didn't ask me to keep my mouth shut about Little Dumpling until this morning, and I had already told you by then—though I didn't tell *her* that. I probably would have told you anyway. I mean, you are my best friend. Besides, she got to tell someone, so it's only fair I get to do the same."

"Who did she tell?"

"Mrs. McSweeney."

That startled me. Mrs. McSweeney is my grandfather's cousin—which makes her my third cousin, or something like that. Even though we're related, we don't see each other that much. I don't think she and Grampa get along very well. Of course, Gramps doesn't get along with anyone very well. And Mrs. McSweeney does put up with him on occasion. I guess that makes her one of our closest friends.

It's a little pathetic.

"How come your mom told *her*?"

"She and Mom are great pals. Besides, Mom didn't really have a choice. The three of us have dinner together at least once a week, so it would have been almost impossible to keep Little Dumpling a secret."

That stung a bit; Grampa and I had *never* had dinner with Mrs. McSweeney. I wondered if she had never invited us, or if Grampa just refused whenever she did. She might have given up asking before I even came to live with him.

Trying to get my mind off that, I went back to something else Jacob had said. "You're calling the baby Little Dumpling?"

He grinned and reminded me about the note in the basket. "Mom says Little Dumpling is a perfect nickname for him because he's cute as a dumpling. That seems kind of dumb to me. I mean, how cute can a dumpling be? But he is awful cute."

That was when I realized that Jacob's mom wasn't the only one falling for the baby. I didn't say that, though.

I may be weird, but I'm not stupid.

By the time another two days had passed, it was clear Jacob's mom had no intention of *ever* taking the baby to the police, or anywhere else, for that matter.

"I'm starting to get really worried," he told me one afternoon, his fingers tapping against his thumb as if he was trying to send a message in Morse code. "Last night Mom asked me to help her haul my old crib out of the attic so LD—"

"LD?"

"That's what we call the baby for short. Anyway, Mom wanted to set up the crib so he could stop sleeping in her dresser drawer. Lily, she's never going to go to the police!"

"You're, like, outlaws!" I cried, clapping my hands.

Jacob flopped back on the grass. "Great! As if flunking math wasn't enough, now I'm a criminal!"

"You don't understand," I said softly. "It's the same with me and Grampa. After . . . after . . ." I paused, then finally said, "When I needed somewhere to go, social services wanted to send me to a foster home. They didn't think Grampa was suited to take care of me. He disagreed, and he came and, um, took me. I'd already been in a couple of foster homes by that time, one awful, the other really wonderful. I didn't care that it was wonderful—I wanted to be with Grampa. Which is how I ended up here. Now you don't have to worry about me telling about LD, because then you could tell on me, too. So your secret is safe."

"So is yours," said Jacob solemnly. We pressed the palms of our left hands together (it's more sacred that way, because the left hand is closer to the heart) and swore to guard each other's secrets.

About two weeks after LD arrived Jake and I were walking home together when he suddenly said,

"Mom claims she's not worried about anyone finding out about the baby, but I don't believe her."

We had just made it over the little bridge that crosses the stream running through the cemetery. I like to stand in the middle and watch the water flow underneath, but I can't when I'm with Jacob. Being on a bridge makes him too nervous.

I won't begin to describe the rituals he needs to get across one.

"Let's sit here," I said, motioning to a big tree we both like. Once we had settled in, I said, "Okay, why don't you believe her?"

"Because we go three towns over to buy baby supplies!"

"Yep, that's a good sign that she's worried."

"And yesterday when I pointed out to her that everyone around here knows who we are and how many people we have in our family, she said, 'If it comes to it, we'll tell people LD is your cousin. Besides, it might not be for long. His mother could come back any day now.'"

"She doesn't believe that," I said.

"I know! She's totally fallen for the kid!"

"So have you!"

"Have not!"

I laughed, and Jacob couldn't help but smile. "All right, I do kind of like him. I used some of my allowance to buy him this little green rattle. I totally got teased by some older kids who saw me doing it, but when LD shakes it and laughs, he's so cute I can hardly stand it." He paused, then said, "I'm starting to worry that Mom might consider moving just so she can pretend he really is ours."

"You can't do that!" I cried, panic-stricken.

"Well, I don't want to." He looked away. "If my dad came back, he wouldn't know where to find us."

I thought for a moment. "Okay, listen . . . I know you don't believe LD's mother is coming back, but from now on you have to pretend that you do."

"Why?"

"So you can keep telling *your* mom you can't move, because you have to be here in case LD's mother does return!"

Jacob smiled. "Good plan."

"Now you'd better head out. My grandfather is coming."

I spoke too late. Grampa had spotted us and was heading in our direction. He did not look happy.

Jake scrambled to his feet, clearly ready to run. Grampa is only about five and a half feet tall, and to be honest, he's kind of scrawny. But he's got a glare that could bore a hole through an oak.

When he was about ten feet away, he pointed his clippers at me and snapped, "I thought I told you not to hang out with that boy, Lily!"

"We're not hurting anything, Grampa!"

"The hurt's already been done!" Turning his angry eyes on Jake, he snarled, "You'd best git."

"Sorry, Jake," I muttered. "You'd better go."

He turned and ran.

I looked at my grandfather. "Why do you hate him that way?" I asked.

"Ain't him so much," said Grampa. "It's his whole dang family."

"But *why*?"

He didn't answer, just turned and stalked away.

6
(Jacob)

TRANSFORMATION

When I got home, I found Mom having coffee with Mrs. McSweeney, who was bouncing Little Dumpling on her knee. Her shoulder bag, which mostly held her knitting, was beside her on the table. She never went anywhere without it, and I was sometimes amazed at the things she could pull out of it.

Curled up at her feet, casually licking a milk-white paw, was Mrs. McSweeney's cat, Luna Marie Eleganza the Sixth.

Mrs. McSweeney always brought Luna with her when she came to visit. This made me happy, since we don't have a pet of our own. I loved to stroke the cat—she had the silkiest fur I had ever felt. Her tail was so fluffy it looked like an ostrich plume, and her nose was as pink as peppermint candy. Her ears, too, were pink, especially when there was light shining through the thin skin.

When I first met Luna, she had been named Luna Marie Eleganza the *Fourth*. Mrs. McSweeney claimed the reason for the name change was that the cat had since used up two more of her nine lives.

"Well, if it isn't himself!" Mrs. McSweeney exclaimed when I came in. She spoke in a thick Irish brogue that I had come to love. "Come here and give your old darlin' a kiss, will ya now?"

Mrs. McSweeney's full name is Eloise Elvira McDougal Smirnov Rodriguez Chang McSweeney. The last four names were the result of outliving four husbands.

"Which was quite enough for any woman," she had told my mother on more than one occasion. "Any more after that and I'd've felt I was takin' more than my share, if you know what I mean."

Though she appeared frail, Mrs. McSweeney could wield an ax—she still cooked on a wood-burning stove—with amazing power and accuracy.

"It's the bread," she had told me when I was six and staying at her house while my parents took a weekend away. Just as I was thinking I needed to find some of this bread and eat it—I was, after all, only six—she clarified by adding, "Nothin' like kneadin' bread to strengthen the arms—especially if you have fourteen children, bless the little darlin's, and are making the bread for all of them."

When I was seven, she let me try kneading a batch of bread dough myself. I quickly understood why she had developed such sturdy muscles! That was the same year she let me watch as she beheaded one of the chickens she kept in the backyard and then prepared it for Sunday dinner. She had carefully explained each of the internal organs as she removed them from the body cavity, taking care to point out the eggs that were in various stages of development.

I had adored her ever since, though I continued to regard her with a combination of love and wary awe.

"I've got a committee meeting at church tonight, Jake," Mom said. "I'll tuck LD in before I go. He's a good sleeper, so you shouldn't have any problem. If you do, call Mrs. McSweeney. She can be here in a jiffy."

"And glad to do it," agreed the older woman.

I sighed, but the truth was I didn't really mind. I like having the house to myself every once in a while.

Mom left for her meeting about two hours later. When she was gone, I went to my room and took out one of my grandfather's books. Considering how scary his stories could be, this wasn't really wise—especially given the fact that I was pretty much alone in a house that would make a good set for a horror movie. But I couldn't resist.

One of the things I like about the Always October stories is that despite the fact of them being so weird and scary, somehow my grandfather always managed to weave in an idea called "tikkun olam." Mom told me it's a Hebrew phrase about "repairing the world." She likes the idea and tries to live by it (even though we're Methodist, not Jewish). I think it's one of the reasons she felt so strongly about taking in Little Dumpling.

Arthur also believed it was important to act on this idea . . . which is kind of odd considering the way he broke his own family.

Anyway, when I finished the first story, which involved strange creatures from another dimension kidnapping orphaned children, I shuddered and put the book away. The story had made me uneasy enough that I decided I should check on Little Dumpling.

The baby was sound asleep, his pudgy fingers curled around his green plastic rattle. Looking at him, I almost thought the teasing I got from those kids who saw me buy the thing had been worth it.

"G'night, LD," I whispered.

After returning to my own room, I took out some paper and began trying to draw Syreena, the tall, bat-winged woman in my grandfather's story. Outside, a soft rain pattered against my window while the April wind rustled through the new leaves on the oaks that surround the house. Eventually the rain stopped. The clouds shifted and the light of the full moon came streaming through my window.

I lost track of how long I had been drawing, so I wasn't sure how much time had passed when I was pulled back to the real world by a thump from LD's room.

Putting down my pencil, I went to check on the baby.

I opened the door, then stopped in my tracks.

In the crib where LD should have been, wearing the same yellow duckie pajamas he had gone to sleep in, lay a creature with bright green fur, the beginnings of a snout, and enormous pointed ears that curled over his head.

Had the baby turned into a monster? Or was this some horrible substitution?

Torn between fascination and terror, I moved toward the crib.

The furry baby opened its eyes and smiled at me, displaying a huge mouth full of glistening fangs.

I reversed course and backed toward the door. "Mom?" I called. At least, I tried to call her. My voice didn't seem to be working. I tried again. This time my voice worked better than I expected. *"Mom! You'd better get in here!"*

Then I remembered: she wasn't there.

What was I supposed to do if there was an emergency? Oh, right—call Mrs. McSweeney! And what was I going to say? "The baby just got all furry and grew fangs. I'm not sure what to do about it. Can you come over?"

She would think I had lost my mind.

I looked back at the creature in the crib. Still clutching its rattle, it held out its arms in the classic "pick me up" gesture that Little Dumpling always used. But where LD had tiny, clear fingernails, this thing had sharp black claws.

I had no ritual for dealing with a situation like this.

When I didn't move, the baby beast started to cry. Not a tantrum; just a small, sad whimper. The tears rolling out of its big eyes disappeared into its green fur.

I hardened myself against the sight. Who knew what the little monster might do if I picked it up? Part of me felt I should just turn and run. But the wretched thing continued to stare at me with those big, pleading eyes. It reached for me again.

I shook my head.

It flung itself to the mattress and wailed as if I had broken its heart. "Jay-Jay," it sobbed. "Jay-Jay!"

My eyes widened and my heart melted. LD had never talked before, but it had to be him calling for me like that!

I hurried to the crib and scooped the poor, terrified little guy into my arms. He buried his face against my chest, still sobbing, and I realized he was as frightened as I was. Maybe more so.

I moved to the rocking chair, sat, and began to rock. LD continued to wail. Desperate, I started crooning the lullabies my mother had sung to me when I was little. I started with "Too-ra-loo-ra-loo-ral" and made it through Brahms's "Lullaby" and "Tell Me Why" before the baby stopped fussing.

I looked down at him. The kid was cute, even in monster form.

What is it about babies? I wondered for the umpteenth time.

Still looking at the furry bundle in my arms, I had another thought: *I wish Lily was here. She'd know what to do with a baby monster.*

I sat up, earning a squawk of protest from LD. Why hadn't I thought of Lily to begin with? I had to call her.

I immediately realized two problems. (1) I didn't know her number—heck, I didn't even know if the Carkers had a phone. (2) Even if I found the number, what if when I called, I got Gnarly instead of Lily? I decided if that happened, I should just hang up.

Mom keeps a phone and phone book beside her bed. I carried LD to her room and put him down next to the pillow. He whimpered a bit but didn't raise a major fuss. I turned on the lamp on Mom's nightstand.

It didn't take long to find a "Carker," but the initial after it was *A*, not *G*. I thought it must be the wrong Carker until I realized Gnarly was probably a nickname. (I mean, who would name a kid Gnarly?) I checked the address. Thirteen Cemetery Lane. Had to be the right place!

I took a deep breath, gave the nightstand five taps, then punched in the number. It rang several times. I was about to give up when I heard Lily say, "Carker residence. Who's calling, please?"

"Thank goodness!" I said. "I was terrified I would get your grandfather."

A long silence followed. Finally she said, "It's nice to hear from you, Juliet, but I don't understand why you're calling."

I pulled the phone from my ear and stared at it.

Who the heck was Juliet?

7

(Lily)

◇ ◇ ◇

INTO THE CLOSET

It took Jacob longer than it should have to figure out that I called him "Juliet" because I didn't want my grandfather to know who I was talking to! For a smart guy, he can be a little slow on the uptake.

He finally got it. "Sorry!" he said hastily. "I don't want to get you in trouble, Lily. But I really, really, *really* need to talk to you."

"Can't it wait until tomorrow, *Juliet*?"

"No, it can't! The baby just turned into a monster!"

I could hardly keep from laughing. Trying to remain serious, I said, "Oh, Juliet! I know this is your first time being a big sister, but you have to under-stand that this happens sometimes. The baby is probably just teething."

"No, Lily, *you* don't understand! I'm trying to tell you that LD just turned into a monster—as in, he grew fangs and fur. I think he's bigger, too. I'm afraid he's gonna bust out of his pj's!"

I was starting to get angry. Jake and I had invented some great imaginary games, but call-ing me at home was too much. I carried the phone into the hall. Keeping my voice low but still worried about my grandfather overhearing, I hissed, "Listen, *Juliet*, this could be fun but you *can't* call me like this. We can start the game tomorrow."

"This isn't a game, *Herbert*! Do you think I wanted to take a chance on your grandfather picking up? I called because LD has turned into a monster with fur and fangs and he's still cute but also sort of ter-rifying and my mother isn't here and I don't know what to do so I called you because you're supposed to be my best friend!"

When Jacob gets excited, he talks like punctua-tion had never been invented, so this sentence made me think maybe he was serious.

"Wow," I said. "If that's true, it's cooler than a goblin's heinie!"

Normally he would ask how cool a goblin's heinie

was supposed to be, and how I knew. Now he just said, "It's true! And it's not cool, it's terrifying!"

The tremor in his voice startled me. I was silent for a moment, then said, "Listen carefully, because I'm giving you one last chance. If you tell me, right now, you are making this up, I will forgive you. If you tell me it's real, I will believe you. But if you tell me it's real and later I find out you were fooling, we will never, *ever* be friends again. So . . . are you talking true, or not?"

I held my breath, half wanting him to confess it was a game, half wanting him to say it was real.

"Lily, if this is a lie, then Frankenstein can fart in my face every morning for a hundred years."

It might seem stupid that I believed him, but I did. I mean, I'd been waiting for something like this all my life. "Well," I said, "I suppose it's because of the full moon."

I heard a groan from the other end. "I'm such a dolt! Do you think if I put him someplace dark, he might change back?"

"I dunno. In stories usually just having a full moon in the sky is enough to make whatever thing is going to happen, um . . . happen! But maybe it's different for babies. Was he in the moonlight when it started?"

"Definitely! It was pouring through his window

right onto his crib."

"Okay, that's useful. Is he in the moonlight now?"

"Good grief, I really am a dolt! He's smack-dab in a patch of the stuff."

"Okay, try moving him."

"All right, hold on a minute."

I heard a little howl, a high-pitched sound that sent shivers down my spine. "Was that LD?" I asked when it stopped.

"Yeah, he woke up when I took him off the bed. Boy, my mother is kind of a slob. There's nowhere in here to sit. I'm going back to my room."

"Can you take the phone with you?" I asked, afraid he was going to end the call.

"I'll try. I'm not sure how much range it has. All right, I'm in the hall. Can you still hear me?"

"Yep. You should be out of the moonlight now. Any change in the baby?"

"Nothing."

"Maybe you have to give it a few minutes."

Another pause, then, "I'm back in my room now. Hey, LD's ears are smaller. He's turning back!"

"Excellent! Man, I wish we had cell phones so you could send me a picture. Is he still changing?"

"No," said Jacob with a moan. "It's stopped. He's still all furry."

I thought fast. "Maybe you need complete darkness. Try taking him into a closet. Make sure you leave the light off!"

"Lily, I am *not* getting into a pitch-black closet with a baby monster. Who knows what he might do to me?"

"Why, Juliet, you're not afraid of a little baby, are you?"

I felt bad saying it, because I knew Jake hated that kind of argument (mostly because he was doomed to lose). But we didn't have time for a discussion. I was afraid Gramps might yell for me to get off the phone at any minute, and I *had* to know how this turned out.

"All right," he grumped, "I'll give it a try."

Though I was glad Jacob had called to ask for advice, the situation was driving me nuts. I wanted to *be there* so badly it hurt.

Of course, that assumed it was really happening . . . which I hoped it was, because otherwise I would have to have a huge fight with Jacob and then never talk to him again as long as I lived.

"All right, I'm in the closet."

"Is the dark having any effect?"

"How should I know? I can't see a thing. Anyway, I don't think—"

I was starting to explain that he should use his sense of touch when a sudden crackle of static burst against my ear.

"Juliet? *Juliet*?"

Nothing.

I stared at the phone in horror.

Had we simply lost the connection?

Was Jacob playing with my head?

Or had something much worse just happened?

8

(Jacob)

A VOICE IN THE DARK

W hen the phone went dead, my first thought was that I had gone out of range.

Then I heard a crackle—not from the phone, but from the darkness around me.

Even worse, the closet suddenly smelled wrong. The familiar odor of dirty socks was gone, replaced by something damp, wild, and disturbing.

Scary as that was, I didn't actually scream until a deep, raspy voice said, "Ah, good—we have made contact!"

Then I let out a shriek that made the baby howl too.

I groped frantically for the doorknob, found it, discovered it would not turn.

"Do not be afraid," said the voice, which seemed to come from a great distance. "We will not hurt you. We can't even reach you yet."

Part of me thought, *Well, that's a relief.*

Another part thought, *Yet?!?*

And still another part thought, *WE???*

"Who are you?" I cried. "What do you want?"

"My name is unimportant. What I *want* is for you to promise to take care of the baby."

"I'm doing that already!"

"Good, I am glad to know that. Guard him well. But remember, he is not yours! I will be back next month."

"What?"

But the voice was gone. Suddenly the doorknob, which I was still clutching, turned in my hand. The door swung open and I bounded out of the closet. My stomach clenched as I realized I hadn't touched the door three times before I opened it! I started back inside so I could fix that mistake, then decided that was insane. A pain in the gut from skipping the ritual was better than getting back in that closet! I was already shaking so violently, you could have used me to mix paint.

A pudgy hand patted my face. I looked down and

realized LD was now totally human. He rested his head on my shoulder. For some reason that calmed me a little. Patting his back, crooning wordlessly, I carried him to his room. The moon was still shining through the window, so I put him in the rocker, then pulled the crib out of the light. For good measure, I drew the curtains, too.

As I did all this, I was struck with a new thought: *I should have waited until Mom got home to turn LD back! She's never going to believe me if I tell her what just happened.*

Of course, when Lily had been giving me advice, I wasn't thinking about what came next. I just wanted to get the baby back into his normal form. My thoughts shifted. What about that voice? Where had it come from?

I was at the kitchen table, trying to work this through, when the front door opened and Mom called, "How did it go, sweetie?"

"Fine," I replied, tugging my earlobe and cursing myself for fibbing. But what could I tell her? That the baby had turned into a monster? She'd think I had lost my mind. Suddenly I wondered if I could make it happen again. But how? I couldn't just say, "Let's put the baby in the moonlight so you can see what happens."

"The baby slept all right?" asked Mom, coming into the kitchen.

Time to get creative. Trying to call up some of my grandfather's ability to spin a yarn, I said, "Well, he did stir a little when the moon rose. I went in to check on him. Gosh, you should have seen him, Mom. He was so cute in the moonlight!"

She looked at me oddly.

"Come on," I said eagerly. "I'll show you."

"I don't want to wake him," she said.

Luck was with me, because we heard a squawk from upstairs.

"He knows you're home," I said. "He probably wants to see you!"

Mom looked at me oddly again but followed me up the stairs.

"You moved the crib," she said, as soon as we entered the room.

"I thought the light was disturbing him. But since he's awake—"

Before she could say anything, I pushed the crib back where it had been and threw open the curtains. Instantly LD was bathed in silver moonlight.

"See how cute?" I said, looking for any sign of a change.

Nothing happened.

LD stretched out his arms to be picked up.

Mom reached for him.

Desperate, I said, "Let's just admire him for a second, Mom! See how the moonlight makes his eyes sparkle?"

"Jacob, are you sure you're all right?"

"Of course!" I lied. Inside I was crushed. It wasn't going to happen.

I didn't sleep well that night, not well at all.

Things didn't look any better the next morning when I got to the cemetery. Lily was waiting for me, and the expression on her face was almost as frightening as a rough voice in a dark closet.

9

(Lily)

◇ ◇ ◇

I GET TO MEET LD

Well, duh, Jacob! Was I supposed to be all happy after you just disappeared that way the night before? I was torn between worry and anger all night long.

Okay, sorry, I should just focus on the story.

So . . .

I was holding both braids and looking serious when Jacob came along the path the next morning.

"What's wrong?" he asked when he saw me.

"I don't know which one to chew! If you were telling me true last night, it will be the thinking braid.

But if you made all that up, and then cut off the phone call to leave me hanging, it's the angry braid for sure. Except first I clobber you. Then I kick you out of my life. And *then* I take time to chew the angry braid."

"Lily, I swear on my grandmother's grave I was telling the truth."

"Let's see if you really mean it. Follow me."

Jacob sighed; he knew what was coming. A few minutes of walking through the grass, which was still wet with dew, brought us to his mother's mother's grave.

"Okay, put your hand on that tombstone and swear. But remember . . . if you tell a lie on your grandmother's grave, the Midnight Terrors will chase you for the rest of your life."

Without hesitation, Jacob put his left hand on the stone, his right hand over his heart, and said solemnly, "I swear on my grandmother's grave that everything I told you last night was true." Then, clearly trying to get ahead of things, he added, "I also swear that everything I'm going to tell you right now is true too!"

Excitement bubbled up inside me. "Great galloping zombies, Jacob! This is the most fabulous thing ever!"

"Easy for you to say. You weren't there!"

"Wish I had been. Hey . . . maybe it will happen again tonight!"

"Huh?"

"Well, in a lot of lycanthrope movies the transformation occurs three nights in a row." (As a fan of the frightening, I prefer the term *lycanthrope* to the simpler *werewolf*.)

Jacob turned pale. "I dunno. Let me tell you what happened next. It was even scarier, but it makes me think I've got a month before it happens again."

I listened to his story. If he was making this up, he was as good as his grandfather! "That's really freaky," I said when he was finished. "I'm glad you didn't pass out from fear on the spot."

"I thought I was going to!"

"I don't blame you. Okay, we need to do some research. Um . . . are you going to tell your mother about this?"

"Do you think she'd believe me?"

"I don't know, *since I've never met her!*"

This was a dig, and I could tell from the way Jacob blushed that he knew it. See, he had never invited me to his house. Of course, I had never invited him to my house, either. The difference was that his mother didn't have anything against me, whereas my grandfather really disliked Jacob. We never talked about it, but I had a feeling that the real reason he didn't ask me over was that he didn't want to admit to his mother he had a friend who was a girl.

"You still can't meet her," he said now.

"Why not?"

"Because she can't know I told you about LD! But I do want you to see the baby. Maybe you'll spot something I missed, something that will give me proof. Hmmm . . . Mom's teaching Friday night. She'll be gone from about five thirty to eight o'clock. Can you come over then?"

I chewed my right braid for a minute, then said, "I'll have to come up with a good excuse to give Grampa. But I think I can do it."

We didn't spend much time in the cemetery over the next week. Instead we were at the library, using the internet to research monsters. We found some really cool stuff, some other stuff that was pretty terrifying, and some stuff that left me wishing you could buy eyewash for your brain. Unfortunately, none of what we found seemed to apply to baby monsters. And what we found when we searched on *baby monsters* was a lot of cutesy junk that made me want to yark.

The one good thing was that we uncovered some useful information on the matter of the full moon.

It seems that despite what happens in movies, in reality the moon is only full one night of the month. Actually, it's only *really* full for about a minute, since the moment of fullness comes when the moon is exactly opposite the sun. Because the moon is constantly moving, for any given spot true full passes very quickly.

I guess the reason for three nights is that it makes it easier for Hollywood to pack a lot of action into a film. This annoys me. People should be more careful when they're writing about monsters!

Jacob's house has seen better days. Even so, I think it's totally fabulous . . . three stories high, with a wide veranda that wraps around the corner on the right side of the front door. Hmmm. *Corner* might not be the right word, because this is where the tower curves out from the main body of the house. The roof of the tower is a cone that stretches several feet above the already high roof. It's cool . . . almost like a rocket attached to the side of the house.

I cannot tell you how much I wanted to see inside that tower!

To be honest, I had been wanting to see inside the whole house from the first time I walked past it, back in second grade. That desire had tripled when I found out that my writing hero had lived there. So I was very prompt and rang the doorbell at 5:35.

"How did you know it was safe?" demanded Jacob when he opened the door. "What if Mom hadn't left on schedule?"

I rolled my eyes. "Do you really think your mother would find it dangerous for you to have a friend over to visit?"

"She would right now! I keep telling you, she doesn't want anyone else to know about LD."

"Well I'm not stupid! I hid in the bushes at the end of the driveway and waited until she pulled out before I rang the bell. So are you going to ask me in, or do I have to stand on the porch all night?"

"Sorry, sorry," said Jacob, swinging the door open.

"This place is ginormous," I murmured as I stepped into the entryway.

"Way too 'ginormous' for two people and a baby monster," replied Jacob.

"Better than being too small for two people," I said. Instantly I felt bad, because it might have seemed I was saying something mean about my grandfather, who took me in when I needed him. "Where's the baby?" I asked, to change the subject.

"In his high chair. Come on."

We made our way back to the kitchen. As soon as I saw Little Dumpling, I said, "Oh, Jacob, he is soooooo cute!"

Despite what Jacob has claimed ever since, I want to make it clear that I did not, repeat did *not*, actually squeal these words.

He scowled. "I knew you were going to get all girly!"

"Oh, shut up. He's cute, and you know it."

"I guess so. He's less cute once he turns green and the fangs come out."

"Can I hold him?"

"If you want."

As soon as Jacob removed the tray from the high chair, LD stretched out his arms. I scooped him up. Without hesitation he cuddled against me.

If you've ever held a baby, you know that special baby smell . . . and I *don't* mean the odor of a full diaper! It's something you get when you nuzzle your nose against the top of a baby's head, and it's one of the best smells in the world. Holding LD close, I plunked down in one of the wooden chairs. Then I bounced him on my knee while I sang my newest song, "The Chipmunk's Funeral."

"It's a good thing he can't understand you," said Jacob. "You'd probably creep him out."

"Ha-very-ha. Hey, do you have a video camera?"

He blinked at the sudden change of topic. "Why? Do you want to me to film you singing to the baby?"

As he said this, LD squawked and held out his

arms to be transferred to Jacob. I took one last sniff of his head, then passed him over. When he was safely snuggled in Jacob's arms, I said, "No, I don't want a video of me singing to the baby! I want to help save your skin, you goof. Think about it! If your mother is out during the next full moon and things go wrong, you're *really* going to need something to show her."

Jacob turned pale. "Yeah, I see what you mean."

"So, do you have one?"

"I don't know. Maybe in one of the junk rooms. Dad kept—"

"Junk *rooms*?"

Jacob blushed. "I come from a long line of pack rats. Wanna help me look?"

"Sure!"

We went up by the back stairway. It took a little while, because Jacob had to touch certain spots along the wall, and holding the baby made it a bit tricky. I kept my mouth shut about that part. But when we reached the top and I looked ahead, I gasped. I couldn't believe how long that hall was! Jacob started forward, but I kind of dawdled, because I was looking at the portraits lining the walls.

Suddenly I gasped. "Jacob!" I yelled. "JACOB!"

10

(Jacob)

◇ ◇ ◇

SPELUNKER

At Lily's cry I hurried back and asked, "Are you all right? You sound like something frightened you."

"Who's that?" she demanded, pointing to one of the paintings.

I smiled, since I could understand why the picture might have disturbed her. "Tia LaMontagne. She was my grandmother, almost." Seeing Lily's expression, I added, "She married Arthur Doolittle but disappeared before they had any kids."

"Disappeared?"

"Without a trace."

"Boy, people in your family make a habit of that, don't they?"

I felt as if she had just stuck a knife in my ribs. Lily must have seen the expression on my face, because she cried, "Oh my god, I'm sorry, Jacob! I . . . "

"Forget it," I said gruffly. "Just tell me why you were so startled."

"Because I've seen her before."

"No surprise. She was pretty famous around here. You probably saw her in some historical article or—"

"Jake, my grandfather keeps her photo on his dresser!"

That *did* surprise me. "Are you serious?"

She nodded solemnly.

"Okay, that is definitely strange."

"That's what Medusa's hairdresser said. Her last words, if I remember correctly. Anyway, I must have asked Grampa about that picture a dozen times but he never answers. I think the question makes him angry." She examined the painting again. "She's fascinating. Beautiful, but kind of . . . strange. She makes me think of a cat."

"I know exactly what you mean. Dad used to say that his own father told him there was a long story behind that painting, and the key to the family mystery. When Dad would beg him to explain, Arthur always told him to wait until his eleventh birthday.

But by the time that birthday rolled around . . ."

I stopped, unable to say more. As if Little Dumpling could sense what I was feeling, he reached up and patted my cheek.

Lily waited a bit, then nudged me and said, "Let's see if we can find a camera."

I nodded. A little farther down the hall I stopped and said, "Junk Room B has the more recent stuff." Shifting LD to my left shoulder, I touched the knob three times, then opened the door. Stepping aside, I said, "After you, madam."

"Dracula's devious dentures!" Lily cried when she saw the array of books, paintings, gadgets, trunks, boxes, artwork, and general clutter. "This all belonged to your dad?"

"Well, it's not fair to blame him for *all* of it. As I said, I come from a long line of pack rats."

She stepped inside, gazing around in amazement. "A *carton* of whoopee cushions?"

"Dad thought they were hilarious."

She pointed to the wall. "Helmets?"

I took a deep breath, then said softly, "Dad was a major spelunker."

"That sounds dirty. Do I need to look it up on Urban Dictionary?"

Despite how I was feeling, that got a smile out of me. "Well, it can be dirty, but not the way you mean.

A spelunker is someone who explores caves. It was Dad's hobby. He loved being underground." I took another deep breath, then said softly, "He never came back from his last trip."

"Jake! I'm sorry. Did he . . . ?"

I closed my eyes. "No one knows what happened. He was exploring solo, which is a major no-no for spelunkers, but Dad was ornery that way. When he didn't report in, they searched the cave he was supposed to be investigating. They couldn't find any sign of him. But whether he found some hidden chamber and got stuck or copied his own dad and just took off on us . . . "

My voice trailed away. After a long silence Lily said, "There are all kinds of stupid stories going around school about what happened. Why don't you—"

I cut her off. "I don't care what they think! And I don't want to talk about it. All right?"

She nodded, looking frightened.

LD began to fuss.

"Give me the baby," she said. "I'll walk him in the hall while you look for the camera."

I passed over LD, glad for the chance to be alone for a few minutes.

11

(Lily)

◇ ◇ ◇

THE PUZZLE IN THE PICTURE

I hurried into the hall . . . and straight back to the painting of Tia LaMontagne. I studied it until LD began to squirm. Then I started walking, jouncing him gently and crooning as I wondered what it was like for Jake to not know whether his father was dead or had simply taken off for a new life.

I stopped in front of the picture of Tia LaMontagne again. Jacob definitely had some odd-looking relatives . . . but then, who doesn't? The thing was, none of them looked as odd as Tia. I paced with LD but kept coming back to that one picture, staring at it and thinking about what Jacob's father had said.

An idea was forming in my mind.

Just then Jacob came out of the room holding a box. "Found one!" he crowed.

I continued to stare at the painting.

"Did you hear me?" he asked, coming to stand beside me. "I found a camera!"

I nodded, then said softly, "Jake, what if your grandfather was giving your dad a clue?"

"Huh? What are you talking about?"

I blushed a little, wondering if I was being foolish. "I just had an idea. Maybe it's crazy, but I think we should try it."

"I repeat: What are you talking about?"

"Your grandfather told your dad there was a long story behind that picture, and the key to the family mystery, right?"

"Yeah."

"Well, what if he was being literal?"

"What do you mean?"

"I mean, *let's look behind the picture!*"

Jacob smacked himself on the forehead. "Good grief! Why didn't I think of that? It might be crazy, but it's the kind of thing my grandfather wrote about all the time. It's definitely worth trying."

I examined the situation. The hallway was at least ten feet high and the portrait was a good three feet wide and four feet tall. The frame added another six inches on each side.

"It's going to take both of us to get it down," I said.

"No kidding," said Jacob. "Wait here with LD. I'll get a couple of chairs from the kitchen for us to stand on."

A few minutes later LD was sitting on the floor, and Jacob and I were lifting the picture off the wall.

"Oh, crud!" Jacob muttered. "You were right, Lily, but it's not going to do us any good!"

I groaned. Two things marked out the area where we had removed the painting. The first was a rectangle, exactly the dimensions of the painting itself, where the wallpaper was bright and unfaded.

The second, smack in the center of that rectangle, was the round metal door of a wall safe. On the front of it was a dial, like the dial on a combination padlock. I wanted to scream. I thought I had been so brilliant working out the puzzle, and all it got us was this.

"I'm sorry," I said glumly.

"Don't be silly," said Jake. "You figured out more than I ever did. Let's set the painting down. We might as well give the thing a try. I read a book once—sheesh, I think it was one of my grandfather's—where a safe like this was so old that the dial just clicked into place."

He spun the dial. It did no good. He twisted it back and forth. Nothing. He let me take a turn. I tried pressing my ear to the safe, hoping to hear some clue-giving click. Nothing.

Jake sighed. That made sense. What was there to say?

Working together, we got the picture back on the wall, which was even harder than taking it down. By the time we were done, LD was fussing for his dinner and I had to head for home.

I didn't sleep well that night. I kept thinking about the portrait of Tia LaMontagne. Something about it was tickling at the part of my brain that loves puzzles.

It took me a week to figure it out. Or, at least, to think I had figured it out. I still needed to actually test my idea.

"When is your mom teaching again?" I asked Jake that afternoon.

"Friday."

"Can I come over then?"

"I suppose so. Why?"

"I want to visit the baby!"

I didn't tell him the real reason—that I thought I had figured out how to open the safe. I didn't want to build up his expectations if I had it wrong. As it was, my own expectations were driving me crazy. I was afraid my brain might explode before Friday got there.

Somehow I managed to live through the week. That evening I again hid in the bushes at the end of Jake's drive, waiting for his mother to leave. She didn't pull out until quarter of six, and by then I was in a frenzy thinking she wasn't going to go after all.

Once she did finally leave, I sprinted for the house. Jacob was waiting with the door open and LD over his shoulder.

"I figured you'd be here," he said with a smirk.

"What happened?"

He shrugged. "LD was fussing. Mom nearly flipped out, because she hates to be late for class. I think she was making him worse because she was so stressed herself. I finally convinced her to just go. The baby calmed down as soon as she left."

"Can I hold him?"

"Sure," he said, passing the warm little bundle to me.

I was surprised. "He's bigger than he was just last week!"

"Yeah, he's growing awfully fast. It's another thing that makes me nervous about him."

I noticed that even though Jacob claimed the baby made him nervous, he was looking at the little guy with obvious affection.

"Come on, get inside. I don't want you standing here if Mom realizes she forgot something and suddenly comes back!"

With a sigh, I followed him in. Little Dumpling was gooing and shaking his rattle. When we were in the kitchen, I said, "Can we look at the painting of Tia again?"

"I suppose so. Why?"

I smiled. "I had another idea."

He looked at me suspiciously but led the way up the stairs. Once we were in front of the picture, I said, "My grandfather has a book of art from the Middle Ages—"

"Your grandfather has an art book?"

"There's a lot more to my grandfather than you think," I snapped. "Now listen. I used to spend a lot of time with that book. It had all kinds of stuff about how to, well, *read* a painting. Artists used to pack a lot of symbols and secret messages into their work."

"What has that got to do with this?" he asked.

"Who painted it?" I replied.

"Tia. It's a self-portrait."

"I was hoping you'd say that. Jake, I think she's telling us the combination to the safe!"

He looked at me as if I'd lost my mind. "What the heck are you talking about?"

"Just follow me. Some of the details in this picture are pretty odd, right?"

"You're not kidding!"

"Odd enough to make me think they must have meaning. Look at her right hand. What's it doing?"

"Pointing to that weird clock-faced moon."

"What time does it show?"

"Five minutes to midnight."

I smiled. "Say it a different way."

He looked puzzled for a moment, then said, "Eleven fifty-five?"

"Good. Now look at her left hand. What do you see?"

"She's extending three fingers."

I grinned. "See? I knew you were smart."

"Stop being a wise guy and tell me what you're thinking!"

"Okay, let's *merge* what the two hands are telling us. Right hand, eleven. Left hand, three. Right hand, fifty-five. Right eleven, left three, right fifty-five. That kind of number sound familiar?"

His eyes widened. "It's a combination! Lily, that's brilliant!"

"I don't know that I'm right!" I cautioned. "It's just an idea."

"Well, it's more than I've had. Stay here while I get those chairs!"

When Jake returned, I put LD on the floor. He sat there, shaking his rattle and watching as we wrestled the picture off the wall again. It was easier now that we'd already done it once.

When the painting was down and safely propped against a wall, we mounted the chairs again.

"You want to try, or shall I?" I whispered.

"Your idea," said Jake. "You get to try."

I thought that was very gallant of him. Fingers trembling, I spun the dial a few times to clear the lock, then turned it right to 11, left until I went past 11 and stopped on 3, then right to 55.

We heard a small click.

"Bingo!" said Jacob as I pulled open the door.

Inside were two things: a wooden box and a small brown envelope. The box was dark and highly polished. The envelope was oddly lumpy. Jake lifted them out of the safe; then we climbed off the chairs and sat down.

"Box first," I said. I realized my voice was shaking with excitement.

Jake nodded and opened it. Inside, nestled on a bed of midnight-black velvet, was a silver disk about three inches across. A series of twenty or thirty symbols, none of them familiar to me, had been engraved around the outer edge. Within that ring were four circles, each about the size of a penny.

They had been marked with black enamel (or something) so that one circle was solid black, two were half black and half silver, and one was only a thin outline, so that the circle's interior showed all silver. They were equally spaced, with the black and the silver circles opposite each other. The two half-black circles—also opposite each other—had their silver sides pointing outward, toward the edge of the disk.

Mounted at the very center of the disk was a black arrow, something like the hand of a watch. Jacob put a finger against it. The arrow moved easily, clicking into place each time it pointed at one of the symbols.

"What is this thing?" I asked.

"Don't have a clue," he replied. "It's cool, though."

He slipped it into his shirt pocket—it just barely fit—and we turned our attention to the envelope.

"Your turn," Jake said, handing it to me.

Working slowly, I started to loosen the flap on the back.

"Why are you taking so long?" asked Jake impatiently.

"We might need to reseal it. I've had a lot of practice doing this with mail from social workers and teachers."

When I finally had the flap loose, I said, "Hold out your hand."

Jake did as I asked, and I turned the envelope over.

An old-fashioned key fell into his waiting fingers. It had a long barrel and a flat head, making the shape a little like a hangman's ax. The "blade" had notches cut out to match whatever lock it went to.

I felt a chill ripple down my spine.

"The key to the family mystery?" I whispered.

"I don't know about that," replied Jake softly. "But I'm pretty sure it's the key to the top floor of the tower."

"What's up there?"

"My grandfather's office."

"You don't mean it's been locked ever since . . ."

"Pretty much. Dad told me that Gramma Doolittle used to go up there the first year after Arthur disappeared. Then one day she locked the door and never went up again. He said he thought she threw the key away. I wonder if he was wrong." He smiled at me. "Shall we give it a try?"

12

(Jacob)

◇ ◇ ◇

THE TRUE KEY

"Wowza!" Lily exclaimed when we entered the guest room, which takes up the second floor of the tower. "This is beautiful!"

"Thanks," I said, accepting the compliment on Mom's behalf. She keeps the room in perfect condition, as if overnight company might drop by at any time. Lace curtains cover the window. The four-poster bed is topped by a beautiful handmade quilt she swapped a large weaving for. The inner wall is dominated by a huge painting.

Lily instantly went for the painting.

"Fantabulastic," she said, in a hushed voice.

The picture is strange, by most people's standards, so it was no surprise Lily liked it. It shows a huge mansion at night, the towers lit from behind by a full moon. A light shines from one window. A dragon is coiled around one of the towers.

"It was painted by Tia," I said.

"I wonder if it has any secret messages," replied Lily.

"Not that anyone has ever hinted at," I said. "Dad told me about the picture in the hall—I just never figured it out. Come on, let's try this key."

I had moved to the door that opened on the stairs to the next level. When Lily joined me, I passed her the baby, then inserted the key in the lock.

It turned easily.

The door swung open without a sound.

The stairwell was dark, but not so dark you couldn't see a scattering of cobwebs. I started up the steps.

"Wait a minute, Jake," said Lily. "There's something weird here."

"Huh? What are you talking about?"

"I'm not sure. Something doesn't look right to me. Wait, I've got it! Look at the cobwebs."

"So? I'll get something to take them down if you want, but there aren't that many . . ."

My voice trailed off.

"Exactly," said Lily softly. "There aren't that many. I don't know how many cobwebs are likely to build up over a quarter of a century, but I bet it's more than we're seeing right now. Someone has been coming up here."

"But not recently," I said, "or there wouldn't be any at all."

"Like, maybe not for two years or so?" asked Lily gently.

I looked at the stairwell again. Had my father worked out the puzzle in Tia's picture and found his way up here?

"Let's keep going," said Lily.

I nodded and led the way.

"It's glorious!" gasped Lily when we entered the tower's top room.

I had to admit she was right. The curved walls had big windows that featured a great view of the cemetery. Between them stood bookshelves crammed with my grandfather's books as well as a massive collection of supernatural and horror fiction from other writers and at least two hundred books on myth, legend, and folklore.

The centerpiece of the room was an enormous desk.

"I've heard about this," I said, going to stand

behind the desk. "After Arthur's career took off, he had it handmade especially for this room."

Ten feet long, the desk faced the windows and was curved to match the curve of the walls. On top of it sat a primitive computer. I guess Arthur had abandoned his typewriter a year or two before he abandoned his family.

A light coating of dust covered the desk's surface. Running a finger through it, Lily said, "If this is twenty-five years' worth of dust, then I'm Dracula's daughter."

The desk had seven drawers—a center drawer, right in front of where you would sit, and three drawers on either side of the kneehole.

"Shall we?" I asked.

"How can we not?" Lily replied with a grin.

We started with the center drawer. It contained nothing except the usual writer's tools—pens, pencils, erasers, paper clips, a box of staples, and so on.

The drawers on the right side were all empty, as were the top two drawers on the left. But when I opened the bottom drawer on that side, Lily murmured, "Pay dirt!"

Carefully I lifted out the items we had discovered: two notebooks and a sheaf of papers.

"Maps!" cried Lily, grabbing the papers. "I bet your grandfather drew these to help him keep things straight as he wrote more stories about Always October. He should have published them in one of the books. That would have been cooler than Frankenstein's pink pajamas!"

She looked at them more closely, then scowled.

"What's wrong?" I asked.

"The place names are all in some kind of code." She set them aside. "Let's look at the notebooks!"

The first one was facedown. I turned it over and felt a chill run along my spine. Written on the front in my father's clear, distinct handwriting were the words *Always October*. But when I opened it, I felt the same frustration that Lily had in looking at the maps. It was written in code! I flipped through it, hoping to find something I could read, and toward the end, I did. It wasn't part of the notebook itself, rather a handwritten note that had been slipped between two of the pages. The words struck my heart like a hammer:

The mystery calls. Though it breaks my heart to go, I can stay no longer. Forgive me, wife. Forgive me, son. I have done the best I could.

With love and regret, Arthur

"It's your grandfather's farewell note," whispered Lily.

"Has to be," I said, forcing the words past the lump in my throat. "But *what* does it mean? Is it a suicide note?"

Lily shook her head. "Hard to tell. The 'mystery' *could* mean the world beyond this life. But it could just as easily refer to some earthly mystery instead."

We opened the second notebook. It was also in code. However, even in code it was clear that this was written by the same hand that had done that farewell note.

Lily gasped.

"What?" I asked.

"I should have spotted it with your father's book, but it just hit me. Don't you recognize those symbols?"

I felt like an idiot. "That silver disk!" I cried. I pulled it out of my pocket.

"It's a code key!" said Lily excitedly. "This is what your grandfather was talking about—*it's the key to the family mystery!* It's got to be the way to translate those notebooks. Oh! I just realized something. Hand it to me, will you?"

I passed it over. Lily ran her finger around the edge, and I saw her lips moving as she counted the symbols.

"Twenty-six," she said triumphantly. "Same as the letters in the alphabet."

It seemed so simple. But it wasn't. The obvious answer was to match the top symbol to "A" and then just go around the dial matching the rest of the alphabet. We tried that with the first few words of my father's notebook and got total nonsense.

"It's here," said Lily firmly. "I'm sure of it. You know I love this kind of stuff, Jake. And I'm good at it. Will you let me take it, and one of the notebooks, and see what I can do?"

I hesitated. This was definitely a job for Lily's puzzle brain. But I didn't really want to pass it over to her. It didn't feel right somehow.

"Let me work with it tonight," I said. "If I don't get anywhere, I'll hand it over to you tomorrow."

Her face fell, but she nodded and said, "Okay, that's fair."

The next day I handed the code key, my father's notebook, and three of the maps to Lily.

"Take it," I said bitterly. "I almost broke my brain trying to figure it out. I hope you have better luck than I did!"

Then I went to the library and used a school computer to check the exact date of the coming full moon. I wanted to know in advance when LD was likely to make his next transformation. It was a relief when I discovered it would occur on a Friday night, since I knew that if LD did have another transformation, I would be too wired to go to school the next day.

Things got more complicated that same afternoon, when Mom said, "I've decided to go to the National Fibers Conference, Jake. I hate to do it, especially now, what with the baby and all. But it's my best chance to pick up some new commissions and we really need the money. Mrs. McSweeney has offered to stay with you and LD while I'm gone."

I blinked, then asked, "When are you leaving?"

"I head out next Friday and get back late Sunday night. Jacob? Are you all right?"

"Sure," I said. "Fine."

That wasn't true, of course, but I couldn't figure out any way to tell her that I suspected LD might turn into a monster again that same Friday night. When I thought about it, I decided maybe it was just as well Mom wouldn't be here. If anyone could handle a baby monster, it was probably Mrs. McSweeney. She was as tough as anyone I'd ever met.

Two nights after Mom told me about the fibers conference, something started howling in the distance after the sun went down.

"What was that?" I cried the first time I heard it.

"Probably just a neighbor's dog," said Mom,

looking up from her loom. "Or maybe a coyote," she added after a moment, plucking a strand of blue yarn from the pile she was working with. "I've heard they've started to move back into the area."

When I asked Lily if she had heard the howls, she nodded vigorously, adding, "Grampa says he thinks it's wolves. I like the sound."

Then she sang a brief song about the wolf eating Little Red Riding Hood.

The howling continued, louder and closer every night.

13

(Lily)

✧ ✧ ✧

MIST IN THE MAUSOLEUM

We heard the howling too, and I could tell that it was making my grandfather nervous.

As for me, all I could think about was trying to crack the code. I knew the secret was in that silver disk, but I couldn't tease it out. I tried matching every other letter to the ring of symbols, going *A*, *C*, *E* around the edge and then starting over with *B*, *D*, *F*, and so on. I tried doing the alphabet backward. I was positive, or at least almost positive, that the symbols matched the alphabet. But how, and in what order?

The one thing that puzzled me was that the moon

symbols—the two full and two half circles—would pop up in the written pages sometimes.

It took me longer than it should have to figure it out, but I finally cracked the code on Wednesday night when I realized that the moon figures were signs, telling me where to set the code key!

For example, when the black circle appeared in the notebook, I would set the arrow so that it pointed toward the black circle on the code key. The symbol in the outer ring just above that became *A*, and the alphabet marched around the code key in that order. When a different moon symbol appeared, say the half moon that bulged to the right, I would reset the arrow, and the symbol it pointed at then became the new *A*.

Even after I figured this out, the work was slow and painstaking.

It was also spine tingling.

I couldn't wait to report to Jacob the next day. What I had read was so sensational, I had a hard time keeping the top of my head from blowing off!

"What is going on with you?" asked Jacob when we got to the cemetery the next afternoon. "You've been twitchy as a mouse at the Cat Convention all day."

I took a deep breath, then said, "I think it's real."

Jacob scowled at me. "*What's* real?"

"*Always October!* I think it's real, Jake! I know your father thought it was real. He figured out how to open the safe, just like we did. He cracked the code and read your grandfather's journal. I don't know what's in there for sure, since I only had your dad's to work with. What I do know is that your dad started trying to find a way to get to Always October, because he believed that's where your grandfather went. He talks about someone named Mazrak. It's kind of spooky. He says things like, 'Mazrak says blood calls to blood' and 'Am I on the right track, or simply losing my mind?' and . . ."

I hesitated.

"And what?" demanded Jake.

"The last entry—I skipped ahead, because the translating is really slow work—the last entry says, 'Mazrak wants me to go to the cave.'"

Jake turned pale.

The next day in school, Friday, I watched Jake grow more anxious with every passing hour. He blew the math test, which was no surprise. I mean, really, how could a boy with a baby monster on his hands concentrate on how many quarters Eugene owed Penelope if she sold him thirty-two percent of her lemonade stand? Even so, it did nothing to improve his mood.

When school was over, we returned to the mausoleum, but Jacob was too nervous and restless to talk. Finally he said, "Sorry, Lily. I gotta go home."

"I understand. But meet me here tomorrow morning, okay? I won't be able to rest until you tell me what happened! I might even sleep out here, so I'll be ready no matter how early you come over."

"Do you *really* sleep out here?"

"Sure. It's very restful." I let out my best spooky laugh, hoping to get a smile out of him. He just rolled his eyes, uncertain whether I was kidding or not.

"I'll come over as early as I can," he promised, then added gloomily, "assuming I live through the night."

"I'll keep my fingers crossed."

I meant that very sincerely. I didn't want to lose him. I didn't tell him *that,* though. It was a little too mushy.

I also didn't tell him that I really did intend to sleep in the mausoleum . . . or at least stake the place out for a while. I was sure it was connected with what was happening at his house, and I hoped I could gather some useful information. An hour or so after I had supposedly gone to bed for the night, I slipped into my jeans and flannel shirt, crawled through my window, and headed for the mausoleum.

The full moon was enormous, silvering the dew

that already coated the ground.

I could hear the howling in the distance.

About halfway to the mausoleum I heard something else: a roaring and shouting from the direction of the main gate. Turning, I saw an enormous creature racing in my direction!

I know every tombstone in that cemetery, so it was easy for me to get a sense of the creature's height, and let me tell you, he was BIG.

Only he wasn't the one doing the shouting. That was coming from *another* enormous creature who was chasing *him*.

Look, I like weird stuff as much as the next person. More, actually. But I'm not crazy, and I knew the best thing for me at that moment was to get out of the way. But where? Were the creatures I had already spotted the only ones here, or had the whole cemetery been invaded?

I considered turning back and running for the house, but that would take me closer to the creatures. So I ran forward, instinctively heading for the mausoleum where Jacob and I had our clubhouse.

The door was open. The moment I entered, I knew things were as bizarre in there as they were out in the cemetery. Instead of being black as a coal bin at midnight, the place was filled with a thick, gray mist. The mist itself was laced with lines of flickering purple light. The air smelled clean, the way it does after a nearby lightning strike. I flinched the first time one of the purple lines touched me, but it did no more than send a tingle over my skin.

Terrified, but also excited, I groped my way forward.

I didn't scream until a figure stepped out of the mist, grabbed me by the arm, and hissed, "What are *you* doing here?"

14

(Jacob)

◇ ◇ ◇

WHAT CAME THROUGH THE CLOSET

As I sat at the kitchen table that Friday night, sneaking tidbits of food to Luna, I wondered if I should warn Mrs. McSweeney about what might happen. Problem was, I couldn't figure out how to bring it up without sounding like I had gone bonkers.

Maybe she would just sleep through the whole thing.

The thought wasn't all that comforting.

Of course, that was assuming it was actually going to happen.

I wondered if I would hear that voice again. Well, not if I had to go back in the closet to do so; I had no intention of doing *that* a second time. But I kept thinking about what the voice had said about the baby not being ours. I knew he wasn't ours, not really. But the note in the basket certainly made it seem as if he had been left on our porch by his mother. Was the note a fake? Had LD been kidnapped? If he didn't belong in our world, it would be good if his people could come for him, wouldn't it? Was that what the voice intended to do?

I hated that idea, and I knew Mom would totally freak out. On the other hand, we didn't really have a right to the baby. And what about when he became a teenager? They grow hair and get weird all on their own. Who knew what would happen if you added a monthly monster transformation into *that* mix?

These things were tumbling through my mind as—an hour after Mrs. McSweeney had tucked LD in for the night—I quietly set up the camera and tripod in the little guy's room. True to my father's style, the camera was top quality. By plugging it in so it didn't rely on battery power, then setting the image quality to a lower resolution, I could record for nearly four hours before the cartridge was full.

I couldn't decide if I should stay in the room or not. Part of me wanted to be as far from here as possible. Another part felt I should be present to witness whatever happened.

I decided to stay but moved the rocking chair next to the door, in case I needed to make a quick escape.

Then I settled in to watch.

Under the circumstances, I didn't think it would be possible to fall asleep. Somehow, I did. I don't know how much time passed before a noise woke me.

I rubbed my eyes, then blinked. The room was oddly bright. After a moment I realized the light came from the full moon shining through the window. At the same time a series of snorts from LD's crib brought everything back to me. It was monster time!

I hurried to the crib.

Green fur had sprouted again all over the baby's sleeping form, his ears were larger than ever, and he had to be two or three inches taller than when Mrs. McSweeney had put him to bed.

I decided I needed a close-up, so I went to the camera to adjust the settings. Though I tried to be quiet, my movements woke Little Dumpling. The baby opened his eyes, blinked, then scrambled to his feet—an infant monster in duckie pajamas that were splitting at the seams. As I had the sudden thought that I hoped he wouldn't outgrow his dia-per, he clutched the bars of the crib, threw back his head, and howled.

Answering howls sounded from outside the house.

A cold shiver raced down my spine. Then I heard another set of noises, this time coming from the closet!

I turned. A sliver of light had appeared under the closet door. That was disturbing, since I knew the light bulb in there wasn't working. Even more disturbing, thick tendrils of smoke, glowing red and smelling of sulfur, began curling out.

The doorknob rattled as if being turned from the inside. The rattling stopped, replaced by a pounding so fierce that the door bulged outward.

The smell of sulfur grew thicker.

"Up!" pleaded a voice. "Up! Up!"

LD was urgently stretching his furry little arms in my direction. In one hand—or was it a paw?—he was holding that green rattle. I quickly adjusted the camera to a wide view so that it took in both crib and closet, then raced to get the baby.

"Up! Up! Up!" he cried.

His obvious fear melted my heart, and I hoisted the little guy into my arms, desperately hoping he wouldn't sink his still-sprouting fangs into my neck.

"I think we should get out of here, kiddo," I said.

"OUT!" agreed Little Dumpling.

I backed toward the hall. Before I had gone three steps, the closet door burst open. Inside was an orange-skinned, red-eyed, fang-mouthed monster. Visible only from the waist up, the bare-chested, scaly creature was bathed in red light and surrounded by billows of curling smoke. Raising an enormous, muscle-bound arm, he pointed a thick finger at me and said, "I'm glad to see you were ready. Please bring me the baby."

Despite the harshness of the creature's voice, his words were calm, even pleasant. I might have considered doing as he asked, despite the way he looked, if LD hadn't locked his arms around my neck, screaming in terror.

My stomach twisted. If the baby had shouted, "Daddy!" I could have handed him to the monster in the closet with a clear conscience and left the two of them to enjoy their reunion while I got my butt out of there. But the way LD clung to me, howling and trembling, made it impossible to consider that.

I would have got my butt out at that point anyway, taking the baby with me, except my legs had stopped working. The only thing that kept me from melting into a puddle of terror was that the monster in the closet didn't seem able to move either. Well, that wasn't quite true. He was moving but appeared to be struggling against some invisible barrier.

"You will need to bring me the baby," said the monster. "He must return home, and I cannot yet enter the room."

I heaved a sigh of relief. I wasn't sure how long "yet" would last, but at least I had some breathing space. And even though the monster sounded like a grizzly bear might if it learned to speak, his tone had remained reasonable. But why was Little Dumpling screaming and trembling this way?

"Bring me the baby!" ordered the creature in the closet. This time his voice held a sharper edge.

"NO!" screamed Little Dumpling, tightening his hairy arms around my neck. He dug in his claws a bit as he did. "NO! NO! NO!"

As if things weren't bad enough, at that moment the window slid up and another monster thrust his head into the room!

That was too much. My legs suddenly working again, I ran for the door.

It slammed shut in my face.

Little Dumpling howled in new terror.

Ignoring the fact that I had missed the lamp and the back of the chair, I touched the doorknob three times and tried to turn it.

It was frozen in place.

I struggled with it for a moment, then pivoted and pressed my shoulders against the wood, realizing I didn't want my back to the monsters.

Looking to the window, I saw that the new arrival was deep blue. His head was bald, but he had a bushy black beard, so long that it disappeared from sight beneath the sill. A single eye stared at me; a black patch covered the spot where the other eye should have been. Looking directly at me, the newcomer growled, "If you wish to live to see morning, come with me!"

Though I was sure I wanted to live to see morning, I was *not* sure that going with this guy was the way to do it. Little Dumpling was no help. Furry face buried against my shoulder, he whimpered, "No, no! Bad, bad, bad!" But whether he was referring to the first monster, the second monster, or life in general at that moment, I couldn't tell.

The monster in the closet—the orange guy with red eyes—turned toward the monster in the window. "Do not interfere, Keegel Farzym! You know the baby is ours!" Turning back to me, he bellowed, "Bring . . . me . . . that . . . child!"

A terrible ripping sound filled the air as the monster thrust his right arm into the room, tearing through whatever invisible force had been holding him back. The smell of sulfur grew stronger. The monster's hand—enormous and orange, its long fingers tipped with fierce black claws—stretched toward me.

I heard a pounding on the door and feared it was

yet another monster until I heard Mrs. McSweeney shout, "Jacob! Jacob, what's going on?"

Frantic, I turned again, grabbed the doorknob with my free hand, and twisted with all my might. "Mrs. McSweeney!" I cried. "Mrs. McSweeney! Help!"

She stopped pounding on the door. For a terrible instant I feared she had fled, but almost at once I heard her chant some strange words I could not understand. She stopped, and I heard her try to work the knob.

"Jacob!" she cried. "Try it from your side!"

The knob still wouldn't budge. I wanted to use both hands, but LD was clinging to me so tightly, I couldn't put him down to try.

Bracing one foot against the wall, I yanked with all my strength.

Nothing.

"No, no, no!" whimpered Little Dumpling again as he tightened his grip on my neck. "Bad! *Bad!*"

That horrible shredding sound repeated. Glancing over my shoulder, I saw the orange monster thrust his other arm into the room. He leaned forward, stretching both hands toward us.

"Mazrak will break through in seconds!" bellowed the blue monster, the one called Keegel Farzym.

Mazrak! That was the name Lily had found in my father's journal, the one who had wanted him to "go to the cave." Who was he? Was he responsible for my father's disappearance? Turning toward the orange monster, I screamed, "What did you do to my father?"

"Bring me the baby and I'll tell you!"

"Jacob, do *not* give him the baby!" cried Mrs. McSweeney through the door.

"If you don't want Mazrak to capture you, get over here *now*!" roared Keegel Farzym.

My head was spinning. Mazrak must know what had happened to my father. But I could not imagine handing the baby over to him.

"Jacob, do as he says!" cried Mrs. McSweeney.

"Do as *who* says?" I screamed.

"Keegel Farzym!"

Mazrak's anger was growing, his shouts getting louder, his red eyes blazing with rage. Suddenly the window didn't seem like such a bad idea—or wouldn't have if not for the fact that to get to it, I would have to pass uncomfortably close to the closet and Mazrak's grasping hands.

"Hurry!" bellowed the monster at the window.

"Do it, Jacob!" cried Mrs. McSweeney.

I bolted forward. Mazrak lunged for me, but the invisible barrier still held him from the waist down. I bounded over the bed to the window. Mazrak roared with new fury.

"Give me the baby," ordered Keegel Farzym.

His voice was urgent but surprisingly gentle. Even so, I hesitated—until LD twisted in my arms and reached toward the bearded creature. Deciding to trust the baby's instincts—I figured he should know more about monsters than I did—I passed the baby to Keegel Farzym. He tucked LD under his right arm.

The baby almost disappeared beneath the monster's enormous beard.

Grasping the sill with his left hand, Keegel Farzym swung sideways and said, "Climb on my back!"

"I can't go with you!"

"You would rather stay here with Mazrak?"

Another roar from the closet, followed by more ripping sounds, banished my doubts. With a yelp of terror, I scrambled through the window and onto Keegel Farzym's back.

I had scarcely placed my hands on his shoulders when he leaped to the ground, which was about twelve feet below. The jolt of landing shook my teeth but didn't seem to bother Keegel Farzym, who immediately loped away from the house.

I heard a ferocious roar from behind. Looking over my shoulder, I saw Mazrak's face at the window.

"He's broken through!" I screamed. "Faster!"

Little Dumpling began to wail.

Keegel Farzym's pace was handicapped by the fact that he was clutching Little Dumpling at his side and had me clinging to his back. So when I glanced over my shoulder again and saw Mazrak squeezing through the window, I feared it wouldn't be long before the orange beast caught up with us.

I felt an insane urge to kick Keegel Farzym's sides and shout, "Giddyap!" Only I didn't know whether that would encourage him to run faster or simply to turn around and kill me. I sank my fingers into his beard—the coarse black hairs were as thick as my mother's yarn—and held on for dear life.

Keegel Farzym circled the house, barreled along the driveway, and turned onto the road. The night was misty. Wisps of fog, made bright by the full moon, swirled as high as the monster's knees.

I heard a howl, then another. Then a pack of wolves leaped from out of the darkness. I flinched, bracing myself for their attack. It never came. Instead they ran alongside Keegel Farzym, who gasped, "Welcome! Welcome, children of the night!"

A moment later I saw where we were heading. I should have guessed anyway. The cemetery lay dead ahead.

Mazrak was only steps behind us now, still roaring his anger.

"Geer-up, Hai!" shouted Keegel Farzym.

At these words the wolves turned away. Glancing over my shoulder, I saw them form a half circle in front of Mazrak. They crouched and growled, as if daring him to try to get past them.

The orange monster bellowed a curse. Then he spread his arms and began to chant. His voice, deep and powerful, gave me chills. After a moment he slammed his hands together, making a sound like a small explosion. Even as far away as we now were I caught a whiff of something unpleasant. The wolves uttered a series high-pitched yelps, then bolted into the darkness.

"You can't escape me, Keegel Farzym!"

The words were terrifying—though not as terrifying as the knowledge that if the orange monster managed to catch up with us, I would be the first thing within his grasp.

Reaching the cemetery, Keegel Farzym raced through the gate. He waved his arm. The gate, which had been rusted open for as long as I could remember, slammed shut.

Howling with renewed rage, Mazrak grabbed the iron bars and shook them like a prisoner in a jail cell. He shouted more words I couldn't understand. Orange light crackled around his hands, and the gate burst open again.

Mazrak was in but again Keegel Farzym had bought us precious time. Leaping over marble headstones, ducking to avoid low branches, my bearded blue mount wove between patches of bright moonlight and dark areas where that same light caused the shadows of tombstones to stretch ahead of us like graves waiting to be filled.

I could tell Keegel Farzym was getting tired. He ducked behind the Crawford family tombstone, which was enormous, and leaned against it, gasping. Still clinging desperately to the monster's beard, I held my breath and hoped Little Dumpling would stay quiet.

Mazrak snorted and growled off to our left. "You can't hide from me!" he bellowed. "I'll sniff you out, wherever you are."

Little Dumpling whimpered.

"Shhh," I hissed.

The baby fell quiet.

From the sound of his shouting, Mazrak was getting farther away. I thought we were safe.

Then Little Dumpling sneezed.

With a roar, Mazrak turned and came crashing toward us.

Keegel Farzym leaped to his feet. Only by grabbing another handful of beard did I manage to avoid slipping to the ground. He bolted toward the mausoleums. As he did, I realized he planned to go inside one.

"Don't!" I cried. "We'll be trapped!"

Ignoring my warning, Keegel Farzym shot into the very mausoleum Lily and I used for our hideout.

The door slammed shut behind us. Keegel Farzym pivoted toward it and chanted, waving his hands. A soft blue glow appeared around the doorframe. I had the feeling he was trying to seal it, to keep Mazrak out.

He turned again. The inside of the mausoleum should have been pitch-black. Instead, it was roiling with a gray mist, lit by jagged lines of bright purple that were shooting through it like tiny lightning bolts. Little Dumpling laughed and tried to catch one. I tried to stop him, afraid that he would get zapped. As I did, I brushed against one of the lines myself. It prickled, but not unpleasantly.

Mazrak had reached the mausoleum and was pounding on the door, his voice angrier than ever. Keegel Farzym started to run again. I braced myself for the collision with the back wall.

When it didn't come, I felt a new wave of fear. *Where's the wall?* I thought. Then, more importantly, *Where are we?*

The light shifted from the gray mist to something that spoke more of moonbeams in a forest. When we had gone a little farther, I heard a pleasant sound to our left. It took me a moment to realize it was a waterfall.

Clearly, we had left the mausoleum.

"Where are we?" I cried.

"Always October," panted the monster.

Always October! The statement was both thrilling and bewildering. But before I could ask Keegel Farzym to explain, we spotted something that caused both of us to cry out in shock.

15

(Lily)

◇ ◇ ◇

THE HIGH POET

When that hand reached out of the darkness and grabbed me, I shrieked and nearly fainted.

Then I realized it was my grandfather.

"What are you doing here?" I asked, unintentionally repeating his question.

There wasn't really time to discuss the matter because the roaring was getting closer. I pressed myself to the back wall of the mausoleum. No, that's not quite accurate. I *tried* to press myself to the wall. Only there *was* no wall. I just kept moving. That was scary. On the other hand, it meant we could still run from the approaching monster.

Grampa had figured that out too. "Let's skedaddle!" he cried.

We ran until the sounds were far behind us, then stopped beneath a huge tree—a tree larger by far than any in the cemetery. Mist curled around our knees as we stood gasping for breath. It was only then that I realized that Grampa had brought his pickax with him. He clutched it as if he intended to use it on the first thing that came near us.

As our breathing slowed, he turned to me and asked, "What were you doing in that mausoleum?"

Before I could figure out what to say, Jacob showed up, riding on a big blue monster. Clutched in the monster's right arm was a furry baby who I assumed must be Little Dumpling. Well, that settled one thing—Jacob had been telling the truth about the baby turning into a monster!

Not that by this time I had any reason to doubt him. . . .

"What are you doing here?" cried Jacob when he saw Gramps and me.

"Never mind that now," growled the monster he was riding. "We must keep moving until we reach someplace safer. I don't know who you two are, but you had better come along. You can explain why you're here later." He squatted and said to Jacob, "Slide down. I don't need the extra burden!"

Jake slid off the monster's back. The moment his feet hit the ground, the monster took off at a slow trot. By running, Jake, Gramps, and I were able, just barely, to keep up with his long-legged stride.

About the time that a stitch was blossoming in my side, we entered a boggy, foresty place. The mist was thicker here, and waist high. The ground squelched beneath our feet. The scraggly branches of the trees looked like clutching hands eager to grab and hold us.

It was wonderful.

The blue monster stopped beneath another huge tree. The ground surrounding it was rumpled by thick roots, and through gaps in the mist I could see that it was covered by fallen leaves painted in a thousand shades of yellow, orange, and red. The smell of October, which I love, was rich in the air.

I started to ask a question. The monster held up his right hand, which was the size of a small frying pan, cautioning me to silence. He was clearly concentrating. I realized he was listening for any sound of pursuit.

After a moment he nodded and said, "With luck, we've left Mazrak in Humana."

I knew the name Mazrak from the material we had found in the tower room. The very mention of it made me tremble. But the other word . . . "Humana?" I asked.

"It is our name for the world you come from," said the monster. Turning to Jacob, he said, "I tried to seal the gateway after we came through. If I managed it properly, Mazrak will have to go back to your closet to return to Always October."

"Do you think he'll go straight back?" Jake asked nervously. "My babysitt— My friend was still in the house. I'm worried he might hurt her."

"He's not after anyone else, but he *will* be dangerous if someone tries to stop him. His only interest is in the baby, and his main concern right now will be to get back here as soon as possible. Truly, I fear we have not seen the last of him." Turning to Gramps and me, he said, "I believe this would be a good time for you to answer the boy's question, which is mine as well: *What are you doing here?*"

"Suppose you tell us where *here* is first," snapped Grampa. "Not to mention what *you* were doin' in *my* cemetery!"

I flinched. Leave it to Gramps to talk back to a monster!

"My name is Keegel Farzym. I came to your side of the Great Tapestry to protect this baby." The monster looked at LD with astonishing tenderness. "I had good cause to believe there would be an attempt to steal him tonight—as, indeed, there was. I am glad I was able to thwart that. Even so, having the baby back in Always October creates serious problems. There, I have answered your question. Please return the favor."

Gramps scowled but appeared unable to think of a reason to refuse. Lips tight, he said, "I was sittin' at my kitchen table when I heard a big ruckus, lotta shoutin' and stuff. Came out to see what was wrong. Saw you and that other critter runnin' around and felt stupid I didn't bring my shotgun instead of my pickax. Decided to take shelter in that mausoleum, only it was all wacky inside, what with the mist and the light and everything. Didn't wanna go back outside, though, with the two of you still there. I was tryin' to figure things out when Lily here came stumblin' in . . ."

He shot me a look, as if I had some explaining to do myself . . . not only to the monster, but to him.

"I heard the ruckus too," I said quickly. "I came out to see what was going on, just like Grampa."

Okay, that wasn't strictly true. But I didn't think there was any point in getting into a discussion with my grandfather about why I was outside well before the fuss began. Besides, my brain was buzzing with the idea that Always October, which I had read about in Arthur Doolittle's stories, was actually real—and that we were actually there. I was trembling, and I honestly can't say whether it was from fear or delight.

Gramps picked up the story. "It was not more than a few seconds after Lily showed up before I saw *you* headin' toward us. My only thought then was to get away. So we started to run too."

"Actually, what we tried to do was press ourselves against the wall," I put in. "Only it wasn't there!"

"Right," said Gramps. "*That* was when we started to run. The missing wall was pretty dang weird, but at least we had somewhere to go. We had stopped to catch our breath when you showed up. So that's our story. Now why don't you tell me just what this is all about!" With a squint, he turned to Jacob and added, "Or can you answer that question, boy?"

"I have no idea what's going on," said Jacob, his fingers tapping against his thumb faster than I'd ever seen before. Turning to Keegel Farzym, he asked, "What are you going to do with us?"

"I wish I knew," the creature replied. He looked a bit cranky.

"Are you going to kill us?" asked Jacob.

The monster's laugh sounded like rocks dropping on a kettle drum. "If I wanted you to die, I would have left you with Mazrak!"

As if frightened by this, LD called "Jay-Jay!" and reached out for Jacob. To my surprise, the blue monster, who was nearly twice Jacob's height, handed the baby down to him. I could tell that it calmed LD to be in Jacob's arms. Oddly enough, I could see that it also calmed Jacob to cuddle him. I noticed that LD was still clutching his green plastic rattle.

Patting the baby's back, Jacob said, "Why did you bring us here?"

Keegel Farzym raised the shaggy brow that topped his good eye—the action looked like a giant black caterpillar humping up—and said, "We were being chased by a furious monster intent on stealing the baby and probably doing you great harm in the process. Did you have someplace safer in mind?"

Jacob shivered. "Not really. But who are you? Why did you save us? *Did* you save us? Why was that other monster after us? *What is this all about, anyway*?"

The blue monster chuckled at the barrage of questions. Then a serious look crossed his face. His nostrils flared and he stuck out his jaw, displaying his lower fangs, which were about two inches long and glistened in the moonlight. Extending an enormous hand, he said, "I am Keegel Farzym, the High Poet of Always October."

Jacob hesitated, then shifted LD so he could hold him with his left arm. He stuck out his right hand. "My name is Jacob Doolittle," he said as his hand disappeared within Keegel Farzym's grip. "Pleased to meet you. I guess. I mean, *am* I pleased to meet you?"

Jacob was blithering. I couldn't blame him. I mean, how often do you have to shake hands with someone who is eight feet tall and blue?

I cleared my throat.

"This is my friend Lily," said Jacob quickly. "And her grandfather, Gnarly—uh, Mr. Carker."

Keegel Farzym nodded solemnly and again held out his hand. His knuckles were the size of golf balls and he had rough pads on his palms. Even so, his grip managed to be both firm and gentle. Since he could easily have turned my hand to jelly if he wanted, that was a relief.

That handshake made me feel better about the monster, and about our situation.

He shook my grandfather's hand next. I tried to read Grampa's expression, but his face was blank, not showing fear, or excitement, or . . . well, not showing anything. I wondered what was going on inside his head.

LD squirmed to be let down. Jacob lowered him gently to the ground, where he began trying to grab the mist.

"As to your question of whether you are pleased to meet me," said Keegel Farzym to Jacob, "I would hope the answer is yes. Most monsters would consider it a great honor."

"They would?" asked Jacob.

I kicked his ankle to let him know he sounded more surprised than was polite.

Keegel Farzym nodded solemnly. "Poetry is very important in Always October. I am also the grandfather of Dum Pling, who is a very important child."

"He is?" asked Jacob and I simultaneously.

I resisted the urge to punch his arm and say "Jinx."

Jacob narrowed his eyes suspiciously. "How did you know we call the baby Little Dumpling?"

Sounding surprised himself, Keegel Farzym said, "I had no idea what *you* called him. Dum Pling happens to be his name."

He made it sound like two words, a first name and a last, which made me mad.

"You name your kids things like Dumb?" I asked. I probably sounded sassier than I should have, given the size of the creature I was talking to.

Keegel Farzym shrugged, an oddly human gesture. "In the secret language of monsters, *bob* means 'the sound of a large dog puking.' This does not make us think that when you name someone Bob, you are calling him dog barf. In our language, the word *dum* means 'sweet.' The baby's name, translated into your language, means something along the lines of 'sweet William.'"

I glanced at Little Dumpling. He was squishing

mud between his hairy toes and eating a bug.

"So what makes him so important?" demanded my grandfather.

"Are not all babies important?" asked Keegel Farzym. "Does not each carry seeds of possibility that may change the world for good or ill? But in more than most, this is true of Dum Pling, on whose tiny shoulders rests the fate of Always October— and perhaps Humana as well."

"You keep talkin' about Always October," said my grandfather. "But that's just a place this kid's grandfather made up for his stories."

"On the contrary, Mr. Carker, it is a place that Arthur Doolittle *described* for his stories, after he learned about it. And now you are here." Extending his arms, he said grandly, *"This* is Always October. Here, twilight lasts for half a day, the moon is almost always full, and the sun is rarely seen. It is the home of the folk you call monsters, the place that haunts your dreams at night, the realm that whispers to you when you remember something frightening yet wonderful. In short, it is the world you fear but cannot bear to stay away from."

Following the sweep of his gesture, I realized that until now I had been too distracted to notice that even in the moonlight the trees were glowing with all the colors of autumn. A carpet of leaves rustled beneath our feet. The smell of fall hung sweetly spicy in the air.

"It's autumnalicious," I whispered.

Little Dumpling blew a spit bubble and gurgled happily.

Looking at him, Jacob said, "If Little Dumpling is so important to Always October, how did he end up on my doorstep?"

"Ah. Therein lies a tale. And within that tale lies the root of our problem. Come, we have a long way to go before we reach our destination. Walk with me and I will tell you some of it—though the main part must wait until we reach the Council of Poets."

Scooping up Little Dumpling, Keegel Farzym started out again. Glancing over his shoulder, he said, "Stay with me. And if you value your lives, do *not* stray from the path!"

Jacob, Gramps, and I trotted after him. Thick mist swirled around our legs.

"Isn't this wonderful?" I asked, leaning close to Jacob.

"You're crazier than I thought!" he whispered back. Despite his words I noticed that he was smiling.

Silver moonlight filtered through the branches above us.

An occasional leaf, bright and perfect, fluttered down from the trees.

In the distance, something howled.

I shivered. Without saying anything, Jacob and I moved a bit closer together.

I was as happy as I've ever been in my life.

Despite Keegel Farzym's promise to tell us more, the High Poet said nothing for the next several minutes. Little Dumpling grew restless and squirmy, stretching his arms back for Jacob. Once Jacob was carrying him, he stretched toward me. For the next several minutes Jacob, Keegel Farzym, and I passed the baby around as we walked.

Grampa continued to mutter uneasily.

The path was soggy, but firm enough to keep us out of the surrounding swamp. Sometimes it became too narrow for us to travel side by side, and we would be forced to drop into single file. Usually Grampa went last, but a couple of times Jacob took that position. I could tell, mostly by glancing at his hand to see how his fingers were moving, that being last made him nervous. I think he was terrified some monster might rise from the murky water and grab him from behind . . . that he might disappear without the rest of us even knowing he was gone.

Jake tended to worry about things like that.

Here in Always October his worries actually made sense.

The full moon shimmered on the dark water and silvered the mist that wound around the twisted trunks of the great trees. An occasional ripple indicated some unknown thing slithering beneath the swamp's surface. Eerie cries sounded in the distance.

"What's making that howling?" asked Jacob from the end of the line.

"Just children playing," replied our monster guide. "Lovely sound, isn't it?"

"Yes," I said. "I really like it."

Twice we crossed paths that twisted away among the trees. They were scary but somehow fascinating. I found myself longing to follow them, to see where they led.

"Don't," warned Keegel Farzym without even looking back. "Stay with me."

"How did you know what I was thinking?"

Jacob and I asked the question at the same time. Another jinx moment I had to let pass.

"It was an easy guess," rumbled the High Poet. "Those paths are woven over with spells to lure you in."

"Why?" I asked.

Keegel Farzym shrugged. "It differs from path to path. Usually it's because something terrible waits at the other end, hoping to catch the unwary."

The strip of dry land was wider here, and Jacob moved up beside me. I saw him swallow before he asked, "What *kind* of terrible something?"

"That also differs from path to path," replied Keegel Farzym softly. "Best not to speak of it, really. Therefore, the last thing I will say on the matter is this: if you should venture onto one of those paths, I cannot protect you."

"Well, ain't that convenient?" snorted Grampa.

The High Poet shook his shaggy head. "It is ancient law, enshrined in rhyme:

"To each monster safe his home,
  Where he may set the rules,
  And none may therefore venture in—
  Not even to spare fools."

A few minutes later we saw a distant cliff. At the top of the stony height loomed a dark mansion. A single light shone in its tower window.

"What's that?" I asked.

"Cliff House," replied Keegel Farzym. "It is home to the Library of Nightmares. From topmost tower to deepest dungeon it is a very scary place."

Jacob leaned close and whispered, "If *this* guy thinks the place is scary, it must be downright terrifying!"

"I know. But doesn't it kind of make you want to go there?"

He sighed and handed me the baby.

A few minutes later we had to go single file again.

A few minutes after that I turned to talk to Jacob. He was nowhere in sight.

16

(Jacob)

THE DREAM EATER

When the trail narrowed once more, we were forced to revert to single file, this time with me at the end. We had walked this way for maybe ten minutes when our route was crossed by another of those fascinating paths. I paused to gaze into it.

As I did, I felt my fear melt away.

Without intending to, without realizing what I was doing, I stepped forward. The instant I set foot on the path, I was filled by a desperate need to explore it. What I felt wasn't mere curiosity. Whatever was drawing me on was something deeper, stronger, far more compelling.

125

I'll only go a little way, I thought, feeling oddly brave. *I just want to see what's down there.*

That feeling of bravery was delicious in itself. Fear had been so much a part of my life since Dad had disappeared in that cave that to finally be without it was like having a huge weight fall from my shoulders. Though I intended to take just a quick look along the path, then turn back, I wanted this feeling to go on.

As I continued, the path became too fascinating to abandon. I knew if I followed it long enough, I would find the answer to an important question, a question I didn't even realize had been bothering me. Twice I thought, *I really need to go back and catch up with the others!* But each time I actually tried to turn back, my heart ached with a horrible sense of loss.

"Just a little farther," I told myself both times. "A little farther and *then* I'll turn around."

Except I knew it wasn't true. Deep inside, I knew I had to discover what was at the *end* of the path.

The farther I went, the stronger grew the feeling that something wonderful, something important, was waiting for me.

It wasn't until the path led me into a large clearing that I realized what a fool I had been.

And by then, of course, it was too late.

Across the center of the clearing stretched a great web. Its silvery strands, thick as yarn and intricately woven, shimmered in the moonlight.

In the center of the web, its reddish-black body divided into two great lobes by an absurdly slender waist, was a spider the size of a coffin. Its eight black legs were thick as a man's forearms where they arched out from its body, but tapered down until they were toothpick thin at the ends. As for the creature's face, though you couldn't actually call it human, neither was it truly spiderlike, since it jutted forward on a solid neck and was framed by oily curls of lavender hair.

Arrayed across the upper part of that face were four enormous eyes. The outer two looked like basketballs made of black glass. The inner two, merely fist sized, had yellow-gold irises and pupils like a cat's.

They were gazing directly at me.

Beneath the eyes gaped two large holes—nostrils, I assumed.

Below the nostrils stretched a mouth so wide, it seemed the creature's head would split in half if it smiled too broadly.

The sight was so terrifying I could hardly breathe.

And that was before the creature *did* smile (the head didn't split, which would have been a relief) and murmured in a low, feminine voice, "Hello, little one. I was hoping you would make it all the way here. It takes a brave boy to do that. I *like* brave boys."

"Really?" I asked, trying not to stammer.

The spider creature's smile grew broader. "Oh, yes indeed. They're much tastier than the cowardly ones."

My heart began to hammer, and I knew she was wrong about me being brave. I wanted to turn and run. No, I *ached* to turn and run. The problem was my body had frozen in place, unable to move. As soon as I thought that, I realized it was not actually true; even without trying, I knew I could walk *toward* the spider creature.

"What's your name, boy?" she asked in her dulcet tones.

"J-J-J-Jacob," I stammered in reply.

"Ah, that's a lovely name. And I am called Octavia. Now tell me, J-J-J-Jacob, what brings you here on this beautiful night?"

"I j-j-j-just wanted to see what was at the end of the path."

She smiled again. I wished she hadn't.

"I'm so glad you like my path. I worked very hard to make it. I've found that boys, especially, can't resist it."

"Can I go now?"

Her laugh was low and musical. "You're so sweet!

No, I don't think it's time for you to leave. It's been a while since a boy came to visit, and I've been . . . lonely. Besides, you have something I want."

I was silent, too terrified to speak.

"Don't you want to know what it is?" she asked, sounding as if my silence had hurt her feelings.

I shook my head.

"Well, I have to tell you anyway. It's one of the rules. Come closer and I'll whisper it in your ear."

Though everything inside me was screaming that I must turn and run, run now, run fast, my body refused to obey my commands.

I took a step forward.

Then another.

Octavia lifted her first set of legs and placed them gently on my shoulders. I wanted to close my eyes and block out the sight of her. I found that I couldn't. I had no choice but to look at her mouth. It was surrounded by coarse, stiff hairs, each as thick as a pencil. In front glistened a pair of curved black fangs, about a foot long. Attached to the sides of her mouth were two things that looked like small arms.

Pulling me still closer, she said softly, "Even though you wouldn't ask what I want, I'm going to tell you."

I was surprised I could hear her over the pounding of my heart.

Drawing me so close she could put her mouth to

my ear, she whispered, "Your dreams, boy. *I want to eat your dreams!*"

I shuddered, and my mouth went dry with fear.

"Not just your night dreams," she continued. "I'm going to eat your other dreams, too . . . your hopes, your goals, your desires, your ambitions." She sighed, then said softly, "Boy dreams are *so* lovely. They're like green sprouts just unfurling, all tender and delicious!"

She drooled in anticipation, a dark-green trail of saliva that sizzled when it fell to the leaves below.

I flinched away.

"Don't struggle! That will only make it hurt. If you stay still, I won't have to silk you." She smiled and added, "Of course, we *can* do it that way if you prefer."

I was too frozen with terror to respond.

Octavia lifted the armlike things that sprouted from the sides of her mouth and placed them against my head.

She inserted the moist, pointy tips into my ears and began probing inward.

I was about to pass out when someone shouted from behind me, "Let the boy go, you monster!"

It was Gnarly!

The Dream Eater screamed in rage, then cried bitterly, "Can't I ever have a meal in peace?"

"Let him go, or I bury this pickax in that fat belly!"

Still clutching me by the arms, the Dream Eater scrambled up her web, moving backward with astonishing agility. Soon my toes were dangling about six feet above the ground.

"Don't think you can get away by doing that," shouted Gnarly. Pulling a pair of pruning shears from a pocket of his coveralls, he began snipping at the finger-thick strands that anchored the web to the tree at the right side of the clearing.

Octavia squealed with new fury, her green spittle flecking my face. It burned where it touched me.

"Drop him, or this entire web is comin' down!" shouted Gnarly.

"He's mine!" cried the Dream Eater. "He answered my call and followed my path and came to my home, and therefore by right and by rule and by rhyme and by rune he is mine, mine, *mine*!"

Gnarly clipped several more strands. The web sagged. Octavia screamed again, a sound like a handful of broken glass being dragged across a chalkboard. Gnarly grabbed a fallen branch, thrust it into the web, and began to shake it, bellowing, "Let the little idiot go!"

"His dreams belong to me!" shrieked Octavia. "And I am sooooo hungry. It has been too long since I feasted on the brains of a boy."

"If it's brains you want, you got the wrong kid!" Gnarly's voice was closer now, and I twisted in Octavia's grip to see where it came from. To my astonishment, he had started to climb the tree to which the right side of the web was anchored. He was clipping the silvery strands as he did.

Octavia's web sagged worse than ever.

"Stop!" screeched the spider creature. "Stop! *Stop*!"

"Not until you let the boy go!"

"All right, take him!"

With that, Octavia flung me away. My arm caught in her web, pulling a large section of it with me as I arced through the air. I landed hard, and it knocked the breath from my lungs. I didn't mind. I would have gladly fallen several feet farther—would have leaped from a cliff, actually—to escape Octavia's grip.

Gasping raggedly, I scrambled toward the path, trying to scrape off the clinging webbing.

It wouldn't come.

A cry from behind made me turn back. The Dream Eater had leaped to the ground. She was advancing on Gnarly. The old man held his pickax before him. Swinging it back and forth, he snarled, "Don't make me hurt you!"

Octavia laughed.

I wanted to run, I really did. But I couldn't leave

Gnarly to face Octavia on his own.

She continued toward him, waving the armlike things at the sides of her mouth.

Gnarly held his ground. "I swear I don't want to hurt you," he said, tightening his grip on the pickax. "Jest let me and the boy go, and we'll call it done."

"He came to me. He answered my call and he came to me and he was mine until *you* interfered. I let him go, as you demanded while you were destroying my beautiful home. But someone has to pay a price for that. *Someone* has to die!"

I knelt behind Gnarly and scrabbled in the dirt. The soil was soft and loose, so it didn't take long before I had a double handful. Darting to Gnarly's right, I flung the dirt at Octavia's eyes—not the black, glassy ones, but the bright yellow ones at the center of her face.

She screamed with pain.

"Now!" I cried. "Kill her now, Gnarly!"

"Don't be stupid!" snapped the old man. "Come on, let's git while we can. Move, boy. *Move!*"

He turned and ran from the clearing, me hot on his heels. I expected that once the Dream Eater had cleared her eyes she would pursue us, and I was gut certain that with those eight legs she could move with terrifying speed. I figured it would be only moments before she was right behind us, so I was surprised when her voice began to fade. However, the last thing I heard chilled my blood. "I cannot leave my lair, but do not think you are safe! Someone must pay for what you've done. Someone must pay!"

Suddenly her voice changed, took on a hollow quality, almost as if she were speaking from a deep well somewhere. Yet despite that it was distinct and clear, terrifyingly so:

> *"Hear me now, as I prophesy:*
> *For what you've done, someone must die.*
> *Till that happens, here you'll stay,*
> *So do not think you've got away!*
> *October holds you in its grip*
> *Till price is paid for homeward trip!"*

Was that just meant to scare us? Or did her words carry truth?

When Octavia's cries seemed sufficiently far behind, Gnarly and I paused, gasping for breath.

"Thank you," I said when I could speak again.

"Aw, hell, kid. I knew Lily would be upset if you got lost."

I felt as if I had been slapped. Changing the subject, I said, "Why didn't you kill that monster after I threw dirt in her eyes?"

Gnarly sighed in exasperation. "Don't you know it's bad luck to kill a spider? What in tarnation do they teach you in that school, anyway? And if killin' a regular spider is bad luck, can you imagine the bad luck you'd git for killin' one the size of your sofa?" He shuddered at the thought. "Come on. Lily is waitin' to see if you're alive."

Blushing with shame over having let myself fall into Octavia's trap, I followed Gnarly back to the others. Neither of us spoke of Octavia's curse, though it continued to ring in my mind.

I would not have felt quite so bad if I had realized that I carried with me an unexpected treasure.

17

(Lily)

◇ ◇ ◇

THE UNRAVELERS

When Jacob and Grampa emerged from that horrid path, I hurled myself forward and flung my arms around Jake's neck. I wanted to tell him how relieved I was that he was back. Unfortunately, all that came out was "I can't believe you did that! What were you thinking?"

"Don't blame the boy too much," murmured Keegel Farzym. "I should not have let him fall to the end of our line. Octavia's lure is nearly impossible to resist."

"You're burned!" I cried, looking at Jake more closely. "What happened?"

He touched his face and winced. "Spider spit," he said ruefully.

I shuddered. At the same time, Little Dumpling, who was in Keegel Farzym's arms, lunged toward Jacob. The High Poet knelt to bring the baby within reach of his "big brother." I let go of Jacob, and Little Dumpling climbed into his arms. He nestled there, pressing his face to Jacob's neck and whimpering a bit.

I went to my grandfather. "Thanks," I whispered, giving him a hug.

"Somebody had to do it," he muttered. I held in a little laugh. Though Grampa would never admit he was proud of something he had done, I knew better.

"I am sorry I could not come to your aid, Jacob," said Keegel Farzym. "But as I told you, there are rules about these things. Octavia's domain is a place I am prohibited from entering. Fortunately, the same magic that keeps me out keeps her in, so it is a place that she cannot leave. It's also good fortune that we had Mr. Carker with us. Otherwise . . ."

He shuddered and did not finish his sentence. Instead, he reached toward Jake, who flinched away.

"Hold still!" commanded the High Poet. He studied Jake for a moment, then said, "Hmmm. You'd better pass the baby to Lily."

I could tell it wasn't easy for Jacob to let go of Little

Dumpling, but he did as Keegel Farzym ordered. I watched his fear turn to relief as the blue monster pulled away the webbing that still clung to him.

When Keegel Farzym had removed all the webbing, he held it up to the moonlight, then began chanting in a strange language. The webbing started to glow, looking as if it had been spun from pearls. The High Poet selected a pencil-thick strand of the luminous, silky stuff and let the rest drop to the ground. Clamping the thumb and forefinger of his other hand just beneath the spot he held, he slowly drew the webbing through that pinching grip. The stuff sizzled and crackled. Shining drops of what I can only guess was some kind of magic began to fall at his feet.

After he had drawn the webbing through his fingers, the High Poet coiled it. He handed the coil to Jacob, saying, "This is incredibly strong. It may come in handy at some point. At the very least, it should serve as a reminder to stay on the path."

Jacob nodded mutely.

"Can I feel it?" I asked.

Jake passed the webbing to me. It was silky and smooth, and not in the least sticky. I thought how wonderful it would be to have a sweater made from such stuff. I handed it back. Jake seemed at a loss for what to do with it. Finally he lifted his shirt and wrapped it around his waist.

His tummy was cute.

Keegel Farzym nodded in approval, then said, "Let us continue our journey."

"Where, exactly, are we going?" I asked.

"We must consult with the Council of Poets on what to do next."

"How far is it?" asked Jacob.

"It's not the distance, it's the danger," replied Keegel Farzym. As if to prevent further questions, he began walking faster, requiring the rest of us to trot to stay with him.

After a few minutes we heard an odd popping. As we got closer to the sound, I realized it was caused by bubbles rising through the murky water and bursting as they reached the surface.

Keegel Farzym muttered something under his breath. When he stopped, I asked, "What was *that*?"

"A spell to keep the Verm from rising."

"The Verm?" asked Jacob.

The blue monster gestured toward the troubled water. "The Verm is the creature making those bubbles. They're farts, actually. Trust me, we'll be happier if he doesn't realize we're here."

When we were well past the lair of the Verm, I said, "Keegel Farzym, I think it's time you tell us what's going on."

The big monster stopped. A bat flew overhead.

His hand moving faster than my eye could track, the High Poet snatched the creature from the air and popped it into his mouth. He chewed for a minute, then spat out a bone, all the while staring into the distance. Finally he said, "Always October is in great danger."

"I'm sorry to hear that," I said. "But what does it have to do with Little Dumpling?"

"A great deal, if my theory is correct. Not only with Dum Pling, but with you and every human in your world. Not in the sense that it is your fault, but in the sense that you are all in danger too."

"Now what's *that* supposed to mean?" snapped my grandfather.

Keegel Farzym sighed. "How long Always October has existed is a mystery. We know neither where it came from nor how it came to be. Our Poets and Magicians have many theories. My own is that we monsters are a creation of you humans."

He spat out another bone. Little Dumpling, who at the moment was curled in my arms, snatched it before it could hit the ground. He began to chew on it, making little *nom-nom* sounds of pleasure.

"Here is my belief. At some point long ago, perhaps hundreds of years, perhaps thousands, human imagination . . . the combined imagination of *all* humans . . . became so powerful that it created a place to manifest and hold the fears that come with being alive. This was the beginning of Always October."

I shivered, and it wasn't because of the cool breeze that rustled through the leaves, making the trees seem to whisper to one another.

Keegel Farzym sniffed, as if checking the wind for any hint of our pursuers. Apparently satisfied, he went on.

"As the number of humans, and thus the sum of all human fears, continued to grow, so did Always October."

"So shouldn't all the monsters here be, well . . . fearsome?" I asked.

Immediately I wondered if I should have stayed silent. What if my question turned out to be an invitation for Keegel Farzym to demonstrate how scary he really was? (When I thought that, I realized that the first five letters of *demonstrate* are D-E-M-O-N. It was a weird thought but I can't help it. That's how my brain works.)

To my relief, the High Poet smiled and said, "Ah, but there is an element of fear that can be exciting, almost playful. Why else would human children so often ask for scary stories? Believe me, the terror is here . . . you'll find it in monsters like Mazrak and Octavia. But the shivery fun is here too."

Little Dumpling kissed me sloppily, then stretched his furry arms toward Jacob, who hoisted him onto his shoulders. Grabbing Jacob's ears, LD howled at the moon. It was a tiny, quavering sound, yet scary nonetheless. Even more frightening was the answering howl from the nearby darkness.

Keegel Farzym placed one enormous finger against his blue lips, leaned toward the baby, and hissed, "Shhhhh!"

LD made a spitty sound, as if annoyed, but fell silent.

"We should move on," said Keegel Farzym. "I will explain more as we walk."

Despite this, it was several minutes before he spoke again, and then only because Grampa said, "That was all very interesting, Mr. Monster, but you still haven't explained what it has to do with that baby fuzzball."

Pausing in his stride, Keegel Farzym turned to face us. "You are correct, Mr. Carker. However, I would prefer to wait until we reach the Council of Poets to deal with the specifics of that matter. For now, suffice it to say that something happening in Always October could damage, perhaps even destroy, the weaving that binds our worlds together, and I believe the child is key to preventing it."

I glanced at Jacob, who had cuddled LD closer

when Keegel Farzym said this. Turning to Keegel Farzym, I said, "What would happen if the weaving is damaged?"

"To be honest, no one really knows. I am leader of a group that fears it would be not merely bad, but catastrophic. We believe Humana and Always October are woven together by deep bonds of fear and imagination—bonds that, though sometimes troubling, are necessary for both worlds to thrive.

"This idea is rejected by the Unravelers, a group of monsters who wish to separate our worlds by undoing the Great Weaving that binds us together. We fear that if they succeeded in severing the threads that connect us, it would destroy this world even as it plunges yours into a vortex of unrestrained fear."

Keegel Farzym lifted Little Dumpling from Jacob's shoulders and hoisted him into the air, which placed him a good ten feet above the ground. The baby laughed and tried to grab the moon. Keeping his eyes on LD, Keegel Farzym said, "The Unravelers say it is time for Always October to grow up. They do not want a 'parent world' of humans who created us and need us. Instead they wish to be totally independent. My own belief is that we are connected at such a deep level that this Unraveling our opponents desire would, if success-ful, be fatal for both worlds."

He turned his face to the moon, as if searching its glowing surface for the words to explain. At last he said softly, "We are woven of the same stuff, we monsters and you humans. Our world may have sprung from your imaginations, but that very fact binds us to you, and you to us. Humana and Always October are like the warp and woof of a tapestry. You cannot separate one from the other without destroying both."

Lowering Little Dumpling, the High Poet tucked the baby into the crook of his arm and chucked him under the chin. With a rueful smile, he said, "Even if this Unraveling could be accomplished without the destruction of both worlds, think of what would be lost."

"What?" I asked.

"We fuel your imaginations, and you fuel ours. You terrify us, in a pleasant way. Really, some of your art and music are quite horrifying." The High Poet shuddered, and I wondered what art or music he might be thinking of. "We return the favor, of course," he continued.

"Favor?" snorted Grampa.

"Certainly," said Keegel Farzym. "A little fear gives life some spice. Why else would you celebrate Halloween as you do? Why else would people love scary movies so much?"

LD gurgled happily and blew a spit bubble.

Gazing fondly at the baby, Keegel Farzym said, "It goes both ways, naturally. After all, without humans, what would monster children dream of to frighten them during the day?"

He shook his head, causing his great black beard to swish back and forth. "I'm making this seem too light. Always October exists to provide an outlet for your fears. And you desperately need that."

"Why?" I asked.

"When fear rules, growth stops. A little fear can be like fuel, but great fear can stop everything . . . or lead to great destruction. Brave choices and bold acts move all good things forward. Without Always October to hold your excess fears, the old darkness that has never gone away, the darkness that remains deep in the human heart, would become a looming danger."

"What darkness is that?" Jacob asked, his own voice hushed.

"Fear of the unknown. The terror of what lurks outside the cave when you are huddled in for the night; the wondering about death and what comes after; the knot in the gut that comes from dread of the outsider, of anyone who is different . . . these things will rise and drown you. The worst of your wars come from fear. The terrible things you do to hold each other down, lock each other out, come from fear. Knowing that, can you imagine the result if Always October were to vanish and the amount of fear in Humana suddenly doubled? Tripled? Increased tenfold?"

I wasn't sure if the High Poet actually expected us to answer that question.

It didn't make any difference. Before any of us could speak, something burst out of the ground in front of us.

18

(Jacob)

SPLOOT FAH

When the ground erupted, I jumped backward in alarm. My foot slipped on a pile of wet leaves, causing me to land on my rump—which put me at about eye level with the pair of monsters in front of me.

They stood only about three feet tall, but those three feet were terrifying. Perfectly identical, they had green skin, goggling eyes the size of lemons, and pointy noses. Their fingers and toes were splayed flat at the ends, making each like a minia-ture shovel. These were tipped by fierce-looking black nails, almost claws. Both creatures had on tight-fitting brown garments, something like those things high school wrestlers wear. Their bare arms and legs were lean and tightly muscled. Their heads were topped with short brown fur.

Staring at me intently, curiously, they took another step forward. I scrambled back, only stopping when I bumped into a big tree. I pushed myself as tight as I could against the tree, bracing for their attack.

Moving in unison, they stepped still closer. As they reached for me, Keegel Farzym said sharply, "That's enough, Sploot Fah. Leave the boy alone."

The creatures spun around. "Why?" Their voices were high, but also raspy. "I only want to examine him."

"I said to leave him alone," repeated Keegel Farzym sternly. "That should be sufficient. What do you want anyway?"

"To get to the root of things!" cried the creature to my left.

"Which is my job and my joy!" exclaimed the one to my right.

Keegel Farzym sighed. "I'm sorry he frightened you, Jacob. He's harmless—"

"Am not!" they cried indignantly.

"All right, have it your way," said Keegel Farzym. "You're fierce and terrible. But admit that you cannot harm the boy as long as he is with me."

"Of course not," said the one on the right.

"I had no wish to harm him," said the one on the left.

"I was merely curious," they said together. "Something about him fascinates me."

"What are they?" I asked.

"Not *they*!" cried the creatures, whirling on me. "Sploot Fah is a he! A *he*!"

I looked at them, confused. "But there are two of you. . . ."

"No, no!" they cried, hugging themselves in delight. "There is only one Sploot Fah! But *inside*, Sploot Fah is so big, so wonderful, so amazing, it takes two bodies to hold him!" Flinging their (or his) arms wide, they (or he) cried, "Sploot Fah is a much of a muchness!"

"You're twintastic," Lily told the creature (or creatures), coming to stand beside me. "But that still doesn't tell us what kind of monster you are."

"He's a monster of ego," said Keegel Farzym wearily.

"This is not so!" cried the one on the right.

"'Tis a monstrous lie!" added the one on the left.

"Sploot Fah is a digger . . . "

"A tunneler . . . "

"A seeker . . . "

"A finder . . . "

"A lover of darkness . . . "

"And deep places . . . "

"Of secrets . . . "

"And hidden things!"

"Sploot Fah is an annoyance, a prankster, a lover of mischief, and a master of naughtiness," interrupted Keegel Farzym sharply.

"Yes, yes, that is all true!" cried Sploot Fah happily, crossing his hands on top of both his heads and doing a little dance of joy. "But Sploot Fah is also a helper, a holder, a kindness, and a friend when a friend is needed."

"You have not been around long enough for me to be sure of that," said Keegel Farzym. "All I know is that you love mischief . . . and this is *not* the time for mischief."

"Why not?" cried one of them. "You have a baby with you!"

"And babies love mischief," continued the other.

Suddenly they paused in their string of babble. They looked more closely at the baby, then at each other, then at the baby again.

"Oh my!" they cried in unison. "Is that Dum Pling?"

The one on the right: "Sploot Fah thinks there is a *story* here."

The one on the left: "This definitely needs getting to the root of."

"Tell Sploot Fah, High Poet . . ."

"What are you doing here with *that* baby?"

"That is more than you need to know," snapped Keegel Farzym.

"Fine!" cried both parts of Sploot Fah. "Do not speak civilly to me. I have other things to do anyway."

Sniffing in disgust, the creature(s) dove back underground.

"Do we have to worry about him telling Mazrak where we are?" asked Lily.

It was a smart question. I wished I had thought of it myself, but I was still pretty shaky from the way Sploot Fah had focused on me.

"I think it unlikely," said Keegel Farzym. "Sploot Fah is an annoyance, but he seems to be of good heart. Now come along—we need to keep moving."

The path forked and divided many times. We had left the swamp, though the transition had been so gradual I had hardly noticed it. Much as I tried, I could not keep track of the choices Keegel Farzym made about which branches to follow. Worse, several times the High Poet took us completely off the path. It was harder to walk when he did this, because the forest blocked most of the moonlight. Also, the trees were massive, and the leaf-strewn ground was ridged by their great roots—which were all too easy to trip over.

"Boy," muttered Lily at one point. "I hope nothing happens to Keegel Farzym. Without him, we'd be in big trouble."

Then she started singing "Cannibal Bunnies Go to the Fair."

It seemed like a bad song choice to me.

At last we reached a large clearing. At its far side a sheer cliff stretched hundreds of feet straight up. The clearing itself was a perfect half circle, formed by the trees at either end growing right up to the base of the cliff.

Tucked against that cliff, smack in the middle of the open space at its base, was a cozy-looking stone hut with a thatched roof.

Keegel Farzym led us to the hut. Handing me the baby, he said, "Stand here, all of you. And don't move. I need you to stay close to the door for what I'm about to do."

Holding Little Dumpling tight to my chest, I nodded.

Keegel Farzym walked about twenty feet to our right. Starting at the base of the cliff, he paced out a half circle that perfectly matched the larger half circle formed by the trees beyond him. When he reached the end, he turned and retraced his steps, muttering to himself and making strange gestures. On the third pass he took something from a pouch at his side and sprinkled it in front of him as he went.

When he had made five passes in all, he returned to where we waited and said, "Stay here while I go inside to dismantle the traps. Be cautious. Speak to no one. Above all, do not cross the line I just made!"

He opened the door, ducked his head, and stepped into the hut.

The door swung shut behind him.

After a moment Lily reached for the baby.

"Just promise not to sing to him," I said, passing LD to her.

Lily made a face, then started bouncing the baby and telling him how wonderfully strange he was.

"Good!" said LD. Then he patted her cheek and blew a spit bubble.

Gnarly, standing a foot or two away, muttered uneasily.

I gazed out at the dark forest. *How much, exactly, did my grandfather know about this place?* I thought. *How did he find out about it? And how much had my father figured out before Mazrak lured him to that cave?*

Ignoring my instructions, Lily started to sing

about the three bears eating Goldilocks for breakfast. LD got so excited, he began shaking his rattle. When the song was finished, he reached for me.

I was glad to have him in my arms again. Something about holding him—about trying to protect him—felt solid and right to me. That was the one thing in the world—two worlds, actually—that I knew right now: I had to take care of the baby.

That's one of the ideas that crops up in my grandfather's stories over and over again. You have an obligation to protect and care for beings that are smaller and weaker than you are. It's part of that "tik-kun" thing, I think. My mother believed in the idea, intensely. It's part of why we kept Little Dumpling.

Time dragged on. Was it possible Keegel Farzym had brought us here for some purpose other than saving us from Mazrak? The High Poet was a monster too, after all. Who knew how he thought, what he might be planning? What if he was going to leave us out here just for the fun of it? Heck, he hadn't come to help when Octavia had captured me, spouting some nonsense about it being against the rules. And what had he been doing when he was pacing out that half circle in front of the hut? Was that line to keep other creatures out . . . or to keep Lily and Gnarly and me in?

As my mind conjured up horrible fantasies, I

noticed a horrible reality: eyes had appeared in the darkness around us—*glowing* eyes that hung at all levels, as if the creatures they belonged to stood anywhere from a foot to twelve feet high.

Then I saw a flickering light that was definitely *not* an eye approaching. I pressed back against the hut. Lily joined me. Little Dumpling began to whimper. Gnarly moved to my other side. Clutching his pickax, the old man whispered, "Hang on, kids. We won't go down without a fight!"

Soon I saw that the flickering light came from a torch. The torchbearer drew near enough that he could be seen, then stopped just outside Keegel Farzym's line.

A flood of astonished relief washed over me.

"Dad!" I cried, my voice thick with joy. "Dad, I'm here!"

"Jacob! Thank goodness! I've been searching for you for hours! Come on—bring the baby and we'll go home."

"I can't believe you found us! How did you get here?"

"Later, Jacob. We don't have time right now. Hurry!"

I started toward him. LD howled in fright.

"Jacob!" cried Lily. "I don't know if we should do this."

Ignoring her, I continued forward. I had taken only three steps when the door behind us opened and Keegel Farzym roared, "Jacob, what are you doing?"

"Getting out of here!"

"Jacob, do not cross the barrier! *That is not your father!*"

I hesitated, frightened and confused. It had to be my father standing there with the torch, waiting to take us home.

It *had* to be.

But if it was Dad, why didn't he come to get me, instead of just standing there?

Keegel Farzym bellowed a word I could not understand. Instantly the line he had so carefully walked began to glow.

"Hurry, Jacob," called my father. His voice was urgent now, almost angry.

I took another step forward.

"Jacob!" yelled Keegel Farzym. "If you pass that barrier, I cannot protect you!"

Again I hesitated. LD was squalling now, squirming in my arms and reaching back toward the High Poet.

"Hurry, Jacob!" ordered my father. "I can't come to get you. Keegel Farzym has set a barrier against me."

"How do you know that?" I asked.

"I'll explain later. *Hurry!*"

Something was wrong. I don't know how I knew, but I was as certain of it as I was of the weight of Little Dumpling in my arms. I took a step back, feeling something inside me that had already been broken break a little more.

"Hurry!" snarled my father.

I took another step backward.

"COME HERE, YOU LITTLE IDIOT!"

As the words exploded out of my father's enraged face, his face itself changed. His eyes reddened. His skin turned orange. Clothes splitting, the man exploded into Mazrak.

I screamed but once again found that I could not move.

Mazrak lunged toward me. As he did, Keegel Farzym's protective barrier blazed into a wall of purple light. Mazrak struck it. A crackle of energy threw him backward and he thudded to the ground, howling in rage. But other than angering the monster, the fall had no effect; he was back on his feet in an instant. Raising his arms, he began to chant, his voice low, ferocious, and terrifying.

The purple light of the barrier grew dim, as if losing strength.

Mazrak walked toward it, still chanting.

How long I would have stood there, unable to move, I don't know. What saved me was Lily grabbing me from behind and pulling me back.

"Jacob!" she screamed. "Jacob, come with me!"

We stumbled and almost fell. Fortunately, Gnarly was right behind her. He put his arms out to support us. Then he helped Lily drag me to the hut.

At the door, Lily plucked Little Dumpling from my arms, then followed closely as Gnarly pulled me inside.

The door slammed shut behind us.

I collapsed to the floor, sobbing.

So I was not the first to spot the place's unexpected occupant.

19

(Lily)

◇ ◇ ◇

THE WORLD BELOW

Pulling Jake away from Mazrak was the scariest thing I'd ever done (at least, until then). I still have nightmares where I see the rage on that horrible monster's face as he realized we were about to escape him.

But in the hut I saw something that lifted my heart.

"Mrs. McSweeney!" I cried. "What are *you* doing here?"

Jacob gasped and looked up.

"Well, what do you think, darlin'?" she said. "I came to help!"

My grandfather snorted. "I shoulda known you'd be mixed up in this, Eloise."

Mrs. McSweeney made a tutting noise. "When a monster invades a house where I'm tending the young ones, I don't have much choice, now do I, Abraham?"

"But how did you *get* here?" asked Jacob, wiping tears from his eyes.

"*I* brought her, of course," said a sharp female voice from somewhere near my feet.

Looking down, I saw Luna Marie Eleganza the Sixth lounging next to Mrs. McSweeney's shoulder bag, which she had set on the floor. The cat extended a pure-white paw and began to lick it.

"Did that cat just talk?" asked my grandfather.

"As a matter of fact, I did," said Luna, not bothering to look up. "Do you have a problem with that?"

"I never heard you talk before," said Jacob.

"I don't, on our side of the Tapestry. Things are different here."

"What did you mean when you said you brought Mrs. McSweeney?" I asked.

"Oh, cats can cross over to Always October anytime they want," said Mrs. McSweeney. "That's usually what's going on when you know a cat is in the house but can't find it—he or she has simply gone to Always October."

"Of course, we don't generally bring our people with us," put in Luna, sounding a trifle smug. "But herself here is a bit different."

Mrs. McSweeney, looking serious now, said, "I've known who Little Dumpling was since the night he showed up on your doorstep, Jacob. That's why I urged your mother to go to that conference and made it clear I would stay with you. I wanted to be there on the night of the full moon in case anything happened."

"If you knew, why didn't you say anything?" asked Jacob.

"Do you think your mother would have taken me seriously if I did? I already have a reputation for being slightly strange. Besides, I've been sworn to silence about certain things." She sighed. "As it worked out, the situation was far worse than I expected. When I heard that uproar in the baby's room, and then couldn't get in, I knew things were bad. Then everything went silent, which was even worse. The door swung open, but the room was empty. I raced to the window and saw Mazrak running across the lawn. I snatched up Luna—"

"A bit roughly," put in the cat.

Mrs. McSweeney scowled down at her. "It *was* an emergency, dear." Returning her attention to the rest of us, she continued, "I knew they were goin' to Always October, and knew I had to get here too. But if Luna made the crossing from Jacob's house, I had no idea where we would end up. So we hurried home, because crossing from there brings us here to the Council Chamber, and that way I could at least warn the Poets about what was happening."

"How did you know Always October existed to begin with?" I asked.

"That's another story altogether, and a fairly long one. Right now let's concentrate on finding a way to get you home. We need to be back before Jacob's mother or there's goin' to be hob to pay."

She looked at Jacob appraisingly. "Actually, there's going to be hob to pay when your mother sees those marks on your face. What in the world happened to you?"

"He had an encounter with Octavia," said Keegel Farzym.

Mrs. McSweeney raised her eyebrows.

"Now don't give me that look, Eloise," said the High Poet. "I warned them about staying on the path."

She made a little snort, as if she thought that was pretty inadequate, then said, "Did you at least get some silk out of it?"

"A lot, actually," said Jake.

"Well, that's something," she muttered.

I was getting impatient with all this. "Can't Luna take us home?" I asked.

Mrs. McSweeney shook her head. "It would be lovely if she could, dear. Alas, it's a one-cat, one-person arrangement. I'm her person, so she can bring me here. No one else—well, no other human—gets to travel on that ticket."

Luna looked up from licking her paw. "I am *not* a ticket!" she said sharply.

"Just a figure of speech, darlin'," said Mrs. McSweeney.

"The McSweeney is right," said Keegel Farzym. "It is urgent to get you back, for more reasons than you yet understand. Nor would it work for the cat to take you back right now even if she could. There is something you must do *before* you return."

"What?" I asked.

"All will be revealed in a few minutes. Let us move on."

"Now just a ding-danged minute," snapped Grampa. "You're chivvyin' us along awfully fast, Mr. Monster. I'd like to know how come you didn't come out to git the boy yourself."

The High Poet sighed. "I entered the hut ahead of you for two reasons, Mr. Carker. The first was to disarm the traps meant to protect this entrance to the Council Chamber . . . traps that would surely have ensnared the three of you. The second was to work a *new* spell to prevent the enemy from following once I got you inside. This new protection won't last long, but it should help. Unfortunately, once that spell was in place, I could not pass back *through* the door without destroying the very protection I had just created."

"I s'pose that makes sense," said Grampa grudgingly.

"I don't care about that!" cried Jacob, still struggling to control his voice. "What I want to know is how Mazrak was able to look like my father!"

Keegel Farzym frowned. "That is hard to say. I do not know all that our enemies are up to, or all that they are capable of. Perhaps Mazrak spied on your family long enough to mimic your father's appearance."

"My father was gone long before LD came to live with us."

"I did not say the baby was the only possible reason for Mazrak to spy on you. Other things about your house remain of interest to us. Now come. The Council awaits."

As he said this, a door creaked open. A faint blue light appeared in the back wall, which I now realized was actually formed by the cliff. Dim as it was, the glow provided enough light for us to make our way forward.

We stepped onto a stone stairway that spiraled

downward. It was lit by that same blue glow, which made my friends look slightly monstrous themselves. The light, such as it was, turned out to come from a fungus growing in patches along the walls and on the ceiling. It was lumpy and wrinkled, and smelled like wet forest.

LD reached and patted one of the lumps. It burst with a loud pop, causing him to cry out and bury his face against Jacob's neck. Then he laughed, twisted in Jacob's arms, and reached for another.

"Best not to touch the lumnifung," said Keegel Farzym gently. "It's delicate."

"Want!" wailed Little Dumpling as Jacob pulled his arm down. "Want!"

I noticed that his vocabulary seemed to have increased since we entered Always October. Reaching out for him, I murmured, "Hush, sweetie, and I'll sing to you."

Jacob passed me the baby, and I began my song about the children the witch in the gingerbread cottage had cooked before she'd met Hansel and Gretel. It's one of my favorites—I have a separate verse for each child I've invented.

As I sang, I wondered whether the baby might turn back into his human form now that we were out of the moonlight. He didn't, for reasons we would soon learn.

The stairs brought us to a stony, circular chamber, about fifteen feet high and fifteen feet across. I had no idea how far underground we were now.

Ahead of us, across the stone floor and dimly visible in the blue glow, was another door, this one made of rough wood held together by thick iron straps. Nailed to its surface were various signs and symbols, some carved from wood, others made from metal. Keegel Farzym put his hand on the door, then spoke some words I could not understand.

With an ominous creak, the door swung open.

Following Keegel Farzym, we stepped into a huge chamber. It was lit by seven flickering torches, each burning in a different color. The flames ranged from a vivid red through yellow and green to a deep royal purple. Twisting roots—some fine as thread, some thicker than my arm—thrust through the ceiling and the moist earthen walls. Patches of toadstools dotted the floor.

I loved the place instantly.

Wonderful as the space was, the creatures who occupied it were even more fascinating. Five in all (or, at least, so it seemed just then), they sat in a half circle around a curved wooden table that was nearly level with my chin. Two more chairs stood empty. One, bigger than the rest and carved with strange designs, was at the center. On the table in front of that chair rested a crude hammer that looked as if it had been made by jamming a thick wooden handle directly into a chunk of stone. Beside the hammer was a flat rock.

A large tapestry covered the wall behind the table, its woven image showing a moonlit swamp through which prowled the silhouettes of mist-shrouded creatures.

Not one of the five monsters seated at the table looked like any one of the others. Even so, they did have three things in common: they were large, they were strange, and they were frightening.

"Pretty! Hello!" cried Little Dumpling, reaching toward them.

The face of the monster farthest to our right was hidden within the shadow of a large hood. I wondered if the creature wore the hood because it was too horrible to look at. It was the first to speak, saying in a low, surprisingly pleasant voice, "Welcome back, Poet."

My grandfather gasped. Looking up at him, I whispered, "What is it, Gramps? What's wrong?"

"Nothin'," he said, shaking his head. "Nothin', Lily."

The look in his eyes told me that he didn't mean it.

What was he hiding?

20

(Jacob)

THE COUNCIL OF POETS

When we entered the Council Chamber, the feeling that I had stepped into one of my grandfather's books skyrocketed. As in his stories, everything was strange and scary yet somehow made you *want* to be there. What really upped that feeling was the fact that I had already seen three of these monsters on the cover of his last collection of short stories—the one published just before he disappeared.

Mrs. McSweeney put her hand on my shoulder. LD gurgled and patted her fingers, clearly glad she had joined us. Luna coiled around my feet. For some reason I felt well guarded.

"You do not come alone, High Poet," remarked the slimy green creature sitting at the far left of the group. He was one of the ones I had recognized. Just as my grandfather had described, his voice had a gurgling quality. "In fact," he continued, "you have returned with a small crowd."

"That was not my plan," rumbled Keegel Farzym. "But when reality meets intent, intent is what gets bent."

"Tch," said a furry something sitting just to the right of the center chair. "The High Poet should not indulge in doggerel."

Keegel Farzym walked around the table and settled into that center chair. He picked up the hammer, thwacked it on the flat rock, and said, "I declare this meeting of the Council of Poets to be in session." He glanced to his right and sighed. "Ed, are you here?"

"I'm here," replied a gloomy voice from the seemingly empty chair next to the slimy green guy.

Keegel Farzym sighed again. "You know that the rules specify you must appear to us for the meeting to be official."

A grumbling sound came from the chair. Slowly a form took shape. It was so horrible that I cried out and turned away. I heard Lily gasp and noticed that even the other monsters were averting their eyes.

"Satisfied?" asked the gloomy voice.

"That will do, Ed," said Keegel Farzym. "But you know it was necessary." After another moment passed, he said to us humans, "It's safe to look now."

I turned my eyes toward the table.

Ed's chair appeared to be empty once more.

"Allow me to introduce my comrades," said Keegel Farzym. "In the chair farthest to your left is Bu-Blasian."

The slimy green creature nodded his head in greeting. Green droplets fell from his brow to the table in front of him.

"You can call him Bubbles," suggested the gloomy voice from the chair next to him.

"Shut up, Ed!" snapped Bu-Blasian.

Keegel Farzym sighed yet again. "The chair next to Bu-Blasian is occupied by Invisible Ed. He is called this because he spends most of his time out of sight, as an act of courtesy to the rest of us."

"You mean he's too ugly even for other monsters?" asked Gnarly, who seemed to have no idea of what the word *rude* meant.

"Hah!" snapped Ed. "*You* might think so, human. The truth is, I'm so beautiful, it embarrasses them."

Keegel Farzym rolled his enormous eyes. Gesturing to his immediate right, he said, "And this is Syreena."

I shivered. I had been trying to draw Syreena on

the first night LD transformed into a monster.

Unmistakably female, Syreena was nearly as tall as the High Poet, and very slender. She wore a form-fitting scarlet dress and had long, jet-black hair that set off her snow-pale skin. Her deep, hollow eyes were oddly beautiful. A pair of glittering fangs protruded from between her lips, and from her back rose a pair of ice-white wings that looked as if they belonged on the ghost of a giant bat.

"Pleazzzed to meet you," she murmured, nodding slightly.

Turning to his left, the High Poet gestured to the furry monster and said, "This is Bloodbone, sometimes known as Fang."

"Or, on occasion, Rover," put in the hooded monster at the end of the table.

Bloodbone growled deep in his throat. I couldn't tell if this was a greeting or a response to that last comment. Bloodbone didn't have a face that I could make out. All I could see was a pair of large, intelligent-looking eyes peering out from the mass of shaggy brown hair that filled the chair. Also a shiny black nose.

Between Bloodbone and the hooded monster sat a golden-haired woman who had only one eye. It was centered above her nose and bigger than a tennis ball.

Other than this, she was quite beautiful.

"I am Iris," she said, not waiting for the High Poet to introduce her. She nodded a greeting, causing her golden hair to flow forward.

Taking control of the situation again, Keegel Farzym said, "And at the end of the table is Teelamun."

The hooded monster nodded, much as Iris had.

Turning to look directly at us, Keegel Farzym said, "Step forward, please, and introduce yourselves to my fellow Poets."

Lily and Gnarly looked at me, as if to say, *You got us into this—you go first.* Swallowing hard, I took a step toward the table and said, "My name is Jacob Doolittle."

"And it was to your home that Dum Pling was delivered?" asked Iris, the one-eyed monster.

"Yes. I found him on our doorstep."

An uneasy murmur rippled among the Poets.

"Those marks on your face look fresh," said Iris. "Did you acquire them since you arrived here in Always October?"

I nodded, then said, "I had . . . an encounter with someone named Octavia."

Iris glanced at Keegel Farzym, and I saw him wince. I wondered if she, like Mrs. McSweeney, thought he should have done a better job preventing that situation.

"Before you leave, we will provide some ointment that will help heal them more quickly," she said. Her face grew serious. "While I am glad you escaped her clutches, I must ask this: Did she pronounce any, um . . . *curses* on you when you got away?"

I felt my face grow red, which made the burns hurt all the more. "She said someone has to pay for us getting away."

"Pay . . . how?" persisted Iris.

I swallowed hard. "She said someone has to die before we can return home. But it was just a threat, wasn't it? She can't hold us here, can she?"

Keegel Farzym looked grim. "I wish you had told me this earlier."

"Nothing you could have done, Poet," said Iris. Turning to me, she said, "Answer me this, Jacob: Did she say it was a curse or a prophecy?"

I thought for a moment. "Prophecy," I said at last.

"Well, that's better than a curse, at least," said Bloodbone.

"Yes," said Iris. "Let us hope that, like most prophecies, it is not quite what it seems."

"And you others?" asked Syreena.

Lily and Gnarly stepped up beside me. "I'm Lily Carker," she said. "And this is my grampa, Gnarly."

Gnarly nodded and wheezed something that sounded like a greeting.

"And how is it that you two are here?" asked Bloodbone, sniffing as if he smelled something suspicious.

"Grampa and I live at the cemetery. We sort of got here by accident," said Lily. Then, looking straight at Keegel Farzym, she said, "When are you going to tell us what's going on?"

Another murmur rippled among the Poets. Keegel Farzym lifted the stone hammer and banged the flat rock. "The girl has a right to ask. I promised to enlighten them. The time has come."

After a few grumbles, the others fell silent.

"As I told you," said Keegel Farzym, "our council is opposed by a group of monsters who wish to unravel the threads that bind our worlds together. Mazrak, the monster who invaded Jacob's home tonight and then pursued us back here, is leader of that group."

"But why do they want LD?" I asked, mystified. "For that matter, why did LD's mother bring him to my house to begin with?"

Keegel Farzym paused. When he continued, his voice was thick with unhappiness. "The baby's mother is named Meer Askanza. Her mate, Gergrik, is part of the group that wants to divide the worlds. Though she no longer dared to say so openly, Meer Askanza disagrees with this. She brought Dum Pling to your world to stop the Unraveling. It was a dangerous journey, but she undertook it to save both worlds."

Iris, the one-eyed monster, added, "As to why she came to your house, we are not sure. The original plan was for her to head for the home of the McSweeney. Obviously, something went wrong."

I turned to look at Mrs. McSweeney, who simply said, "Meer Askanza was pursued and had to change her plans."

Keegel Farzym took a deep breath and bowed his head. I sensed a deep sorrow in him.

"But why would having the baby in our world do anything to prevent this, er . . . Unraveling?" asked Lily.

Syreena fluttered her wings and said, "The baby vas brought to your verld because vile he is there, the Great Unraveling cannot take place. His presence is like a knot that binds the verlds together."

"Couldn't one of you come and do the same thing?" I asked.

She shook her head. "That vould not verk. It has to be the baby."

"This baby and no other?" I asked, holding LD closer.

"This baby and no other," affirmed Invisible Ed.

"Actually, we have no other babies like this one

just now," added Iris. "In fact, we rarely have babies of any sort. They do happen sometimes, but most of us just . . . well, *appear.*"

"Full-grown?" I asked, startled.

She shook her head and smiled. "No, usually in what seems to be our early teens."

I remembered Keegel Farzym saying that Sploot Fah had not been around long. I wondered if that was what had happened with him—if he had just appeared one day.

"Actual babies are rare," continued Iris. "But . . . well, they are another matter altogether."

Keegel Farzym nodded.

"So how do monster babies happen?" asked Lily.

I groaned. I so did not want a lecture on the "facts of life" from a group of monsters! However, Keegel Farzym's answer was not what I expected. Looking uncomfortable, the High Poet said, "This is where it gets complicated. You see, this babe is not entirely of this world."

Lily and I glanced at each other.

"What do you mean?" I asked after a moment.

"Sometimes there is . . . crossover between our worlds. It is not unknown for humans and Octobrians to fall in love. Even, on rare occasion, to have children."

"Are you saying LD is half human?" cried Lily.

The High Poet shook his head. "Not half. One-quarter. A generation has passed since the romance that led to his existence. But human blood does indeed course through his veins. That is why he appears human most of the time in your world. It is his natural aspect for Humana. That is also why he retains his Octobrish form here . . . it is his natural aspect for *this* world."

Bloodbone spoke up, saying, "Of course, here in Always October he will turn *human* on the one night of the month when there is no moon."

"Naturally," agreed Keegel Farzym. "But that is beside the point. The main thing is that his presence in Humana will bind our worlds together. As long as Dum Pling is *there*, the Unraveling cannot occur and the Tapestry will continue to connect us. But every moment that he remains in Always October increases the danger that the Unravelers will act. Therefore, it is imperative he be returned to Humana as quickly as possible."

"Returned and protected," put in Invisible Ed, his voice as gloomy as usual. "He is the last of his line. Should he perish—perish the thought—there will be no defense left against the Unraveling."

"I don't understand," I said. "If Dum Pling being part monster and part human binds the worlds together when he is in our world, then why doesn't it do the same thing when he's here in Always October?"

"A reasonable question with a simple answer," said Teelamun. "As the High Poet told you, the bloodline is not an even divide, and Dum Pling is only one-quarter human. That is not enough to bind the worlds when he is here. The fact that he is three-quarters monster, yet maintains a human aspect, is what makes his presence in *your* world such a powerful link."

It was only the third time Teelamun had spoken, and though I had been uncertain the first time I heard her, now I was sure: The deep, clear, pleasant voice was definitely female.

I nodded. "So we need to get him home as quickly as possible, right?"

"Correct," burbled Bu-Blasian.

Keegel Farzym shook his head. "Correct, but incomplete. To return to Humana is going to be far more difficult than it was to cross to Always October."

"And then, of course," said Teelamun, "there is— the other thing."

21

(Lily)

◇ ◇ ◇

THE SILVER SLICER

It wasn't just Jake who got nervous at that moment. I saw the Poets glance at one another uneasily, then heard an odd tapping. I realized it was Invisible Ed, drumming his fingers on the table.

Syreena was the first to speak. "The thing is, it vould be best if Dum Pling vere not allowed to transform for the next few years."

"Why?" I asked. "It's cooler than the Wolfman's new hairdo when he does!"

Syreena looked at me sharply. "For vun thing, it vill frighten the poor child more and more until he is old enough to understand vat is happenink!"

I nodded. "I see what you mean."

"That is not the main reason," said Teelamun, impatiently. "The *main* reason is that the energy given off by his transformation would enable the enemy to open a portal to your world. That is how Mazrak came through tonight. Unless you want another visit from him or one of his friends, you *must* prevent Dum Pling from reverting to his Octobrish self."

"And how are we supposed to do that?" asked Jacob.

Again the monsters glanced at one another, looking even more uncomfortable than before. Finally Keegel Farzym said, "The *method* of preventing the transformation is simple. However, there is a side effect that . . . complicates things."

"Oh, fer Pete's sake, git to the point," snapped Grampa.

"There is a . . . bracelet. If brought into contact with the baby on a daily basis, it will collect the Octobrish energy building in his body. With that energy absorbed and the bracelet removed, the rise of the full moon will have no effect on him."

"And what happens to that stored-up energy?" asked Mrs. McSweeney, giving me the sense that she knew certain rules about how these things work.

Keegel Farzym took a deep breath, then said, "There are two possible outcomes. The first is simple: If the bracelet is not being worn, moonrise will activate the accumulated energy and the bracelet will explode. This will be fairly damaging to anything within ten feet of the bracelet. It will also mean there is no way to prevent the baby's transformation in the month that follows. Ergo, the bracelet must be worn."

"Well, that ain't gonna work," said Gramps. "It can't fit the baby and then fit someone else!"

Keegel Farzym smiled. "You assume a nonmagical item, Mr. Carker, in which case what you say would be true. Fortunately, this bracelet has the quality of adjusting its size to fit whoever wears it. Thus it will fit Dum Pling when placed on his wrist, and also any human who chooses to wear it, no matter how big or small."

"Very clever, Poet," said Mrs. McSweeney. "And I'm quite sure I can convince Jacob's mother to keep the band upon the babe if I tell her it's a good-luck gift from his unofficial grandmama."

Jacob spoke up. "You said there are two possible outcomes. One is that the bracelet explodes. What's the second?"

"It's that the bracelet is being worn, and the energy is transferred to whoever is wearing it."

"And what will happen to that person?" persisted Jake.

"He will discover his inner monster," said Teelamun grimly.

"Only it won't be inner any longer," added Invisible Ed. "At least, not on those nights."

Jacob nodded. "I had a feeling you were going to say that."

"You mean the person wearing it will turn into a monster?" I asked eagerly.

"Precisely," said Keegel Farzym.

"That's slicker than the Creature from the Black Lagoon," I muttered.

"What difference will it make?" asked Mrs. McSweeney. "Won't the same energy still be released?"

The High Poet shook his head. "No, Eloise. Instead of *radiating* energy, as would Dum Pling if he were to make the transformation, the human who wears the bracelet will *absorb* the energy."

"In other verds, the energy goes in, rather than out," said Syreena. "Thus it vill be undetectable."

"You'll need to keep a careful eye on the bracelet," put in Iris. "The timing must be exact, as the window of opportunity will be small."

"And just how are we supposed to know when the time is right?" asked Jacob, who was now ghost pale. I knew what he was thinking—that since he was the one who actually lived with Little Dumpling, he was the obvious candidate.

Bloodbone shrugged. "When the bracelet glows, the time is right."

"Well, that's a relief," muttered Jacob.

Little Dumpling reached up and patted him on the cheek.

Grampa, Mrs. McSweeney, and I moved closer to Jake's side. As we did, I thought I saw a movement in the wall to the left of the table. I blinked and started to point, but whatever I had seen was gone.

"I never wanted a little brother, you know," said Jacob gruffly.

"Who does?" asked Iris, winking that single enormous eye. Though it was clearly meant to be a friendly gesture, it made me shiver.

"Little brothers can be a terrible annoyance," agreed Bloodbone, nodding his shaggy head.

"True," said Teelamun from beneath her hood. "But then, so can first children. And what would happen if parents never had *them*?"

I heard Jacob draw a deep breath. "All right," he said. "I'll do it. Give me the bracelet."

I was so proud of him, I thought my heart was going to burst. To my surprise, for the third time an uncomfortable looked passed among the monsters.

"We do not have the bracelet," said Teelamun at last.

"Well then where in tarnation is it?" asked my grandfather.

"It rests in the care of Flenzbort," said Bloodbone. "You will have to go to her home in Dark Valley to retrieve it."

He tipped back his head and unleashed a mournful howl.

"This will not be an easy journey," said Keegel Farzym. "However, Teelamun and I will accompany you."

Jacob's reply was interrupted by a hideous squalling from the wall to the left of the tapestry. Turning toward the sound, I saw a small, furry creature emerging from a hole about four feet above the cavern floor. It hissed and snarled furiously, as if it were being born against its will.

Once free of the opening, it floated across the room, twisting and writhing as it came.

"Hold still or I'll squeeze harder," said the gloomy voice of Invisible Ed . . . which was when I realized he must have been the one who extracted the creature from the wall to begin with.

A moment later he deposited the newcomer on the table in front of Keegel Farzym, who reached out and grabbed the creature with both hands. "Hold still!" thundered the High Poet.

The furry thing ceased its struggles.

"Well done, Ed," said Keegel Farzym.

"Half the credit goes to Lily," replied Ed. "I noticed her catch sight of something behind me. That's how I realized Squeak the Sneak was there."

"Spleeblebort!" spat the creature on the table.

I had the feeling this was meant to be a great insult, though whether it was directed at Ed, me, or the room in general I couldn't tell.

Now that Keegel Farzym was firmly holding the creature, it was no longer a blur of thrashing, squirming limbs and fur and I was able to get a good look. A male, clearly. About a foot and a half tall. Dressed in a blue jacket and brown trousers. The parts not hidden by clothes were covered with orange fur. Though he stood like a tiny man, his face was surprisingly catlike.

"What are you doing here, Squeak?" asked Keegel Farzym.

"What I always do," replied the catman with a hiss. He was busy straightening his clothes and barely glanced at the High Poet.

"You mean spying?" asked Bloodbone sharply.

"I was *listening*. I am curious. I like to know things."

"And what do you do with the things you know?" asked Teelamun. "Sell them to the enemy?"

"Can't a creature be curious for curiosity's sake?

I watch and I listen because things are there to see and hear." Turning to Keegel Farzym, he added, "Will you *please* take your hands off me? You are offending my dignity."

"I will offend more than your dignity if you do not answer our questions," said the High Poet gruffly. "However, I will let you go. I would make you promise not to flee, but I know what your promises are worth. Instead I will remind you of how fast Bloodbone can move, and how little you would like to be in his clutches instead of mine."

As if to reinforce the point, Bloodbone growled and showed his fangs.

"I take your meaning," said Squeak.

Keegel Farzym opened his enormous blue hands.

The little catman shook himself as if trying to remove the feeling of the High Poet's grip. "I hate being grabbed," he muttered.

"And ve hate being sssspied on," hissed Syreena.

"It's too bad you're all being so nasty," said Squeak. "I came to bring you some information I got by looking and listening elsewhere."

The table grew quiet.

"What is it?" asked Keegel Farzym at last.

"I don't think I should tell you," said Squeak, running a hand—well, it was sort of half hand, half paw—over his head.

Keegel Farzym's fingers twitched, as if he were longing to squeeze the information out of the creature.

At that point Luna leaped onto the table and stood next to Squeak. Whisking her enormous plume of a tail, she said coyly, "Not even for me, big boy?"

Squeak blinked and looked flustered.

"I'd consider it a personal favor," said Luna, coiling around him.

"R-r-r-really?"

"Uh-huh."

"All right. I wanted to tell you anyway," he said, looking at Keegel Farzym.

"Why?" asked the High Poet.

"Because I'm scared."

"And what could possibly scare the fearless Squeak?" asked Teelamun.

"The end of the world," he said, his voice soft.

"What do you mean?" asked Keegel Farzym.

"I know what the Unravelers plan to do. I've seen their machine."

Jacob, Grampa, Mrs. McSweeney, and I all stepped closer.

"Their machine?" Jacob asked.

Squeak nodded. "They call it the Silver Slicer. They plan to use it to sunder the Great Tapestry so that Humana and Always October will be forever divided. Poets, I fear as you do that this would mean the end of us all. That is why I came to tell you of it . . . and would have done so sooner had I not been treated so rudely!"

"Thank you," said Keegel Farzym gravely. "I regret your rough reception. Had you revealed yourself at once, rather than spying while we spoke, your greeting would have been somewhat more gentle."

"I am what I am," said Squeak, scratching behind his somewhat pointy ear with his right paw-hand. "Now listen, there is more you must know. The reason the Unravelers are so anxious to get Dum Pling is not simply because his presence in Humana will help bind the worlds."

"What other reason could there be?" asked Teelamun.

Squeak looked uncomfortable. Taking a deep breath, he said, "They plan to use him to help power their machine."

A gasp rose from the Poets. I heard Jacob cry out beside me.

"So it is even more urgent than you thought that Dum Pling be returned to Humana," continued Squeak. "And it must be done quickly. They plan to act at the dark of the moon and will do everything they can to obtain the baby before that time."

"But that is only two nights away!" gasped Iris.

"Why do you think I risked my life to come tell you?"

Keegel Farzym nodded. "You have our thanks, Squeak." Turning to us, he said, "We must move quickly. The baby is in even greater danger than we imagined. Therefore, I now ask: Jacob Doolittle, will you accept this burden, to obtain the bracelet and shield the child?"

Jacob looked at Keegel Farzym, then at each of the other monsters (except Invisible Ed, of course).

They stared back at him with intent, worried eyes.

He looked down at Little Dumpling. I couldn't tell what he was thinking, but at last he looked up and said, "I accept it willingly."

I felt a little thrill of pride in my friend.

The monsters stood, placed their hands on their foreheads, and bent forward. "The Council of Poets salutes you!" they said in unison.

They resumed their seats, save Keegel Farzym, who said solemnly, "This burden will be heavy for Jacob to bear. Therefore we now ask of you, his traveling companions: Will you help this boy as he guards the Woven Worlds? Will you vow to care for and protect this baby and to find ways for Jacob, his Prime Protector, to remain safe on the nights of transformation?"

"Now just a ding-danged minute!" said Grampa. "Why don't you tell us what the boy is gonna turn into first?"

"Alas, Mr. Carker, that is a mystery that will only be resolved on the night of his first transformation," said Keegel Farzym.

"Each man has an inner monster all his own," burbled Bu-Blasian.

"Each voman, too, you silly, soggy sexist," hissed Syreena.

"Sounds like buyin' a pig in a poke to me," muttered Gramps.

It sounded to me as if Jacob would be far from the first human to turn into a monster, which was interesting. As I was thinking about this, Teelamun rose from her seat and said, "Abraham, I ask you personally: Will you help? This is a matter of great urgency."

My grandfather glared at the hooded monster. "How do you know my name?"

"You know the answer to that," she replied gently. "I've been watching your face. You've known since you entered this chamber."

Grampa blanched and his lips trembled.

With a sigh, Teelamun raised her long, slender hands—so pale they were almost bone white—and lifted her hood.

22

(Jacob)

THE BATTLE FOR THE BABY

As Teelamun revealed her face, Lily's grandfather made a noise that sounded a little like a sigh, a little like a whimper.

As for me, I gasped so loudly it made LD flinch. But how else should I have reacted to seeing Tia LaMontagne, my grandfather's first wife . . . the oddly beautiful woman whose portrait hung in my upstairs hallway?

Despite the years that had passed since she'd painted that self-portrait, Tia had aged but little. The main change was a pair of Bride-of-Frankenstein white streaks that shot through her flame-red hair.

"Is it really you?" whispered Gnarly. His voice held so much pain, I actually felt sorry for him, something I would not have thought possible.

"Yes, Abraham," she said softly, "it's me."

"But what . . . how . . ." His voice caught.

Lily moved to his side to take his hand.

"This is not the time," said Teelamun. "If we survive what is to come, I will explain everything when we have some privacy. For now, for the sake of old friendship and more, I ask your help in caring for Dum Pling." She lifted her head for a moment, then said softly, "He is my grandchild, Abraham."

Gnarly closed his eyes and swallowed hard. I wasn't sure, but I thought I saw a tear trickle from beneath one of those closed lids. He started to ask a question, then stopped himself. After a long moment he said gruffly, "I'll help."

"I now ask this pledge of all of you," said Keegel Farzym. "Do you swear to help Jacob guard and guide the baby, help him protect the bracelet, and help him remain safe and undetected on the nights of his transformation?"

Though I was terrified by what I had committed myself to, when Gnarly, Lily, Mrs. McSweeney, and even Luna said in unison, "We do!" I felt a surge of warmth and of being not alone in a way I had not experienced since my father's disappearance.

Again, the other monsters rose. (I couldn't see Invisible Ed, but I assume he stood, too.) Making that same gesture of hands to foreheads, they bowed and said, "Humans, we salute you!"

When they had resumed their seats, Keegel Farzym said, "We must return you to Humana as quickly as possible. Alas, the only way to return now is through the Library of Nightmares."

"Poet!" cried Squeak. "You can't do that! The path is far too dangerous!"

"Can you suggest another route once they leave Dark Valley?" asked Syreena sharply.

The little catman thought for a moment, then shook his head.

"Then the route is clear," said Invisible Ed, his voice even gloomier than usual. "They must take the tunnel behind the tapestry to depart our chamber. Doing so will bring them to the surface a mile or so from the Black Bridge of Doom."

"Black Bridge of Doom?" I asked. My voice quavered and my fingers tapped against my thumb so fast, they were almost a blur.

"Doom is the name of the river it crosses," said Syreena, waving a careless hand. "It's poetic, really. Hardly anyvun dies there these days."

"On the far side of the River Doom you must pass through the Forest of the Lost," said Bloodbone.

"Another poetic name, I assume?" said Luna, who had leaped down from the table and was now twining around my feet.

"Very witty, kitty," said Iris. "However, I regret to tell you that this is a place where people really do get lost. *Seriously* lost. Most never come out," she added, a huge tear rolling out of her enormous eye.

"We will need to be particularly careful there," said Keegel Farzym, looking directly at me. "I presume I do not need to mention that you must never leave the path?"

I blushed and nodded earnestly.

"After that you will make your way to Teardrop Hill," said Bu-Blasian.

"Which I suppose is shaped like a Teardrop?" asked Gnarly.

"Actually, it is," replied Syreena, fluttering her ghostly wings just a bit. "However, you will not be able to climb it. To reach the other side, you must instead go under, via the Tunnel of Tears. Doing so vill bring you to the Veil of Tears, vhich is in the exact center of the tunnel."

"I thought a vale was a valley," said Lily. "How can there be a valley in a tunnel?"

"You are thinking of another vord, though it is pronounced in the same way. *This* veil is the kind that obscures, as a veil vorn over the face. You vill understand vhen you come to it. Vithin, you vill meet the King or Queen of Sorrows. You must listen to that monster's story before you vill be allowed to pass."

"Assuming you make it through the tunnel, you will have reached Dark Valley, where Flenzbort lives," said Iris.

"Who, or what, is Flenzbort?" I asked.

"Flenzbort is a trickster," said Teelamun. "She will not—cannot, actually—grant the bracelet until we pass a test. In many ways this will be our greatest challenge. Luckily, Keegel Farzym and I will be with you."

The High Poet nodded. "Once we have obtained the bracelet, our journey will be nearly over. On the far side of the valley is the path that leads up the back side of Nightmare Hill. At its top stands Cliff House, home to the Library of Nightmares. As I'm sure you will recall, we saw it in the distance on the way here."

Leaning close to me, Lily whispered, "We're like the Fellowship of the Ring!"

"More like the Fellowship of the Dumpling," I muttered back.

LD reached up and bopped me with his rattle.

"We will send a message ahead for the librarian to prepare a portal to take you back to Humana," said Keegel Farzym. "With luck, we will—"

His next words were interrupted by a terrible roar. Spinning around, I saw Mazrak burst into the underground chamber. He wasn't alone. Behind him surged a dozen of the most terrifying creatures I had ever seen—except I *had* seen some of them before, on the covers of magazines featuring stories by my grandfather.

LD buried his face against my neck, whimpering in terror.

Without a word Lily moved in front of me, as if to say the monsters would have to get through her before they could touch the baby.

Gnarly and Mrs. McSweeney flanked me. Gnarly held his pickax at the ready. Mrs. McSweeney reached into her shoulder bag and pulled out a knitting needle. At least, it looked like a knitting needle. But it was glowing, which I had never seen a knitting needle do before. Luna stood in front of her, back arched, tail abristle, hissing at the invaders.

Mazrak chuckled. "Your bravery is touching, humans, if somewhat foolish. But our fight is not with you. It is with those who stand behind you." Looking above our heads, he said fiercely, "This has gone on long enough, Keegel Farzym. You have no right to keep that baby. Give him to us or we will take him. Either way, it is time for this to end."

Though Mazrak spoke to Keegel Farzym, it was Teelamun who answered. "That baby had *two* parents. The other was my daughter, who risked all to take the child *away* from those who, through insane pride, would destroy Always October."

"You speak with a petty fear that ill becomes a monster," sneered Mazrak.

"And you act with a recklessness that does not become anyone who is more than beast!" snapped Teelamun. "Meer Askanza's fate is still unknown, but we will not dishonor her sacrifice with surrender."

"Enough!" roared Mazrak. "I'll have the child."

LD screamed and buried his face against me again, clutching my shoulders with his furry little arms. I turned toward the Poets. Clutching LD, I dropped to the floor, then used my elbows to hold myself up so I wouldn't squash him while I rolled under the table.

I was relieved to discover that Lily was right beside me.

As we went down, the Council of Poets rose.

"You dare, Mazrak?" Syreena cried. "You dare come *here*, to invade this place so long forbidden you?"

Suddenly she was in front of the table instead of behind it. Her ghostly wings were still beating when she landed. To my astonishment she shot a gout of flame toward the invading monsters.

"Wow," whispered Lily. "I wish I could do that! I wonder if it came out of her mouth or her eyes."

The battle erupted. Howling like a wolf, Bloodbone leaped over the table. Snapping and snarling, the furry creature shot past Gnarly and Mrs. McSweeney and launched himself at Mazrak's throat. The enormous orange monster swatted him away, but almost immediately Bloodbone was on his feet again, sinking his fangs into the thigh of one of the monsters just behind Mazrak. That monster—purple, half naked, and somewhat trollish looking—screamed and began to beat at its attacker.

Scooting around Mrs. McSweeney, Bu-Blasian held out his hands. Somehow he made a slick of water on the floor in front of Mazrak and his fellow attackers, causing them to slip and grab at each other for support.

Even Squeak joined the battle, leaping atop a monster's head and hissing as he clawed at the creature's face.

Lily and I inched back until we were on the far side of the table, then raised our heads just enough to watch what was happening. Iris now stood on the table directly in front of us. As we watched, she plucked that huge eye from the center of her brow and lifted it above her head. Aiming it at the invading monsters, she cried, "I spy . . . good-bye!"

She squeezed, and a beam of blue light shot out of the eye. It sizzled through the air and struck one of the attackers. The creature screamed and fell to the floor, writhing inside a bloodred force field.

Iris jammed her eye back into her forehead, leaped from the table, and charged into the battle.

Gnarly swung his pickax left and right, holding back a tall green monster whose long arms could not reach him past the arc of the makeshift weapon. Even more startling, with a shake of her knitting needle Mrs. McSweeney blasted out a bolt of energy that sent one of the attacking monsters smashing far against the wall.

"Take that, ya big gobdaw!" she cried triumphantly.

Suddenly, and for no seeming reason, the monster battling Gnarly fell over backward. Gnarly looked startled, then even *more* startled, then nodded and turned and sped back toward the table. Almost instantly Mrs. McSweeney joined him. Soon the two of them were under the table with Lily and me.

"What knocked that monster over, Grampa?" Lily asked.

"That Invisible Ed guy did it. Then he told us to git back here and he'd help us escape."

"Shouldn't we help the Poets?" she asked.

Mrs. McSweeney shook her head. "Right now the most important thing is getting Little Dumpling out of here."

I listened to all this as I continued to watch the battle. Keegel Farzym grappled hand to hand with a monster who matched him in height. However, the creature had four arms, and thus four hands, which put the High Poet at a definite disadvantage. Turning his head toward us, Keegel Farzym bellowed, "Jacob! Get the baby out *now*!"

"How?" I cried.

The answer came not from Keegel Farzym but from a whisper beside my ear: "Follow me!"

It took me longer than it should have to realize it was Invisible Ed speaking.

"How?" I whispered back. "I can't see you!"

With a sigh, Ed grabbed my arm and hissed, "Go to the tapestry!"

As the other Poets formed a line of defense, we crawled toward the weaving. I had to keep one arm scooped under LD in order to support his back while he clung to my neck, so I was doing a one-handed crawl, which slowed us down some.

When we reached the tapestry, Ed began to chant. Though his words were drowned out by the roars, growls, bellows, and shrieks that filled the air behind us, they must have worked, because the image on the fabric shivered, then vanished.

In its place was a glowing blue wall.

"Go through!" said Ed urgently. "Now!"

Glancing back, I saw the High Poet still struggling to hold off the four-armed monster. "Go!" he roared when he saw my hesitation.

"The humans are getting away!" bellowed Mazrak. "And they've got the baby! Press forward! *Press forward!*"

Clutching LD to my chest, I plunged through the blue wall.

23

(Lily)

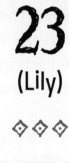

◇ ◇ ◇

TUNNELS

Spurred on by Mazrak's cry of rage, I followed Jake. As soon as I touched the blue wall, my skin tingled all over. I felt myself being pulled forward, as if caught by a giant vacuum cleaner. When the pull, and the tingle, ended, I found myself in complete darkness.

The shouts and screams of the battling monsters had disappeared. All I could hear now was LD sobbing, and Jacob whispering, "Shhh, little buddy, shhhh, shhhh. Everything is all right."

I wondered vaguely if it was a sin to lie to a baby.

"The poor beebums," Mrs. McSweeney said. "He's

got every right to be frightened."

"Grampa?" I whispered. "Are you here?"

"Yeah, I'm here. Not sure I should be. I've got a pickax that wants to bury itself in some monster's belly."

"Do you think we should go back and help?" I asked.

"No," said Jacob firmly. "The Poets wanted us to get LD away from that fight."

"Jacob is right," said Mrs. McSweeney. "Besides, I'm not certain we could go back even if we wanted to."

"Then what do we do now?" Grampa asked.

The answer came from Luna, who said, "I suppose we keep going. I'm here, by the way, though no one bothered to ask."

"Oh, I knew you'd make it through, darlin'," said Mrs. McSweeney. "You were the only one I *wasn't* worried about. Though I suppose we should check on one more thing." Raising her voice a bit, she said, "Invisible Ed, are you with us?"

Silence.

"Probably stayed behind to fight," said Grampa at last. "Useful guy to have on your side, someone nobody can see."

"Then Luna has put her paw on it," said Mrs. McSweeney. "We keep going."

"Go where?" I asked. "How can we tell which way

is forward when it's pitch-black?"

"And what if there are big pits in the floor we might fall into?" Jacob added.

I wished he hadn't thought of that.

"Luna?" said Mrs. McSweeney.

"Do I have to? You know it makes me itch!"

"You don't *have* to do anything, darlin'. But it would be helpful."

Luna sighed, then begin to purr. It was a lovely sound, rich and rumbly. That was no surprise, really. What *was* a surprise was that her pure-white fur began to glow. Soon she looked like a cat formed out of moonlight.

"That is cooler than the breeze from Mothra's wings!" I murmured.

LD, who still had his head buried against Jacob's shoulder, peeked out, then cooed appreciatively and shook his rattle.

The glow wasn't much, but in the extreme darkness it made a huge difference. We could now see that we stood in a narrow, smooth-sided tunnel. How far it stretched ahead we could not tell; the light provided by Luna reached only ten feet or so.

We turned to look behind us. Nothing but a stone wall.

"Craziest dang place I ever heard of," snorted Grampa.

"Crazy or not, there's only one way to go," said Mrs. McSweeney.

Luna took the lead. Switching her luminous, extravagant tail, she started down the tunnel. Jacob and I followed close behind. Grampa and Mrs. McSweeney came last. Every once in a while Mrs. McSweeney would take the baby, cooing at him as if he were the most precious thing in the world. Which, in a way, I guess he was. When she wasn't carrying LD, I could hear her bickering with Grampa. Even though they were arguing, it didn't sound angry, more like the kind of disagreement that occurs between old friends. I began to wonder if they liked each other more than I had thought.

My mind kept going back to the battle in the Council Chamber. I was terribly worried about the Poets. Though we had barely met them, I had really liked them.

The tunnel twisted and turned, but that was no problem now that we had some light. The big question was how we were to get back to the surface. The Poets had said the tunnel would lead us out, but not how far we should go or what we might find along the way . . . not to mention what might be waiting for us if we *did* get back to the surface. How secret was this tunnel? If Mazrak and his crew had won, or fled, would they know where this would let us out?

That question was replaced by a new, more urgent one when we came to a place where the tunnel forked.

"Uh-oh," said Luna. "Now what?"

The rest of us gathered around her to study the situation.

"Maybe both tunnels lead to the surface?" said Jacob hopefully.

"Yeah, and maybe a little pink bunny is gonna come hopping along to show us the way out," snapped Grampa.

I flinched at the harsh words. The uncomfortable silence that followed was broken by Luna, who said, "Stranger things have happened, Mr. Carker. For example, you might find yourself traveling along a tunnel deep beneath the world of monsters with only the help of a glowing cat to show you the way. Oh, wait. I forgot. You're already doing that."

"Never did like cats," muttered Grampa. "Talkin' cats are even worse."

I had spotted something that interested me. Moving closer to the spot where the tunnels split, I said, "Luna, dear, would you come here?"

Tail waving like a banner, she trotted to my side.

"Do you mind if I pick you up?"

"Not at all. I appreciate you being courteous enough to ask."

I bent to scoop the cat into my arms, then lifted her to the wall of the tunnel on the left. I squinted at the stone for a while, then said, "Someone carved a set of symbols here. I recognize them from papers we found at Jacob's house."

"What do they say?" asked Jacob.

I shifted Luna so I had one hand free, which I used to tuck the end of my thinking braid in my mouth. I chewed as I studied the symbols.

Frustration! Without the code key, I could make no sense of them.

"Look lower," said Luna softly.

I crouched down and found additional marks, not carved but scrawled on the rock with what looked like charcoal: SF WUZ HERE.

Spitting out the braid, I read the words aloud.

Grampa snorted but managed to keep from saying anything, for which I was grateful.

"Are there markings on the wall of the other tunnel?" asked Mrs. McSweeney.

Still holding Luna, I went to examine the tunnel on the right. "None at all," I reported.

"We might as well take the tunnel that has the markings," she said. "We don't have anything else to go on."

"I really don't know if they mean anything," I protested. "Heck, they could even be a warning!"

But no one had a better idea, so a minute later we started down the tunnel on the left.

As we traveled, Jake and I told Mrs. McSweeney some of what had happened after we'd arrived in Always October.

We had been going on like this for about ten minutes when we came to a dead end. My gut clenched. "I'm sorry!" I moaned. "I told you I didn't know if those symbols meant anything."

"Wait," Jacob said. "Look!"

I saw what he meant. Gouged into the stone were indentations that looked like handholds. When I put my hand into one, I was delighted to discover that past the front edge the opening dipped down, making it easy to get a solid grip.

"Maybe this is our escape route!" I said.

Jacob sighed. "Even if the handholds lead to a way out, how could we climb it with the baby?"

More frustration!

What made it even worse was that when I looked up, I was sure I saw a glimmer of light. It was as if the light was teasing me, saying, "See? If you could just figure out how to get up here, you would be free!"

When I pointed out the light, Jacob said, "Lovely. But it doesn't solve the problem of climbing with Little Dumpling."

Brainstorm!

"Maybe we could tie him to your back with that webbing Keegel Farzym gave you."

Jacob shook his head dubiously. "I think we should go back and try the other tunnel."

"No, no!" cried a familiar voice. "This is the right way. This is the *only* way. Come this way or die!"

24

(Jacob)

◇ ◇ ◇

A NEW GUIDE

Both parts of Sploot Fah came scrambling down the rock wall. When he was about ten feet overhead, he leaped to the floor, landing directly in front of us.

"Nice kitty!" cooed the one on the right, gazing at Luna.

The cat, who was crouched at Lily's feet, nodded her acceptance of the compliment but said nothing.

"Well, and you must be Sploot Fah," said Mrs. McSweeney.

"I am!" cried both parts proudly.

"Why did you say 'Come this way or die'?" I asked.

"Good way to get attention," said one with a shrug.

"Besides, it's true," said the other. "Sploot Fah *knows* tunnels."

"Sploot Fah *knows* digging."

"Sploot Fah knows many things, including where bad monsters wait for good babies—"

"Also where peoples carrying good babies can get up top safely."

"And you just happened to be here waiting for us?" said Gnarly. "Sounds kinda suspicious to me."

"Perhaps you should tell us more," said Lily gently.

Both halves of the little monster began to speak at once. They stopped, scowled at each other, then began flipping their hands forward. I realized they were playing a game something like Paper, Scissors, Stone. Only instead of phrases like "paper wraps stone," this one involved terms such as "gimwitz crinkles fludgnuks" and "fludgnuks bash borgle!"

When they were done, half the creature sighed and took a step back. The other half, who I guess was the winner, stepped forward.

"Sploot Fah was suspicious about baby," he explained. "Sploot Fah had *questions.* So Sploot Fah followed, sometimes over ground, sometimes under. Then Sploot Fah saw that Mazrak also followed peoples. Sploot Fah don't like Mazrak, because—"

"Because Mazrak is a booger!" shouted the half of Sploot Fah who had stepped back.

The half who was supposed to be doing the talking shot him a glare. The supposedly silent half clamped his hand over his mouth, then turned his back to us.

Nodding in satisfaction, the speaking half said, "Mazrak is bad. Mazrak is mean. Mazrak does wicked things. Sploot Fah kept following, saw other bad monsters join Mazrak. So Sploot Fah knew bad stuff was coming. Sploot Fah knows paths, knows tunnels, and thought peoples would come this way. So Sploot Fah came to help, just in case, because Sploot Fah is GOOD!"

"Done?" asked the other half.

"Done," said the speaker.

The part of Sploot Fah who had been facing away scurried back. "Let's move," they said together.

"But we can't climb this wall with the baby!" I said.

Both parts laughed. "Why climb wall? That would be silly!"

With that, they leaped up, grabbed the same handhold I had first spotted, and hung from it.

A chunk of wall about seven feet high and four feet wide tipped toward us.

"Watch out! Stand away!" cried Sploot Fah.

Both parts leaped down and scurried backward as the massive chunk of stone fell to the floor with a deafening crash.

Little Dumpling screamed with laughter.

When the dust cleared, we saw that where the slab had been was a continuation of the tunnel. It stretched into the distance, now dimly lit by lumni-fung.

"Opening door is tricky part," said half of Sploot Fah.

"No, no," corrected the other half. "Opening door is easy. Opening door *without getting squashed* is tricky!"

"You say true! Now come on, peoples, *come on*!"

"But we need to go *up*!" I said. "To the surface."

"Go up right here and bad things will happen," said one of the Sploot Fahs.

"Very bad things," agreed the other. "Like getting eaten!"

"Sploot Fah's way will get you up and out," said the first.

"Plus you won't be anyone's dinner!" said the other.

So we followed the pair of creatures, or the

creature who was a pair, through the opening. As we did, I took a step closer to Lily and muttered, "I hope we're doing the right thing."

"It's not like we've got an instruction book," she replied. "And Keegel Farzym did seem to think these guys—this guy—were . . . was! . . . annoying, but not dangerous." She frowned, "It's certainly annoying to try to talk about them. Him! I can never figure out which pronoun I should use!"

"I just hope Keegel Farzym was right," I muttered. Then I touched the stone wall beside us three times.

"Wait, wait!" cried both parts of Sploot Fah as we continued forward.

"Now what?" asked Gnarly.

"Where you brought up?" asked half of Sploot Fah. "In a barn?"

Mrs. McSweeney laughed. "Your sainted mother used to say the same thing to you almost every day, Gnarly—for exactly the same reason!"

"Have to close door," explained the other half, to Lily and me.

Looking back, I saw a pair of ropes, one dangling at either side of the opening. Each part of Sploot Fah went to a rope. Once in position, they nodded to each other, then leaped up and grabbed on.

To my surprise the huge chunk of stone rose swiftly and silently, then clicked firmly back into the opening through which we had just passed.

"Easier to close than to open," said the half on the right.

"Safer, too," said the other half, dusting off his hands. "But *now* can go on."

"And I can stop this stupid glowing," said Luna, sounding relieved.

"It was much appreciated, darlin'," said Mrs. McSweeney.

"I'm glad. Even so, I'll expect some extra treats when we get home. That is, assuming we *do* get home."

For some reason, I found the cat's uneasiness one of the scariest things yet.

As we went on, LD grew fussier and fussier. I started to stumble and realized I was exhausted myself.

I suspected Lily's grandfather wouldn't say anything, and I was pretty sure Mrs. McSweeney was tireless. I also figured Lily wouldn't be willing to admit she needed a break before I did. Telling myself it was LD I was concerned about, not me, I finally said, "Guys, I think we should take a rest. It's got to be at least two in the morning by our time, and we've been through a lot."

"We can't stop now!" protested Lily. "We've got to get LD back to our world before the dark of the moon."

"No, Jacob is right," said Mrs. McSweeney. "If

we just keep staggering on, we won't be in shape to handle anything big that comes at us. And even if *you* don't want to rest, that baby needs a break. The little beebums probably needs a diaper change, too . . . though how we're goin' to manage that, I can't think. Mr. Sploot Fah, do you know a place where we can rest?"

"Sure, sure!" said both parts. "Right here!"

They flopped down side by side on the floor, folded their hands over their chests, and closed their eyes.

"That's nice, darlin'," said Mrs. McSweeney, "but what I had in mind was a place out of the tunnel, with maybe a bit of water so we could get a drink and wash up."

Instantly, both parts of Sploot Fah leaped to their feet.

"Fussy, fussy," said one half.

"But Sploot Fah knows good spot," said the other.

"Keep following!" they said together.

We must have walked for another half hour. I almost found myself wishing we had followed Sploot Fah's first suggestion and just lain down on the tunnel floor. By this point Gnarly was helping to carry the baby. He tried to act like he didn't enjoy having Little Dumpling in his arms, but I could tell that he did.

Finally both parts of Sploot Fah cried, "Here we go!" and led us into a side tunnel.

Unlike the main tunnel, it had no lumnifung; by the time we had gone a little way in, it was pitch-black.

"Careful," said one part. "Turn coming up!"

"Keep left hand on wall!" advised the other part. "That way you won't fall in."

"Fall in what?" asked Lily.

"Big Black Pit of Bottomless Despair!" said both parts together.

25
(Lily)

◇ ◇ ◇

BLANKETS, YES; DIAPERS, NO

I almost wished Jake hadn't asked the question. Big Black Pit of Bottomless Despair was the scariest name for a place I had ever heard.

Maybe that was because, in a way, I had already been there. One of the reasons I love my grandfather so much is that he was the one who pulled me out.

"Well, that sounds nasty," said Mrs. McSweeney.

"Nastier than nasty!" said half of Sploot Fah.

"Very bad place to visit," said the other half.

"Perhaps this would be a good time for you to glow, Luna," said Mrs. McSweeney gently.

"Don't do that!" cried the part of Sploot Fah ahead of us.

"Glowing would be very bad," said the part behind.

"Why?" I asked.

"Because it is Big Black Pit of Bottomless Despair!" exclaimed both parts together. Sploot Fah sounded as if he were explaining something to a rather slow child, and I had a feeling he was rolling all four of his big eyes at my question.

"Can you be more specific?" asked Jacob.

In a softer voice, a voice tinged with a note of fear, the one ahead said, "Pit eats light."

"Not smart to feed pit," said the one behind.

So we walked on in the darkness, staying as close to the wall as we could.

"YAY!" cried both parts of Sploot Fah a few minutes later. "We here! And no one died!"

"That's lovely," said Mrs. McSweeney. "I don't mean to sound fussy, but now that we're past the pit, is there any chance of gettin' some light?"

"Sure! Sure!" cried both parts. "Watch!"

I heard Sploot Fah scrabbling around. A moment later a sudden flare of blue light made me blink. The light came from a torch embedded in the wall. The part of Sploot Fah standing beside it cried, "First!"

An instant later another flare of light, orange this time, erupted at the opposite wall.

"Prettiest!" cried the other part.

"Thank you both," said Mrs. McSweeney.

"Not both!" they cried, sounding exasperated. "There is only one Sploot Fah. *Only one!*"

"Well, thank the one of you," Mrs. McSweeney said, her voice a bit tart.

I looked around. The cave was about twice the size of our living room. At its far side shimmered a dark pool, its surface reflecting the stalactites that hung from the ceiling. Gorgeous. As to the cave itself, its walls were reddish with streaks of other colors. It looked quite pleasant, and I was tired enough that I knew I could sleep on a stone floor.

As it turned out, I didn't need to. Sploot Fah—both parts—darted through an opening and returned with armloads of blankets.

"Where did those come from?" I asked.

"From the blanket maker," said one of the Sploot Fahs, looking as if it was the dumbest question he had ever heard.

LD was fussing more than ever.

"He needs his diaper changed," said Jacob wearily. Looking at Sploot Fah, he added, "I don't suppose you have a diaper maker, too?"

"Diaper?" asked half of Sploot Fah.

"What is diaper?" asked the other half.

"Something you put on a baby to catch the pee

and the poo," I said.

"Aaaahhhh!" cried both Sploot Fahs, throwing their hands in the air and running in circles.

"Baby monsters don't need no stinking diapers," cried one.

"Baby monsters need to pee wild! Baby monsters need to pee free!" cried the other.

"Well, I guess that answers that," said Mrs. McSweeney. "I do think it will be all right to let the baby go bare for a while, Jacob . . . though we should probably be careful where we sit."

"Won't he be cold?" I asked.

"I doubt it," said Luna. "He's got as much fur as I do!"

I realized this was true. Jacob had peeled off the baby's yellow-duckie pajamas, and then his diaper—I was impressed by how tenderly he had done this—and the little guy was covered with green fur from head to toe. It was hard to tell he *was* a guy, if you know what I mean.

"Whooo-eee!" cried both Sploot Fahs. "Stinky, stinky baby!"

Jacob carried LD to the stream that ran out of the pool and washed the baby's bottom. While he was doing this, Sploot Fah snatched up the diaper—each half took one corner—and scurried out of the cave. I have no idea what he did with it, but that was the last we ever saw of the thing. Or smelled of it, for that matter. Maybe he dropped it into the Big Black Pit of Bottomless Despair.

Jacob used a corner of one of the blankets to dry the baby's bottom. Then he pretty much collapsed onto the blanket himself. The baby curled up next to him. A moment later both were sound asleep.

"He's goin' to make a fine big brother," said Mrs. McSweeney approvingly. "Luna, darlin', would you keep an eye on things while we rest?"

"Certainly," said the cat, extending a paw and licking it lazily.

"Then I think we could all do with some sleep. Will you be sleepin' too, Mr. Sploot Fah?"

"No, no. Will go ahead," said one.

"Will check tunnel," said the other.

"Will be good guide and guardian!" they said together.

With that, they trotted into the tunnel we had just left.

I lay on my back, staring into the darkness, and rehearsed again the route the Poets had laid out for us. Get to the surface—not even there yet. Once we did get above ground, we still had the Black Bridge of Doom, the Forest of the Lost, the Tunnel of Tears, Flenzbort, and the Library of Nightmares to get through before we could go home.

And what about Octavia's "prophecy" that one of us must die before the others could return home? Could we really survive all that?

Sleep would not come.

I glanced to where Jake was snoring (which was kind of cute). LD was cuddled against him.

How much time did we have to get the baby back to Humana, and to safety?

26

(Jacob)

THE HISTORY OF A MYSTERY

I was woken by Little Dumpling patting me on the cheek.

"Eat?" he asked woefully. "Eat?"

I looked around. Sploot Fah's torches were still burning. How long had I been asleep?

Looking to my side, I saw Lily and Gnarly yawning and stretching, as if they were also just waking.

Mrs. McSweeney, on the other hand, was already up and around.

"Eat!" said LD again, sounding more desperate now.

I felt awful, because there was nothing to feed

him. At least, that was what I thought. Then Mrs. McSweeney, who was standing next to the pool, called, "Bring the baby here, Jacob. Let's see if he'll eat any of this."

At her feet sat a clay pot and two piles of stuff I couldn't identify.

I stood, stretched, then hauled LD into my arms. As I did, both parts of Sploot Fah bounced into the cave, all four arms loaded.

"More food, food, food!" he cried happily. He skittered over to Mrs. McSweeney and dropped what he was carrying in front of her.

"EAT!" cried LD, more eagerly than ever.

"Mushrooms!" said half of Sploot Fah, pointing at the first pile.

"Fruits and roots!" said the other half, pointing at the second.

"Bugs and worms!" he cried together, pointing at the pot.

"I think we'll stick to the fruits and roots, dear," said Mrs. McSweeney gently. "And maybe a few mushrooms. I do thank you for gathering all this. It was very kind of you."

"Sploot Fah *is* kind!" cried half of him, wrapping his arms around himself in a hug of self-delight.

"Sploot Fah is *wonderful*!" cried the other half, flinging his arms wide with joy.

Using the pool to wash things off, we had our first meal in Always October. Other than being shorter, thicker, and blue, the roots were similar to carrots. They actually tasted pretty good.

The fruit was even better—several kinds of berries as well as some apple-like things.

I skipped the bugs and worms.

I tried to keep LD from eating them too, but when I wasn't looking, he crawled over to the pot and dipped his fingers in. When I turned back, he was popping a squirming handful into his mouth.

"LD!" I cried. "Don't!"

"No, no! That is the mash," said half of Sploot Fah.

"It's the monster mash," said the other half proudly.

"Very good for baby monsters!" he said in unison.

"Let it be, Jacob," said Mrs. McSweeney. "I'm sure Sploot Fah knows better than we what's good for a baby monster. Besides," she added, smiling wickedly, "you should have seen some of the things *you* picked up and ate when you were a baby."

"I'd rather you didn't tell me."

Despite Mrs. McSweeney's words, I was glad my mother wasn't there to see what LD was putting in his mouth.

Once we finished eating, we explained to Sploot Fah the route the Poets had laid out for us.

"Yike!" cried the half to my right. He grabbed his head.

"Double yike!" cried the other half, making the same gesture.

"Will you still lead us?" asked Lily.

"Don't know," muttered one.

"Not sure," said the other.

"Black Bridge of Doom isn't too bad," said the half on the right.

"But Forest of Lost is nasty."

"Tunnel of Tears is even worse."

"And after that . . . Flenzbort!"

The two halves of the creature looked at each other and shuddered. I noticed that they didn't even mention Cliff House.

"Well, at least get us out of here and point us in the right direction," I said.

"After that I have maps," said Lily.

We all looked at her. "Maps?" asked her grand-father.

Lily nodded. "Jacob and I found them in Arthur Doolittle's office. Jake let me make copies."

She reached into the pocket of her flannel shirt and took out some carefully folded papers. "If these are accurate, they should help us get where we need to go." She looked at Sploot Fah. "Do you know how to read maps?"

Both parts of the little monster looked highly offended.

"Sploot Fah is not stupid!" said one.

"Sploot Fah has two heads," added the other.

"So twice as many brains as most monsters!" they cried together.

"Let Sploot Fah see maps."

"Sploot Fah will tell you if they are good or not."

Lily handed one of the maps to the half on the right. I noticed she kept the others and figured she was being careful in case Sploot Fah turned out to be less friendly than he was acting so far.

Both parts of the monster flopped to the floor. Lying on his bellies, he spread the map in front of him and studied it. After a while he leaped to all four of his feet and said, "Yep, this shows true! Sploot Fah will guide you!"

"I thought you didn't want to go all the way," said Lily. "What changed your mind?"

"Sploot Fah likes maps," said one of them.

"Besides, got to help Jake protect the baby," said the other.

"What I want to know," I said, "is why my grandfather had these to begin with."

"I can explain something about that," said Mrs. McSweeney.

"Now, Eloise," said Gnarly. "Ain't no need to go into all that."

"I believe there is, Abraham. Jacob and Lily have a right to know what happened in the past, since it affects where they are right now. But we need to get a move on if we're to get back to our world before Mazrak and his gang try to use that Silver Slicer thing they've cooked up. We've got a long way to go, and some dangerous obstacles ahead. So let's get started. As we walk, I'll tell you the history of a mystery."

I picked up Little Dumpling and plopped him over my shoulder. Once he had offered up a good burp we set out.

We had been walking for about ten minutes, Sploot Fah in the lead, when Mrs. McSweeney began her story:

"The Doolittle family came to Needham's Elbow around the time of the Civil War. By 1888 Edgar Doolittle, the oldest son, had made a fortune in munitions and built the big house you still live in, Jacob.

"For a long time the family was what they call 'a pillar of the community.' But, as so often happens, things went downhill after a generation or two. By the time Arthur Doolittle was born, the house—and the family—had seen better days."

She paused to glance at Gnarly. He grunted and

nodded, as if she might as well continue—which she did.

"I knew Arthur Doolittle from the time I was a little girl. He was five years older than me, and, truth to tell, I had a bit of a crush on him. I saw him at both school and church, and he was very handsome. Even better, he was kind. And he had a . . . well, a *spark* about him that most fellows lack. You may not get that, Jacob, but Lily will understand what I mean. Arthur paid no attention to me, of course; when you're fifteen, a mere ten-year-old isn't of much interest. Even so, I watched him pretty carefully." She sighed. "Well, be that as it may. The one thing everyone knew about Arthur was that he was bound and determined to become a writer. Oh, that man could spin a tale."

"How could you know he wanted to be a writer?" I asked, fascinated at this inside look at my grandfather's life. "Writing's awful private, isn't it?"

Mrs. McSweeney laughed. "That's small-town life, Jacob. The post office was inside the general store, so it was no secret that Arthur was mailin' out manuscripts. We knew when he sold his first story—couldn't help but know from the way he whooped and carried on. He was only eighteen at the time, and we were all happy for him. He didn't break through big until he was thirty-five. When he did become a huge bestseller, people were kind of willing to forget what had happened before that."

"Before?" I asked. "What happened before?"

Mrs. McSweeney hesitated, then said, "Tia LaMontagne."

Gnarly let out a little groan.

27

(Lily)

◇ ◇ ◇

TIA LAMONTAGNE

My grandfather looked as unhappy as the Wolfman with a case of dandruff.

Just to be sure, I said, "When you say Tia La-Montagne, you mean that lady monster Teelamun, right?"

"Precisely," said Mrs. McSweeney, "though I didn't know that back then. At least, not at first."

"I didn't know until today," said Grampa bitterly.

Mrs. McSweeney nodded and actually looked sympathetic. "It wasn't something I could tell you, Abraham."

Grampa glared at her.

"I don't understand!" I said. "How can Teelamun

be a monster? She's beautiful!"

Mrs. McSweeney smiled. "Well, dear, if you'll remember, the Poets believe Always October is the place created to hold human fears so they don't overwhelm us. There is little humankind finds more frightening than a beautiful woman."

"Are you kidding?" asked Jake. "People *love* beautiful women!"

"Indeed they do. But love can be dangerous, as almost everyone discovers sooner or later. Men know that a beautiful woman has power over them. And women fear that someone beautiful can steal their man. The French have a phrase, *femme fatale.* It means 'deadly woman.' Stories about the woman whose beauty leads a man to his doom stretch back as far as ancient Greece." She paused, then said, "Thing is, that kind of woman doesn't even have to *intend* harm. Some women just hit a man's heart so hard, it's never the same afterward."

She glanced toward my grandfather. His face was set and grim.

Turning back to Jake and me, she said, "Tia showed up when Jacob's granddaddy was about thirty. He hadn't married yet, though he certainly had plenty of chances."

"He was a stuck-up snob," muttered my own grandfather.

Mrs. McSweeney sighed. "Perhaps you had better

tell this part, Abraham."

Grampa's nostrils flared and his lip twitched, but after a moment he nodded. "I was workin' in the cemetery when it all started. My own grandfather—that would be your great-great-grandfather, Lily—had been runnin' the place, but he was getting kinda old, so he hired me to help out. I had just graduated from high school and was trying to save some money so I could go to the community college."

"Which you should have done," said Mrs. McSweeney. "You certainly had the brains for it."

"Well, that's all past now, ain't it, Eloise? And it's not part of this story, so just hush up." Turning back to Jacob and me, he said, "One afternoon I'm diggin' a grave when I hear this little cry from behind me. Turning around, I see . . . "

His voice broke off and his eyes misted up.

"Tia LaMontagne?" I asked softly.

He nodded. "She was the most beautiful woman I ever saw, Lily. Even so, there was something strange about her. For one thing, she was so pale, she looked as if she were carved out of white marble, like one of those tombstone angels come to life." Grampa paused, and I could tell it was hard for him to go on. At last he said, "When I asked her if she was all right, she reached a hand toward me, then gave a little cry and collapsed."

Grampa went silent. I was itching to know what came next, but we had come to an upward slope that was covered with loose stones, and it took all our attention to climb it without slipping. When we finally reached the top, I said, "So what happened after she collapsed?"

"I picked her up and carried her to the house—same place we live now—and we sent for Doc Dillon. Docs still visited back in those days. Doc said there was nothin' wrong with her, she just needed rest."

He turned away, as if he couldn't bear to say more. After a bit of silence Mrs. McSweeney picked up the tale. "Well, no one thought it was fit for that woman to stay in the house with two men, of course. And since Abraham and I were cousins, he brought her to me. He used to bring me all his problems back then, me being five years older and *considerably* wiser."

"Which is why you had four husbands, you being so smart and all," said Grampa with a snort.

"Only one bad marriage in the lot," replied Mrs. McSweeney serenely. "I simply outlived them all, and you know it." She turned back to Jacob and me. "As I was saying, they brought the mystery woman to me. It didn't take too long for her to recover, and I found her fascinating . . . partly because she

235

wouldn't say word one about where she was from or how she got here. The only thing she wanted was to meet Arthur Doolittle! I might have been jealous if I hadn't found a good man of my own by that time. Well, set that aside. Arthur wasn't that famous yet, so he was delighted to meet a fan, especially one who was quite beautiful. As it turned out, she was more than a fan . . . she was also a brilliant painter. Even better, from Arthur's point of view, she liked painting scenes from his stories. Six months after they met, Tia and Arthur were married."

I glanced at my grandfather. He was staring at the ground.

"Well, a bit of time went on and the two of them seemed truly happy together. Tia never really fit in, of course. Not easy to get accepted in a small town under the best of circumstances, and Tia was just odd enough to make it even harder."

"I know what that's all about," I muttered.

"Then one day she just . . . vanished. It was quite a scandal. From what Arthur testified, the last time he saw Tia, she was in her studio, finishing up a painting. He was up in the tower, working on his new book, not knowing it was the one that was going to make him famous. Lunchtime rolled around and he went down to get her and . . . she was gone.

"Now, some folks wanted to believe he had killed her. But there was no sign of blood and no one ever found a body. Other folks thought she just got tired of living with such a peculiar man. Some thought something stranger had happened, though no one could ever say exactly what it was. All anyone really knew was that she had just vanished." She snapped her fingers. "Like that!"

I saw Jacob shiver.

"Eventually Arthur remarried and had a son. That would be your dad, Jacob. And Abraham here, he recovered too—"

"Did not," muttered Grampa.

"Well, whether you recovered or not, you got married, which is how come Lily is here." Turning to Jacob, she said, "About the time your daddy was ten, your Grampa Arthur disappeared. Not as mysteriously as Tia, since he left a note, though the note itself was pretty mysterious." She closed her eyes, as if searching her memory, then quoted: "'The mystery calls. Though it breaks my heart to go, I can stay no longer. Forgive me, wife. Forgive me, son. I have done the best I could. With love and regret, Arthur.'"

I shivered as I recognized the message we had found in Jacob's father's notebook.

"My dad never told me that," said Jacob, his voice bitter.

Mrs. McSweeney nodded. "No surprise there. Your daddy didn't like to talk about it."

"But why did Tia come to our side of the Tapestry to begin with?" I asked. "And why did she leave?"

"As Keegel Farzym told you, monsters occasionally visit Humana, just as some few humans, like me, sometimes visit Always October. One of their . . . well, *scouts*, I guess you could call them . . . brought back some of Arthur's early stories, the ones where he was trying to create a world of monsters to write about. Tia liked the stories, but he was getting a lot wrong, and it annoyed her. She came to Humana to set him straight and ended up falling in love. She was, in the truest sense, his muse. *A World Made of Midnight* and all the other Always October stories never would have been written without her."

"That doesn't answer the question of why she left," said Jacob. "Especially if she loved him."

Mrs. McSweeney glanced at Grampa, then said, "Tia left because she was going to have a baby, and she felt it would be safer for it to be born in Always October."

"How do you know all this stuff?" I asked.

Mrs. McSweeney smiled. "A woman alone in a strange new world needs a friend to confide in, Lily.

238

Tia chose me to be that friend. It's how I learned about Always October and found my way into the magical world."

"It's also how she got me," put in Luna, who was trotting along at her feet.

"And a great blessin' to me you've been, darlin'."

About that time we reached a tunnel that sloped upward and brought us back to the surface. Even above ground it was still night, though I couldn't tell if that was because we had slept so long or just because it stayed that way in Always October most of the time. At least the moon was full . . . and fully visible, since the forest where we now stood was sparse, the trees small and twisted.

We could hear the River Doom before we saw it.

"Getting close!" said half of Sploot Fah.

"Sploot Fah good guide!" said the other with obvious self-delight.

We emerged from the forest onto a stretch of bare rock about fifty feet wide. In the light of the full moon I could see that the rock ended at the lip of a chasm. I couldn't tell how deep the chasm was. I *could,* however, see that it was hundreds of feet to the other side.

Stretching across that gap was the strangest bridge I had ever seen.

Also the most frightening.

It was a good thing I was carrying the baby at that point, because if *I* thought the bridge was frightening, then I was pretty sure Jacob was about to . . .

28

(Jacob)

THE BLACK BRIDGE OF DOOM

FREAK OUT!

Of course I freaked out.

I have a problem with bridges even when they're short, wide, and sturdy. The Black Bridge of Doom wasn't short, it wasn't wide, and it wasn't sturdy. Oh, and one more thing it wasn't: something on which any sane person would set foot!

"I can't cross that!" I screamed.

The truth was, I had been bracing myself for this moment ever since the Poets had first told us we would have to cross a bridge. I had also been praying it wasn't going to be one of those swaying rope-and-board horrors you sometimes see in adventure movies. I should have been so lucky! The Black Bridge of Doom was not made of rope and boards, or metal, or stone, or concrete, or anything normal like that.

It was made of twigs.

Twigs!

Long black twigs that grew together in a woven mass and stretched from one side of the abyss to the other, a distance that appeared to be longer than a football field.

As if that wasn't bad enough, the wretched thing was only three feet wide, hardly enough to make me feel safe—especially since it had no side rails!

"I can't go on that," I repeated, more softly this time. "Why didn't the Poets warn us it was made for crazy people?"

"If you'll remember, our conversation with the Poets was cut short," said Mrs. McSweeney. "And I'm afraid you'll *have* to cross it if you want to get home."

I stared at the bridge in dismay, flinching as it swung in a gust of wind.

"Why can't you cross?" asked half of Sploot Fah.

"Jacob has a problem with bridges," said Lily.

"But it's a very nice bridge!" cried Sploot Fah's other half. He scampered onto the bridge, ran about twenty feet out, then jumped up and down. I suppose the point was that since it didn't collapse, I should feel safe crossing it. Unfortunately, though the bridge didn't fall, it *did* bend and sway. The sight made my stomach churn. Sploot Fah wasn't that big. If the bridge moved that way under *half* of him, what would it do when I got on?

"Jacob, darlin', we've got to cross that bridge if we're goin' to get you home," Mrs. McSweeney repeated.

"I know, I know," I groaned. "But you'll have to give me time to get ready for it. Maybe you could just knock me out and carry me."

Gnarly rolled his eyes. "Fer Pete's sake, kid, it's just a bridge. Get over it." He blinked, looking surprised at himself, then began to laugh. "That was a good one! Get it? Bridge? Get over it?"

I liked him better when he showed no sense of humor at all.

"We can't delay much longer," Mrs. McSweeney said firmly. "It's possible Mazrak is on our trail."

I drew several deep breaths, tapping the fingers of both hands against my thumbs so fast, it's a wonder my arms didn't go airborne. Then a sound distracted me—LD, shaking that rattle I had bought him.

In that moment I knew, without question, what

would get me across.

"It's my job to take care of Little Dumpling," I told myself firmly. "'And I have to get him to the other side."

I turned it into a ritual. Crossing my arms in front of my stomach so my right hand was against my left elbow, and vice versa, I repeated to myself, "It's my job to take care of the baby. It's my job to take care of the baby. It's my job to take care of the baby."

Each time I said it, I smacked my fingertips against my elbows.

Ten repeats, ten smacks, and I was ready to give it a try. Stepping over to Lily, I reached for LD and said, "All right, let's go."

She hesitated, then said, "Maybe we should bind LD to your back before you cross."

"How?" I asked.

"Octavia's silk would do," said Mrs. McSweeney. "It might be safer that way, Jacob. I'd hate to think of LD lunging for someone else while you're in the middle of that thing."

"I could carry him," offered Gnarly, surprising me a bit.

"Thank you, Abraham," said Mrs. McSweeney. "But I think it's better to have you on defense, in case of attack."

He nodded and tightened his grip on his pickax.

I had decided Lily's idea made sense. Lifting my shirt, I unwound the silk and handed it to Mrs. McSweeney. Lily put LD on my back, and Mrs. McSweeney started wrapping the silk around the two of us. The little guy protested at first, but after a minute or so he settled down.

"I think the binding makes him feel secure," explained Mrs. McSweeney. She stepped back to admire her handiwork. "There," she said with satisfaction. "Snug as a little papoose!"

I swallowed hard. It was time to start.

Half of Sploot Fah was on the bridge already.

Lily went next.

Then it was my turn. Luna Maria Eleganza trotted on beside me, as if to provide encouragement. I needed it, because the bridge instantly sagged beneath my feet, making my stomach lurch. It was like walking on a trampoline, except a trampoline is wide and only a few feet above the floor while the bridge was narrow and spanned a horrifying chasm.

"Good boy!" cried the part of Sploot Fah who was ahead of me.

For some reason I found the approval of the little monster, or at least this half of him, heartening.

I got a good way out before I accidentally looked down.

Instantly, I wished I hadn't. Hundreds of feet

below me the River Doom raced and roared between jagged rocks. The white, foaming water threw up so much spray that some of the rocks were completely shrouded in mist. Even so, I could see long-jawed creatures leaping from the waves. If I could spot them from this height, I knew they must be enormous.

Closing my eyes, I murmured, "I have to get the baby across. I *have* to get the baby across!"

"Jacob?"

Opening my eyes, I saw Lily looking back at me. Her face was etched with worry.

"It's all right," I said, and took another step forward.

"Good boy," said a voice from behind me. To my astonishment, it was Gnarly. "Now just keep goin'. Keep goin'. . . . "

Slowly, painstakingly, I made my way forward.

Everything might have worked out fine if Mazrak and his henchmonsters hadn't come charging out of the forest.

Because my eyes were locked on my destination, I didn't realize they were there at first. But when I heard Mazrak's roar, I turned to look back—and almost lost my balance.

Mrs. McSweeney and the other half of Sploot Fah, the last two of our group to mount the bridge, hurried back toward the rock shelf. The little monster leaped forward and latched onto the leg of one of the attackers, managing to trip it. Mrs. McSweeney pulled out a knitting needle and started blasting out bolts of power. One monster screamed in anger. Another crumpled and fell.

And more emerged from the woods.

"You kids keep goin'!" bellowed Gnarly. "Git the baby away from here!" Then he turned and headed back toward the fight.

LD was screaming and shaking his rattle.

It was excruciating to leave our friends, but getting the baby to safety was the most important thing. I started forward again. Behind me I heard more shouts of pain, and then of rage. Suddenly Gnarly bellowed, "Cover me, Eloise!"

I glanced over my shoulder and froze.

Gnarly was kneeling at the end of the bridge. He had pulled out his clippers and was *cutting the twigs*!

"Jacob, keep moving!" he roared when he saw me looking at him."

I understood his plan at once. It was to sever the bridge so the monsters couldn't follow me and Lily across. So we had to get over quickly. But the fact of standing on a bridge that was, literally, being cut out from underneath me had me once more frozen in my tracks.

"Jacob!" said a small voice. "Brace yourself. I'm coming up."

It was Luna. Even though I was wearing jeans, I flinched as her claws dug into my skin and she began to climb my side. Once she reached my shoulder, she said, "Close your eyes. I will be your guide and we'll take it one step at a time. First one now. *Now!*"

When I still didn't move, the cat nipped my ear. "NOW!" she repeated fiercely.

I took a step forward.

"Good, you're doing fine. Now take another. I'll tell you if you drift toward either side. I don't want to die any more than you do, so you can trust me to guide you true. Just keep walking the way I tell you."

"Faster, Jacob!" urged Lily from ahead of me. "FASTER!"

"I can't!"

"You have to!" Her voice hardened. *"Or are you going to let those monsters get Little Dumpling?"*

That was cruel, but it worked. The thought of failing Little Dumpling pierced my heart, and I knew I must get him across one way or another. I began to move faster, following Luna's instructions. The bridge bounced beneath me, and swayed side to side as well, making it impossible to run, or even trot.

"Almost there," said Luna. "Keep going!"

I opened my eyes. The end of the bridge was no more than twenty feet away! Suddenly I felt it sag worse than ever. Wondering if Gnarly was about to cut it loose, I glanced back. To my horror, one of the monsters had knocked him aside and leaped onto the bridge. Even worse, Gnarly had cut away so many of the twigs, the bridge could not support the weight of the huge creature.

That end broke free from the cliff.

With LD screaming in my ear, I flung myself forward. I sank my fingers into the coarsely woven twigs, but my feet could find no hold. In an instant I was dangling hundreds of feet above the roaring, rock- and creature-filled river, holding on by only my fingers.

Luna still clung to my shoulder. And LD, of course, was strapped to my back.

I looked up.

It was about ten feet to the top.

I looked down.

The monster whose weight had broken the far end of the bridge free had also managed to hold on! He was a couple of hundred feet below me and climbing fast! His movements caused the long ribbon of the bridge to swing wildly back and forth.

Lily stared down at me, her face white with terror.

"Climb, Jacob! *Climb!*"

As if I was planning to let go! Except I did have to let go, with at least one hand, because that was the only way to move up. Taking a deep breath, I closed my eyes and pulled my right hand free of the twigs. My body sagged. The bridge twisted sickeningly.

I stretched, grabbed more twigs, pulled.

Progress! My head was actually about a foot closer to the edge.

Another excruciating pull upward, and then another. My arms ached. My muscles felt as if they were on fire.

About four feet from the top, I ran out of strength.

Lily was on her stomach, reaching down to me. "Come on, Jake, come on! Just a few more feet!"

"I can't," I gasped. "I'm out of strength."

"Nonsense!" hissed Luna. "Keep going. *Keep going!*"

I took a deep breath, reached up, grabbed for another handful of twigs . . . and missed.

My fingers slipped. I began to slide.

Lily screamed, which did nothing to reduce my panic—especially when I realized it wasn't even my situation that had made her scream.

29

(Lily)

TOOZLE

I don't like screaming, I think it's for sissies. But what I saw by the full moon's light tore that one out of me. Actually, I had first felt a brief flash of hope because I saw what Jake couldn't: Keegel Farzym and Teelamun had arrived! They must have been trying to catch up with us ever since the battle in the Council Chamber.

Unfortunately, that hope died quickly. Despite the reinforcements, the odds were against our friends. Mazrak just had too many monsters. So when I glanced up from Jake's predicament and saw that Mazrak's crew had captured our friends and was carrying them back into the woods, out came the scream.

Add to that the fact that Jacob had run out of strength and might not be able to make it to the top, and that LD was still strapped to his back, and that a monster was actually climbing up after them—it was about the worst moment of my life.

The look on Jacob's face as he stared up at me, clinging to those woven twigs with that vast drop to the raging river below, was heartbreaking . . . especially because I knew his greatest fear wasn't even for himself but for LD.

A coldness seized me as I saw him slide downward. Eyes wide with terror he whispered, "I'm not going to make it, Lily."

Then I noticed something that added to my terror—the woven twigs were pulling loose from where they were rooted in the cliff! With a cry, I sank my fingers into the spaces between them. I wasn't so foolish as to think I could hold the bridge if they came loose. But I hoped that if I could take off even a bit of the strain, it would give Jake time to get to the top.

"Lily, don't hold on!" he cried. "If it goes, it will pull you down with us!"

Before I could say anything, do anything, the half of Sploot Fah who had come across ahead of me brushed past my legs and scrambled down the woven twigs as if he were a monkey. Grabbing Jacob's wrist, he shouted, "Hold on! *Hold on!*"

It was enough to stop the slide. Jacob got his fingers back into the twigs. But at the same time the added weight pulled more of them loose from the cliff's edge.

"That was a close one," said Luna, who was still on Jacob's shoulder.

"Got good grip now?" asked the half-Sploot Fah.

"I think so," Jacob gasped.

"Don't think!" cried the little monster. "KNOW!"

Jacob closed his eyes, then nodded. "Yes, I've got a good grip."

"Good. Now hold on."

He let go of Jacob's wrist and scrambled farther down the twisting weave of twigs. Not a hundred feet below him the enemy monster continued to clamber upward. His movements added to the strain on the bridge, and I felt as if my arms were coming out of their sockets.

Once our half of Sploot Fah was under Jacob's feet, he took a good grip on the twigs and yelled, "Now put feet on me and push up."

"Are you sure?" gasped Jake.

"Do it!"

And Jacob did. It was just the extra help he

needed. When he raised himself by another foot, the little monster scrambled up behind him so that he could do it again.

The much larger monster below them roared in anger and climbed even faster.

I screamed again, this time from the pain in my arms and shoulders. I didn't know how much longer I could hold on.

Jacob was near the top, but the big monster was only about ten feet below him and moving fast. Extending a thick, scaly arm, he reached up, grabbed Sploot Fah, yanked him from the bridge. He let go. Sploot Fah fell but managed to snatch at the bridge and caught himself. He scrambled back up and grabbed the monster's left foot. At the same time the monster reached up and latched onto Jake's leg.

Suddenly Luna leaped from Jake's shoulder. I screamed a third time, thinking the cat was going to plummet to her death in the river. Instead, she snagged onto the big monster's shoulder. He bellowed in pain as Luna's claws sank into his flesh. Yowling like a demon, she scratched and clawed at his bald head. Taking one hand off the bridge, he swatted at her, trying to dislodge her. The action made the bridge swing more wildly than ever.

Sploot Fah swung around to the other side of

the bridge, the side facing the cliff, climbed past the monster who was struggling with Luna, and got under Jake's feet again.

Jake looked as if he might faint. But with Sploot Fah supporting him from below, he continued his upward climb. Less than a minute later he scrambled over the top, Sploot Fah right behind him.

Luna launched herself from the monster's scalp, but the beast managed to reach up and snag her leg. She yowled in alarm. Then something whizzed past me—a rock, thrown by Sploot Fah. It struck the big monster on the head. He let go of Luna for just an instant, and she shot up the rest of the way to the cliff. As soon as she was with us, I let go of the bridge.

To my horror, though twigs were snapping and straining, it was still connected to the edge of the cliff.

"Jacob!" I cried. "Help me!"

With LD still strapped to his back, Jacob knelt beside me. Almost instantly, Sploot Fah was there too. The little monster had gathered an armful of rocks and continued pelting the monster, who still clung to the bridge. The beast was only four or five feet below us now, his horrid purple face contorted with fury. He reached up with his powerful arm, seized another handful of twigs, pulled himself even closer.

Sploot Fah bounced another rock off his head. Jacob and I yanked at the twigs, desperate to dislodge them.

"Stop now and I will let you live!" roared the monster.

I tore another twig free.

The creature bellowed in rage. "I . . . will . . . take you to pieces!"

"Head back down!" I cried. "Right now, or I'm pulling out the last of these twigs!"

The monster glanced below him. The end of the bridge dangled a little way above the river. Dark shapes were leaping out of the water.

"There are monsters down there!" he whined.

"There's going to be one more monster down there in a minute," growled Jacob. "You'll do better to get there by climbing down than you will by falling."

"I'd start now if I were you," I added. "I don't know how much longer this bridge will hold, even if we don't pull out any more twigs. Ooops!" I added, pulling out another twig. "There goes one now."

The monster groaned, then began to scramble down the bridge.

"You'll pay for this!" he roared.

My arms were trembling, and I could see the cords standing out in Jacob's neck. But I knew that neither one of us wanted to be responsible for the death of this monster. We just wanted him far away from us. Far, far away.

The creature was sliding down the bridge now, obviously aware that we might not be able to hold it much longer.

Moments later, we saw him reach bottom, let go, and splash into the river.

With a gasp, we released the twigs, not caring if the bridge fell or not. It did, writhing like a three-hundred-foot-long snake as it plummeted toward the river below.

Trembling from the effort, gasping for breath, we continued watching. After a commotion in the water we saw the monster scramble onto one of the rocks. He climbed to the top and looked up, shaking his fists at us.

Our attention was brought back to our own predicament when Sploot Fah, the half of him that was still with us, began to scream . . . not a sound of fear but of deep, aching loss.

"Half gone!" he wailed, gazing across to the opposite cliff. *"Half is gone!"*

He flung himself down next to Jake and began to sob.

"Grampa and Mrs. McSweeney are gone, too," I said to Jacob. The words were like acid in my mouth.

"Mazrak's monsters took them. They got Keegel Farzym and Teelamun, too. They must have been following us, because they came out of the woods while you were trying to get up the bridge."

"So now it's just us," said Jacob bitterly. He forced himself to his hands and knees. "Unstrap LD, will you?"

I began to unwind the silk we had used to bind the baby to his back. I was nearly done when another cry from Sploot Fah made me turn. He had returned to the edge of the cliff and was gazing at the far side. "Sploot Fah gone," he sobbed. "Gone!"

I don't know what it was that alerted me, maybe just a shift in the way he was standing, but all of a sudden I knew what he was about to do. Dropping the silk, I bolted toward him.

"Sploot Fah, don't!" I screamed.

I grabbed him just in time to keep him from leaping into the chasm.

"Let go!" he cried. "Let go! Got to get other half!"

"Not that way," I panted, struggling to draw him back from the abyss, fearing that he might pull me over with him instead. "Your other half is still alive. If you jump and die, then *he* will be alone. You don't want that, do you? He's still with my grandfather and Mrs. McSweeney. They will all help take care of each other."

I had wrestled him a few feet from the cliff but didn't dare let go, as I was still afraid of what he might do. He spoke no more, but his body continued to shake. I wished I could do more to help him. The only thing I could think of was to be there, letting him know he wasn't alone, just as I had done with Jake that day in the cemetery.

"Hurts," he moaned. "Hurts in here."

He put those odd, spadelike fingertips against his chest, and fresh tears spilled out of his enormous eyes.

"Lily," said Jacob softly. "We need to get moving."

I sighed. "Will you still come with us?" I asked the half Sploot Fah.

He sniffed and nodded. "Yes. Still got to help Jake protect the baby. That's the most important thing."

"Thank you, Sploot Fah."

"No, not Sploot Fah. Not now."

"Then who are you?"

"Don't know. Not Sploot. Not Fah. Don't know who I am."

"We have to call you something," Jacob said, his voice gentle.

Our small friend paused, then said, "Call me Toozle."

"Toozle?" I asked.

He nodded. "Toozle is word for squishy stuff left

on bottom of foot after you step on a bug. Feel like toozle now, so that is what you should call me."

"All right, er, Toozle. Will you still guide us? We still need you."

And that was true . . . we did need him. But I also hoped that acting as our guide might help distract him from the terrible pain he was suffering.

The forest we passed through now seemed younger, more springlike in some ways . . . very different from the massive old trees we had gotten used to. Maybe that's why it didn't feel as threatening. Which was stupid. I should have realized by this point that appearance and reality were not necessarily the same thing.

We had gone maybe a half a mile when I heard something that stopped me in my tracks.

"Grampa?" I whispered.

Jake looked at me nervously.

"Didn't you hear that?" I asked.

"Hear *what*?"

"My grandfather! He's trapped. He needs my help!"

"Lily, I don't hear anything."

"I don't care if you hear it or not! Grampa needs help and I'm going to him."

"Trick!" cried Toozle. "Bad trick. Don't listen!"

"No, no, it's him!" I insisted as my heart flooded with indescribable relief. I turned, and with a wild cry of "I'm coming, Grampa!" I dashed into the forest.

"Lily, don't!" I heard Jake shout from behind me.

He was too late. I was already off the trail and into the woods.

Not that I would have stopped anyway.

I really should have known better, especially after what had happened to Jacob. But it was my *grandfather* calling me.

I hadn't gone more than three or four steps when I felt a surge of dizziness. Where was I? Oh, right . . . the Forest of the Lost. But I had just entered. All I had to do to get out was turn around and go back the way I came, right?

Um, not really. I turned, but even though I had taken so few steps, I could see no sign of the path I had just left.

Fighting a surge of panic, I walked toward where I thought I had entered. It didn't take long for me to know I had walked twice as far as I had coming *in* to the wood.

I turned and walked back. "Grampa?" I yelled. "Grampa, where are you?"

Silence . . . then his voice in the distance, calling for me.

I ran in the direction of the call. The forest was dark and shadowy, but enough light filtered in from the full moon for me to see where I was going. I had only run a little way when I heard him again. Only now his voice was behind me.

I turned and ran in the new direction, ran until I had to stop to catch my breath. As I stood, gasping for air, the world seemed to spin and I heard my grandfather's voice coming from two directions at once. With horror, I accepted that it was not him calling after all.

It was the forest.

That was also when I understood, deep in my gut, what a stupid, stupid thing I had done by blundering into this place.

I wondered if there was a way out, some secret trick that would let you find your way back to the path.

If not, would I wander here forever?

As despair overwhelmed me, I heard a deep sobbing not far away. Thinking it was likely another trick, but unable to resist the hope of finding someone to talk to, I headed for it. As I got closer, I dropped to my knees and crept in the direction of the sound.

Sitting beneath a tree, bathed in moonlight, was a hulking figure dressed in nothing but a pair of tattered pants. He had massive arms and bulging calf muscles. I could not see his face, for it was buried in his hands and surrounded by a shaggy mass of hair. It was easy enough to understand why he was weeping. Or was it? Was this another trick of the forest? What if the tears were only to draw some sympathetic idiot (like me) within reach of the monster's hands?

I backed away, trying to move as silently as a bubble on the wind. I failed at that, for the monster dropped his hands and looked up.

"Who's there?" he called in a deep voice.

I didn't answer. It didn't matter. His gaze fell on me almost at once. His face was like a lion's, and I realized with terror that the mass of hair was actually a mane. He stood, then leaped in my direction. I screamed and scrambled backward. It did no good. He was amazingly fast and with two more leaps had reached me.

He pinned me to the ground with one enormous hand.

I screamed again and again.

"Stop!" sobbed the monster. "Please stop! There's no need to fear. I don't want to hurt you. I just want to know if you can tell me how to get out of here."

I shook my head, still too frightened to speak.

He burst into new sobs, his huge, hot tears falling onto my face. "Of course you can't. You're trapped, just like me. Oh, what a fool I was to enter here just because . . . " Suddenly he stopped, looked to his right, then cried, "Yes! Yes, I hear you! I'm coming!"

Releasing me, he bounded off among the trees.

I lay there, staring at the bits of moon I could see through the leaves, and wept bitter tears. I would never get out of this place, never see Jake or LD again. How long could I last in here? Was there food and water . . . or would I meet a slow death from thirst and starvation?

Rolling over, I buried my face in my hands and sobbed until exhaustion claimed me, and I fell asleep. I don't know how much time passed before I was woken by someone tapping me on the shoulder.

30

(Jacob)

TEARS

I stood, staring at the spot where Lily had disappeared into the forest. And then it hit me—this was the Forest of the Lost! And my best friend had just plunged into it.

Now I was standing here with a baby, half of a monster, a talking cat, and a horrible question: should I wait in the hope that Lily might make it back out, or should I press forward?

Time was short, monsters were on our trail, and I had to get LD back to Humana.

But how could I possibly leave my friend?

Toozle was crying again, which didn't help. "Lily

was good girl," he wailed. "Now gone. Gone, gone, gone . . . "

"Stop!" I said. "I have to think."

Toozle sniffled but stopped his sobbing.

I paced back and forth, wracked with uncertainty. I had to get the baby out of here. But how could I leave Lily?

Then I heard her screaming!

Luna sighed heavily and said, "Wait here." Before I could answer, the cat trotted into the forest too!

"Better wait," said Toozle, plopping down beside the path. "Kitty is smart."

Worries—about time, about Luna, and most of all about Lily—gnawed at my guts like a rat chewing its way through a wall.

"I'll count to a thousand," I said to myself. "Then I have to move on, no matter what."

The counting was excruciating, but it gave me something to focus on. Only by the time I reached a thousand, there was still no sign of either Lily or Luna.

So I did it again, very slowly. And again.

How much time had passed? It seemed like hours, but I knew that couldn't be true. So I did some quick math in my head. Counting slowly, one number per second, getting to one thousand takes just over sixteen minutes. I knew I had been counting slowly, but maybe not slowly enough. Call it twelve minutes for each time I went to a thousand. So, thirty-six minutes.

I counted again.

And again.

Now it had been an hour. Probably the longest hour of my life.

I was trying to convince myself that we had to move on—trying, but not succeeding, because it was too hard to think of leaving Lily—when I heard her cry, "Jacob! *Jacob!*"

I leaped to my feet as she came stumbling out of the forest. I was so happy to see her, I didn't even mind when she threw her arms around me.

"Luna did it!" she said. "She came into the forest and found me and guided me out and . . . "

She turned.

The cat was nowhere in sight.

"Where is she?" gasped Lily.

"Can't both escape Forest of the Lost," said Toozle softly. "Kitty cat must have made trade . . . kitty stay in so Lily can come out."

Lily's chin wobbled. She dropped to her knees and buried her face in her hands. "Oh, no," she sobbed. *"Oh, no!"*

I put a hand on her shoulder. She shook it off.

"Lily," I said softly. "We have to move on. If we don't, Luna will have gotten herself stuck in there for nothing. Mazrak is on our trail. Who knows how close he might be?"

Face still buried in her hands, Lily nodded. She gave one last, shuddering sob, wiped her arm across her eyes, and got to her feet. "All right," she whispered. "Let's get moving."

There was no mistaking Teardrop Hill, for in the moonlight it did indeed look like a giant tear. It was tall, and quite steep. Even so, we might have been able to climb it . . . if not for the fact that the stone it was made of was smooth as glass.

At its base yawned a dark opening about nine feet high and six feet wide.

"Tunnel of Tears," said Toozle, stopping about ten feet away and pointing. The fear in his voice was obvious.

"Why don't we go around?" I asked. "It wouldn't be that much farther."

"Not much farther but lots dangerouser. Big traps and bad critters on each side. Tunnel is sadder but safer."

"Why is it sadder?" Lily asked.

"Because it is Tunnel of Tears! You'll see. Come on."

We glanced at each other. Lily shrugged. "No point in waiting."

Side by side, we stepped forward. The instant we entered the tunnel, a wave of loss and despair swept over me. It was if every sorrow or pain I had ever experienced—from the smallest cut I had received as a stumbling baby to the heart wrench I'd suffered when Dad disappeared—had flooded back in one enormous wave of grief. My knees buckled, and I began to weep.

To my right I heard Lily sobbing; I suspected that what tore at her heart right now, even more than the loss of her parents, was the fate of her grandfather. That and her guilt over Luna.

LD, who was still in my arms, let out a wail so filled with grief that it doubled my own heartbreak.

How could a little baby have so much sorrow in him?

Maybe he missed his mother.

Suddenly Toozle flung himself to the floor. He began beating at his own head, screaming, "Half gone! Half gone!"

"Jacob!" Lily cried. "Stop him!"

I thrust the baby at her, then dropped down beside Toozle and grabbed his arms. The little creature was far stronger than me, but his grief made it hard for him to focus his strength.

"Stop," I hissed. "Stop it, Toozle!"

"Half gone!" he wailed, thrashing beneath my

grip. "Half gone, can't go on."

Finally I picked him up and flung him over my shoulder. Still sobbing myself, I started forward. "Come on," I said, between the choking spasms of grief. "We have to keep going."

Toozle beat at my back, still screaming, "Half gone! Half gone!" But his blows were not hard, and I knew he was not trying to hurt me. It was just that he had so much pain, he couldn't hold it in.

I don't know how far we had gone when we came to a wall of silvery mist.

"That must be the Veil of Tears," whispered Lily.

We hesitated for a moment, then stumbled through. We were encircled by mist, a ring about thirty feet wide. Ahead of us, on a throne of ivory, sat the Queen of Sorrows.

She didn't stay seated long. When we came lurching through the mist, she leaped to her feet. A look of horror—horror, but something more, something I did not yet understand—twisted her face.

"By the Eight Wings of Drakus, what have you done?" she cried.

Then she ran straight at us.

I thought it was finally over. We had made it this far, but the Queen was so big, and we were still so shaken by our trip through the tunnel, that I didn't think there was any way we could stop her from tearing us apart.

Still, when she went for Lily and Little Dumpling, I dropped Toozle and leaped forward to protect them. I can't say I was being brave, because I didn't have time to be afraid. It was as if my body moved on its own. I stood in front of Lily with my hands upraised, ready to fend off the Queen or die trying.

Her words, gushing forth on a wave of pain, made me drop my hands and step back.

"My baby!" she wailed. "My baby!"

Her voice throbbed with grief, with horror, with longing.

"Why have you brought him back to Always October? Why have you brought him back to *me*? What kind of monsters are you, to be so cruel?"

LD stretched his arms toward her, crying out to be taken. Plucking him from Lily's arms, the Queen of Sorrows cradled him against her chest, then sank to her knees, weeping.

It was too painful and too private to watch, and I turned away.

After a few minutes the monster's sobs began to fade. I turned back and saw Lily kneeling next to her, patting her back. She had to reach up to do it, because the monster—Meer Askanza, I suddenly realized—was so much bigger than she was.

LD was gooing happily, patting his mother's cheek as her enormous tears dropped to his face.

Toozle stood watching in amazement. He looked

exactly the way I felt: baffled, and uncertain of what to do.

This moment when no one was moving gave me a chance to get a better look at the monster, who was weirdly beautiful. Her enormous eyes were tinted red—though whether this was their natural color or only a result of her weeping I could not tell. Her skin was blue, not quite as deep as a robin's egg, but close. Glossy hair, jet-black, tumbled down her back like a waterfall of ebony. Her hands, clutching LD tight to her bosom, were long and bony. She wore a robe the deep purple of a sky just before full night.

I had been working through something in my head, and suddenly it clicked into place. According to the story Mrs. McSweeney had told us, Meer Askanza was the child of Arthur Doolittle and Teelamun.

That made her my father's half-sister.

Which meant she was my half-aunt—a blood relative!

I was still trying to absorb this when Meer Askanza took a gasping breath and climbed to her feet. Still cradling LD, she said fiercely, "Do you have any idea what it cost me to take this baby to Humana? Any idea what it cost me to leave him there? Do you not comprehend the terrible risk of bringing him back here?"

We looked at each other, uncertain of what to say.

"I could kill you now with very little problem," said my half-aunt. "So you had better answer me!"

Fear loosened my tongue. "You left him on my porch," I said quickly. "My mother and I have been taking care of him, but the night before last—at least, I think that's when it was—a monster named Mazrak came through my closet and tried to kidnap him. Another monster called Keegel Farzym showed up and brought us to Always October to get away from Mazrak. We're trying to get the baby back to Humana. Keegel Farzym was going to help us, but we got separated when Mazrak and some other monsters attacked us."

Meer Askanza's face was hard and angry. "Mazrak!" she spat, making the name sound like a curse word. She turned and went to her throne. She seated herself, still clutching LD, who was shaking his rattle and looking as happy as I had ever seen him.

"Have you met with the Council of Poets?" she asked.

"Yes," said Lily. "They're the ones who told us we must get the baby back to Humana."

Meer Askanza nodded. "What is your path, and what is your plan?"

Between the three of us—me, Lily, and Toozle—we managed to get out a more detailed explanation of what had happened and where we were supposed to go next.

My half-aunt looked troubled at the mention of Flenzbort but nodded. "That makes sense, in a terrible kind of way." She closed her eyes for a moment, then said, "I must tell you my story before you can continue. That is the toll to pass through the Tunnel of Tears: the King or Queen of Sorrows must explain the grief that carried him or her to this place. In turn, you must listen, and absorb some of my pain, and make it your own before you can go."

"So sometimes it's a king, and other times a queen?" asked Lily.

Meer Askanza nodded. "The Ivory Throne is reserved for the saddest monster in all of Always October. I will remain here until someone experiences a grief greater than mine. That may never happen, for my sorrow is vast and deep, and I see no way for it to ease. Indeed, I expect it will only grow worse once you leave, for to have held my babe once more and then be required for the good of both worlds to let him go again will be almost too much to bear."

She drew a deep, shuddering breath, then began her tale. We already knew some of it, of course—that her mother, Teelamun, had come to our world, fallen in love with my grandfather, then returned to Always October to give birth.

However, the next thing she said gave my life one more twist toward the strange: "My brother and I were greeted with great rejoicing."

The sentence itself was simple. What it implied was not.

"Brother?" I cried.

"Yes. I am one of a set of twins."

31

(Lily)

◇ ◇ ◇

THE QUEEN OF SORROWS

I think Jacob actually staggered when Meer Askanza informed him that she was one of a set of twins. I was pretty sure I knew what he was thinking: in addition to having a monstrous half-aunt, this meant he also had a half-uncle who was part monster.

And I thought my family was weird!

I could tell he was too shocked to continue right then, so I picked up the conversation. "Where is your brother now?"

"Hot on your trail, I fear," she replied.

That seemed to point to one candidate. With a shudder, I whispered, "Mazrak?"

"Of course."

Toozle groaned.

The queen glared at him, then said, "Be still while I tell the rest of my story so that you can be on your way. Time is short and the cause is urgent. You may find something of use in what I have to tell you. Whether you do or not, say it I must."

She drew a deep breath, then continued.

"My brother and I were happy little monsters, at least for the first years of our lives. We were doted on by our mother, and by our grandfather, Keegel Farzym. Alas, as time went on, Mazrak became surly and restless. Once we had been close and told each other all our secrets. Now he withdrew from me and wrapped himself in anger.

"Mother told me it was just a stage, but in time I came to realize it was more than that. While I was curious about our background, about being half human and half monster, and longed to see the human world, and to meet our father, Mazrak viewed the situation differently."

"In what way?" asked Jacob.

Meer Askanza sighed. "My twin felt an enormous rage at not having a father. Some of that anger he focused on Mother, blaming her for taking us away from him. But as time went on, his anger turned inward, directed against himself."

"Why?" I asked.

"He hated being half human—hated the division he felt within his heart. He was tormented by this halfness. Sometimes it seemed as if he wanted to tear himself in two, divide the monster self from the human . . . just as he now wants to tear apart the two worlds."

She closed her eyes. "As it worked out, I am the one who has been torn in half."

At a sound from Little Dumpling she shook her shoulders and opened her eyes once more. Caressing his head, she said, "In time Mazrak's anger grew so overwhelming that I began to fear him. Yet he was my twin, my other half, and I longed for him as much as I feared him . . . longed for the closeness we had felt when we were little. So I made a bad choice."

She fell silent. I didn't want to rush her, but I was painfully aware of the passing time. "What did you do?" I asked at last.

Stroking LD's brow, she said softly, "Wanting to be close to my twin, I aligned myself with the monsters gathering around him . . . monsters who agreed with his growing conviction that Always October should separate itself from Humana and become a world unto itself."

LD shook his rattle.

"In time, I fell in love with one of them—rebels

do have their charms—and took him for my mate. A few years after that, I gave birth to Dum Pling."

Meer Askanza snuggled LD closer and sniffed his head, just as I liked to do. Then she raised her eyes. Looking directly at me, the Queen of Sorrows said, "Having a baby changes everything, including how you view the world. Shortly after Dum Pling was born, my grandfather, Keegel Farzym, managed to get a message to me, asking me to meet with him and my mother. I missed them terribly, for I had not seen them since I'd joined Mazrak's band of plotters. So a few nights later I slipped away from our home to the place Grandfather had suggested for our meeting."

She sighed heavily. "I soon wished I hadn't. Though our reunion was joyful, I could tell they were uneasy. When I pressed for the reason, they told me things I did not want to know and showed me things I did not want to see . . . things that convinced me that if Mazrak had his way, it would be the end of Always October."

I noticed that Toozle had edged close to me. He was clinging to the tail of my flannel shirt, completely caught up in the story.

Meer Askanza closed her eyes. "They finally persuaded me that the only way to prevent this was for me to take Dum Pling to Humana and leave him as a link to bind the worlds."

Toozle whimpered in sympathy.

"Couldn't *you* have been the link?" asked Jacob. "You're also part human."

"Naturally I asked the same question! Alas, I am too old. If I had been brought to Humana when I was as young as Dum Pling, I would have assumed human shape, just as he did, and taken my monster form only once a month. But now that my body is long-settled and the Octobrian side dominates, I would not serve to hold the worlds together."

I nodded, thinking how terrible this must have been for her.

"I wanted to stay in Humana with Dum Pling, of course, but . . ." She gestured at her face and body. "Though my mother can pass for human, I cannot. To remain in the human world would have meant remaining in perpetual hiding, living ever in fear of when the 'monster' might be discovered." She shuddered. "It's never pretty when humans discover a monster . . . or even someone they merely suspect of being a monster. My poor little Dum Pling would never have had a normal life with me, never had friends or playmates. We would never have been free of the need to hide, never been free of fear. I don't mean the fear of the dark and what might be hiding in it, but the darker fear of those who would fear us and, given the chance, destroy us because of that fear. With a human guardian he would have a chance for a normal life.

"I resisted the idea with all my heart. But as terrible as the thought of leaving my child was, even more terrible was the idea of having the world to which he was born dissolve around us. Where, then, would Dum Pling be?"

She looked down at the baby.

"This was a terrible thing to ask of a mother. But life sometimes forces us to monstrous choices, asks of us things far more fearful than the simple frights we all must endure.

"My decision was made even harder because I was not entirely convinced my grandfather and my mother were right. But what if the odds were only fifty-fifty? What if the chance was only one in ten that they were right? Should I gamble our entire world to keep my baby with me?" She sighed. "In truth, I *might* have bet the world. But I could not bet Dum Pling's safety. So I agreed to their plan, which was that I would bring my baby to the human world and leave him with my mother's old friend, Mrs. McSweeney."

"How were you going to bring him to our world?" I asked.

"We decided to open a portal in the nearby

cemetery, in the same place where my mother came through to Humana, where she wanted to meet Arthur Doolittle. Now, the easiest time to pass through the Tapestry is at the full moon—not when it's full here, since that is almost all the time, but when the moon is full in your world. Thinking it would be less expected, we chose the opposite time, the dark of the moon. Grandfather and Mother created the portal, and on the appointed night I slipped away from my home, babe in arms."

Jacob spoke up. "If you were supposed to take him to Mrs. McSweeney, how did he end up at my house?"

Meer Askanza's expression soured. "Our plan was discovered. As I was about to pass through the portal, someone burst out of the woods in pursuit. Grandfather and Mother leaped to block him and managed to hold him off as I fled. I made it through but had no idea how many might be after me, how soon I might be caught.

"It seemed likely that if our plan had been discovered, my pursuers would know where I was intending to go. So I made a desperate decision. Instead of heading for McSweeney Monster-friend, I diverted to the home that had been my father's. I left the baby there and returned to the original route, expecting to be apprehended at any moment.

Yet there was no pursuit. Even odder, when I tried to return to Always October, I found that the portal between the worlds had been sealed and I was trapped in Humana!"

Stomach clench! "Where, exactly, was this portal?" I asked uneasily.

"In one of the mausolea in the cemetery close to Jacob's house. They make natural entry points."

"And, um, what would cause the portal to seal?"

"The touch of a human."

My cheeks began to burn. "That was my fault! I went into the mausoleum that night. The wall was glowing . . ."

"That was the portal," confirmed Meer Askanza.

"It was so beautiful I couldn't resist. I touched it. I'm so sorry!"

"No, no! It was a blessing! If the portal had not been sealed, Dum Pling and I might have been captured and dragged back to Always October. If that had happened, the Unravelers might have acted already by now. And who knows what horror might have flowed from that possibility."

I smiled in relief. "I guess that explains the angry voices I heard from the other side!"

Meer Askanza nodded. "I'm sure it does. Of course, even though the sealing of the portal was a blessing, it also created a great problem . . . namely, how was I to return to Always October?"

"How *did* you get back?" asked Jacob.

"I sought shelter with Mrs. McSweeney. Her cat, Luna, carried me home."

I burst into fresh tears. Meer Askanza looked at me oddly, but Jacob distracted her by saying, "I don't understand. I thought that when it came to crossing between worlds, Luna was a one-person cat."

"I am a monster, not a person," replied Meer Askanza, a bit tartly. "The rules are different. Though it broke my heart to leave my child, it was a relief to return home. However, the very moment I arrived in Always October, I felt a strange dizziness and began to . . . fade. When I became aware of myself again, I was on the Ivory Throne, the new Queen of Sorrows."

Her voice broke. Sobbing, she clutched Little Dumpling to her chest. Suddenly she thrust the baby away from her and cried, "Now take him! Take him and return to your own world. If you do not, all I have done, all I have suffered, will be in vain. Take him and *go*!"

Little Dumpling wailed when Jake pulled him from his mother's arms. Standing next to my friend, I gazed down at the baby's furry face and thought how unfair it was that so much should depend on the poor little guy, who had no idea what was going on.

"Go!" urged Meer Askanza. "My brother will be following you, be sure of it. The sooner you depart, the safer Dum Pling—and both our worlds—will be."

I went to Meer Askanza and gave her a hug.

As we started past her throne, she said, "One more thing. Once you exit the tunnel, you will be in Flenzbort's territory. The danger from her will be different from anything you have faced so far. Keep your wits about you. Expect the unexpected. Take nothing for granted. Accept no food or drink. Now go. Go!"

As we approached the far side of the Veil of Tears, LD cried out and reached back.

I heard a wail of despair from his mother.

I saw Jake hesitate, and knew I had to harden my own heart. Grabbing his arm, I said, "We have to go, Jacob!"

Together, we plunged into the mist.

32

(Jacob)

TWO DOZEN DUMPLINGS

Lily and I did not speak for some time.

Toozle, too, was silent. Little Dumpling, however, was whimpering, and cuddled close in my arms. I kept rocking him, murmuring to him soothingly.

When we reached the end of the tunnel, we found ourselves on the upper rim of a small valley. It stretched below us, silvery in the moonlight. To our right a waterfall plummeted from somewhere above us down to a small lake. From the lake flowed a stream that meandered through the center of the valley. Other small streams flowed from the hills that formed the sides of the valley, joining the main stream so that it grew wider and wider, until it finally disappeared under the cliff that rose at the far side of the valley.

At the top of that steep rise of rock loomed our goal—Cliff House, home to the Library of Nightmares.

In the valley itself we saw only one building—a cottage located to the right of the spot where the stream disappeared below the cliff.

I took a deep breath. "Well, that must be the place," I said.

We started down the hillside.

Flenzbort's "cottage" looked more like something out of a fairy tale than a monster movie. Its low walls were half covered with vines. Beds of flowers, pale in the moonlight, lined the flagstone path that led to the green door. Three chimneys broke through its thatched roof, as did the dormers that sprouted from several spots.

"That doesn't look good," said Toozle.

"What do you mean?" protested Lily. "It's adorable."

Toozle snorted. "In Always October any place look that nice probably some kind of trap."

"Trap or not, we have to get that bracelet," I said grimly. "Come on."

We walked up to the door. I knocked. The door

swung open on its own, revealing a room just as charming as the exterior. A cozy fire crackled in the big stone fireplace. All right, the flames were green and purple, which was a little disturbing. Even so, it felt wonderfully inviting, especially after all we had been through.

To our right stood a long wooden table, benches on either side. Behind the table a narrow stairway led up to the next floor. To our left four chairs were grouped around a moss-green rug. Beyond them a large loom held a partially finished weaving.

Directly in front of the fire, her back to us, a heavyset woman was drawing out yarn at a spinning wheel. A basket at her feet displayed a tuft of white fibers. A raven perched on her right shoulder. Another raven, this one walking back and forth on the mantelpiece, croaked, "Come in, come in! It's scary outside, but nice and warm in here. Or maybe it's warm outside and scary in here. I can never remember which way that goes."

We stepped forward. The door swung shut behind us. The woman turned. Her features were definitely monstrous: greenish skin, a warty nose the size of a potato, and pointed ears topped with tufts of fur. Yet something about her round face and warm smile was oddly comforting, despite the fangs. I reminded myself that the Poets and Meer Askanza had seemed to think this was the most perilous stop on our journey and vowed to stay alert.

"Well, here you are! I'd been hoping you would make it soon."

"You knew we were coming?" I asked.

Her smile held just a trace of smugness. "Not much goes on in Always October that I don't know about."

"Oh, don't act so mysterious," said a familiar voice from the basket at Flenzbort's feet. "You heard it all from me."

With that, Luna—the tuft of white fibers had been the tip of her tail—climbed out of the basket and trotted over to join us.

Lily burst into tears. "You made it out of the Forest of the Lost!"

"Very observant," drawled the cat.

"But how did you do it?" I asked.

Luna extended her right front paw and gave it a leisurely lick, clearly in no hurry to answer.

"Luna!" said Lily.

"Oh, all right, here's the story: You can't escape the Forest of the Lost while you're in Always October, at least not by any method I know. Fortunately, I didn't have to stay here. I simply went back to Humana. Once I got there, I had to move to a different place before returning—otherwise

I would have ended up right back in the forest. I didn't know where you'd be when I got back, but I did know you were heading for Flenzbort's cottage. So I decided to come here to wait for you. Not only was it a good place to meet, it let me skip going through the Tunnel of Tears."

"What a lovely reunion," said Flenzbort. "Touches me right in the pancreas. I see you've brought the baby. I assume you're wanting the magic bracelet that will allow you to return him to Humana without having to worry about him becoming a monster once a month, right?"

I nodded. Despite her warm smile and cheerful voice, and the lovely surprise of discovering that Luna was here, I was growing more uneasy by the moment.

"I can't just give it to you, of course."

"Of course not," said Lily. "That would be far too easy. And it's not like the fate of the world is at stake or anything."

Flenzbort's face hardened. "Sarcasm is not welcome here, missy. Unless it's from me, of course. The thing is, there are rules about this sort of magic. Break the rule, break the tool, lose the charm, cause great harm . . . if you take my meaning."

"So what do we have to do to get the bracelet?" I asked.

"Oh, we'll get to that, dearie, we'll get to it. Right now, why don't I see if I can do something for your face. Those burn marks look pretty nasty. I've got some ointment that might help."

My face really did hurt, and the offer was tempting. But I thought about my half-aunt's warning to accept no food or drink, and figured that it might extend to medicine, too.

"Thank you, but I'd rather just get on with things," I said.

"So suspicious for one so young," she said disapprovingly. "Well, why don't you join me at the table for a bite to eat?"

"Oh, we couldn't do that," said Lily. "We don't have much time, and it's important that we get to the Library of Nightmares as soon as possible."

Flenzbort's face sagged into such a sad expression, it almost convinced me to ignore the queen's warning.

"Not even a wee snack? I made something just for you, because I knew you were coming."

"Not even a wee snack," said Lily firmly.

"Not even for you?" she asked Toozle.

"Too sad to eat," said our little companion, shaking his head. "May never eat again. Half gone, can't go on!"

"My, that *is* tragic," said Flenzbort. She sighed,

then added, "Well, I'm going to eat even if you won't. Come sit at the table with me. While we're there, I'll explain what has to happen next."

I glanced at Lily. She shrugged. What could we do? We were in Flenzbort's home, and she had the thing we needed next. We moved to the table. Holding LD in my lap, I took a spot on one of the benches. Lily sat beside me. Toozle sat on the opposite side, his face barely showing above the table's edge. Luna jumped up on the table, took one look at Flenzbort's expression, and jumped back down.

Flenzbort opened a metal door on the side of the fireplace and pulled out a tray. A spicy-sweet aroma made my mouth water. When she placed the tray on the table, I saw that it was covered with cookies.

"In case you change your minds," she said. She took one, popped it into her mouth, and winked at me. "Just to show you they're not poison or anything. Mmmmm! Delicious, even if I do say so myself!"

The ravens fluttered over and perched on the back of the chair. Flenzbort settled her ample bottom into it, then rummaged in the pocket of her dress. "I believe this is what you need," she said, placing a silvery band in front of her.

"Can I see it?" asked Lily, reaching toward it.

Flenzbort quickly closed her own hand over the bracelet. "Not yet! First you must pass a test."

"What's the test?" I asked.

"You'll find out in a little while. At least, I hope you will. In the meantime, why don't you tell me what you've done along the way? I happen to know you started out with two adults and the other half of this little monster. Seems as if you've been a bit careless, misplacing so many members of your group. Oh, well. At least you have your cat back."

"That was cruel," I said.

"Never said I wasn't," replied Flenzbort, taking another cookie.

LD lurched forward and grabbed one of the cookies too.

"LD, don't!" I cried. But before I could stop him, he had popped it into his mouth.

I felt a surge of warmth in my lap . . . then nothing. The baby was gone!

"Oh, good," said Flenzbort with a smile. "We're ready for your test."

I leaped to my feet, furious, terrified, heartsick. "What have you done with my little brother?"

The words startled me, but I realized they were true. No matter what our actual relationship—half-cousin-once-removed or whatever—as far as I was concerned, LD *was* my little brother.

"Oh, settle down," said Flenzbort, her voice as calm as if I had just asked for a fork. "The baby is fine. Well, at least, for now."

"What do you mean, 'for now'?" demanded Lily.

Flenzbort pushed herself to her feet. The ravens fluttered up, then perched on her shoulders. She looked suddenly weary, almost sad. "Come along and I'll show you."

She lumbered over to the rickety staircase. Lily and I followed, Toozle and Luna close behind us.

The stair led up to a long hallway. Partway down it Flenzbort pushed on one of the doors.

"The babe is in here. If you can find him, you can have him. Unfortunately, you only get one chance. Them's the rules and I can't change 'em."

She stepped aside so we could see into the room.

"Oh, no," murmured Lily.

I said nothing, just stared in horror.

On the floor lay at least two dozen Little Dumplings, all of them sleeping soundly.

"Pick the right one and you can be on your way," said Flenzbort. "Pick wrong, and you'll be really, really sorry."

"Why sorry?" asked Toozle.

"Aside from the obvious reason of the world possibly coming to an end? Well, the rest of those sweet-looking creatures are actually imps. If Jacob picks one of them instead of the real baby, he'll never get rid of it. And believe me, having a genuine imp around is guaranteed to make your life truly miserable. Also, the baby will have to go live with the imps. Not a good idea."

"Lovely," I said, trying to stay calm despite my churning stomach. "Can I have help?" I asked, hoping maybe Luna could sniff out the real LD.

"Sorry, got to do this on your own."

"Why?"

Flenzbort shrugged. "Rules is rules."

I looked back at Lily. Biting her lip, she held up both hands, fingers crossed, and nodded at me.

I stepped into the room.

The babies were all sleeping. I wondered why, then realized that if they were awake, I could have counted on the real LD responding to me. That pinged in my heart. He knew me and trusted me. No, it was more than that. I had to accept it—the little guy loved me.

And I loved him.

And now I had to pick him out of the crowd. Well, not a crowd where everyone was different. This crowd was more like one of those puzzles in a kids' magazine, the ones with six pictures that are almost identical but have tiny differences that you're supposed to find.

Except in this case I had some twenty-four Little Dumplings to choose from, not a mere six. And at first they all seemed completely identical. When I looked more carefully, I began to spot small differences. This one had slightly bigger ears. This one had a smaller nose. This one had a tint of red in his fur. But which one was *my* LD?

I felt ashamed to think I had paid so little attention to him during the month and a half he had lived with us—then remembered that for all but a few hours of that time he had looked human.

I looked at the little monsters displayed before me. If I chose wrong, I would be saddled with an imp for the rest of my life. But that was nothing compared to the fact that a mistake might doom Always October to fade into oblivion, even as it doomed my own world to descend into a chaos of fear.

Then an even scarier thought, because it was so personal, hit me. *What would happen to LD if I got it wrong?*

Panic seized me. They all looked so much alike!

As I stood there, staring, I stuck my hand in my pocket.

And suddenly I had an idea.

33

(Lily)

◇ ◇ ◇

TRACK TO THE TOP

I watched in a state of terror as Jacob tried to pick out the real LD. How could he possibly find the right one? It seemed hopeless, as if he would just have to make a wild guess. Suddenly I saw his expression change. He had figured something out.

What?

Pulling his hand from his pocket, he brought with it . . . LD's green rattle.

Brilliant!

At least, I hoped it was brilliant.

Crossing my fingers, I prayed, *Let this work. Please let it work!*

Jake bent over one of the sleeping babies and gently shook the rattle. The baby blinked, then yawned and rolled on its side. The next baby did pretty much the same thing. The next scowled but did not wake up. The next made a tiny cry, then stuck its thumb in its mouth and went back to sleep.

Seven babies and no sign of LD. I began to fret that maybe Jake's idea wasn't so hot after all, then told myself that LD might well be the last baby he came to.

As it turned out, on the fourteenth try he struck gold. As soon as he shook the rattle over that baby's face, its eyes popped open. Looking up at Jacob, he said, very clearly, "Jay-Jay!"

Then he reached for his toy.

Jacob pulled LD into his arms and began to cry.

"Jake did it!" cried Toozle, leaping into the air.

I wondered how Flenzbort, who was standing next to me, would react to Jacob's solving her puzzle. To my surprise, she let out a long breath and murmured, "Thank the Seven Sacred Stars. Maybe we have a chance after all."

Which was when I realized that she was caught in the same weaving that held us all. Had she set this test because it was her nature as a monster and she could not help herself? Or was it simply part of the magic of the bracelet that Jacob must pass a test to obtain it? Whatever the reason, I was glad it was over.

Jacob beamed as he stepped out of the room with LD clinging to his neck. Looking past him, I saw that the fake LDs had all vanished, returning to wherever it is that imps come from.

Flenzbort held out the bracelet. "Well earned, boy. Wear it yourself until you get back to Humana, then put it on the baby. Now, let's get you on your way. Time is running short."

She led us back down the stairs, over to the great fireplace. She smacked the left side of the mantel with her right hand. With a creak the wood slid a couple of inches over, revealing a gap. Flenzbort reached in and fumbled around until we heard a distinct click. As she withdrew her hand, the fireplace pivoted out to reveal a dark opening. Motioning for us to follow, Flenzbort stepped through.

Once we were all inside, she whacked a spot on the wall. With a rumble, the fireplace swung back into place, plunging us into complete and utter darkness. I heard a scratching sound, followed quickly by a flare of light, and realized that Flenzbort had struck a match. The thought made me laugh.

"What's so funny?" she asked, her ugly face made all the stranger by the flickering light.

"It's just that we're so used to torches and glowing moss and all kinds of strange ways to get light that a simple match was a surprise."

"Well, dearie, whatever gets you through the night is what I always say." As she spoke, she moved to the wall and took down an old-fashioned oil lantern. She lifted the glass part—called a chimney, I remembered—and lit the wick. The light was brighter and more steady now, and revealed to our left a wooden cart resting on a narrow set of tracks. It was about the size of something that would hold four people at an amusement park. Painted on its side were the words OLD BETSY.

Flenzbort patted the cart fondly. "This will get you to the top of the cliff faster and more safely than walking." She pulled open a door in its side. When we hesitated, she snapped, "Go on, get in!"

We climbed into the cart, which had a leather-covered seat at each end. Jacob and LD sat on one side; Toozle and Luna and I sat facing them. Between us, at the bottom of the cart, was a board about three feet long and two feet wide. A wooden post, maybe six inches thick and slightly taller than me, rose through a hole in the center of the board.

Gesturing toward the board, Flenzbort said, "Put your feet there and pump. You'll have a good work-out by the time you get to the top!"

Reaching over the edge, she hung the lantern from a peg on the post. Then she pointed to a lever at the side of the cart. "That's the brake. If you need to stop to rest, set it or you'll roll back down and have to start all over again. When you get to the top, set the brake while you climb out. Then reach in, release it, and give Old Betsy here a push. She'll roll back down all by herself."

"Thank you!" said Jacob and I, both at the same time.

"All right, best get going!" said Flenzbort. She smacked the cart on the side, turned, smacked another spot on the wall. The fireplace pivoted and she stepped through the opening, leaving us alone.

"Well, *that* was interesting," said Jacob. "Ready?"

"Ready!"

We put our feet on the treadle and started to pump, my feet rising when Jacob pushed down, his rising when I took my turn. Toozle's legs were too short to help.

The cart moved heavily at first, but within a couple of passes the motion became smooth and fairly easy. Pretty soon we were rolling along at a good clip. Little Dumpling began to laugh. It was nice to hear, even though a baby's laughter sounded eerie in the dark tunnel.

After a moment I realized that the track was curved, so we were circling up through the inside of the hill as if climbing a giant corkscrew.

The walls were whizzing by pretty fast. Even so, I sometimes caught sight of an opening, and more than once spotted a creature sitting inside. I felt a pang of terror when I saw that one cave had a pile of bones in front of it. Flenzbort had acted friendly enough when she saw us off, but what if she resented Jacob solving her puzzle? I hoped she wasn't sending us to be dinner for some monster friend of hers.

When I said something about this, Jake replied, "If so, does that make us Meals on Wheels?"

Despite the joke, or maybe because of it, we pumped faster . . . which might have been a mistake, because a few minutes later we were both panting for breath.

"I need to take a rest," I said.

"Me, too," gasped Jake. "I think it will be all right as long as we don't stop beside a cave." Then he pulled the brake sharply toward him.

Little Dumpling climbed into Jacob's lap. Toozle moaned softly, a sound that echoed eerily through the tunnel. I wondered why he moaned, then realized he was still suffering from the loss of his other half, just as I still ached from the loss of my grandfather.

I was beginning to have an idea about what I might do about Grampa, but I wasn't ready to say anything yet.

After several minutes Jake said, "Ready?"

I nodded. We returned our feet to the treadle, he released the brake, and we began to pump. Within minutes we came to a level spot, then bumped into a vertical pad that clearly indicated we had reached the end of the line.

"Guess the ride is over," said Jake.

He reset the brake and we climbed out.

"Let's not send Old Betsy back down until we see if there's a way out of here," I said.

"Right there!" responded Toozle, pointing.

It took me a second to spot what he meant. Then I saw it: a ladder that led through an opening in the rocky ceiling.

"Toozle, would you climb up and make sure we can get out that way?" asked Jake.

Without a word the little monster scrambled up the ladder. A few seconds later he stuck his head down through the opening and said, "Door at the top. It opens out."

Jake scowled. "I can't climb that ladder holding LD. Help me strap him on again?"

He lifted his shirt and unwound Octavia's webbing. Working quickly, I wrapped it around Jake and the baby until LD was securely in place.

Jacob turned, released the brake, gave Old Betsy a push. The cart rolled away, taking our only source of light with it. Moving carefully through the dark, we made our way to the ladder. Luna batted my leg and said, "Let me ride on your shoulder. I don't like ladders."

I lifted her, relishing the feel of her silky fur, and placed her on my shoulder. It wasn't far to the top, and we emerged through a trapdoor into a small shed. Toozle had the shed door open for us. Enough moonlight came through for us to see that it opened onto the surface world.

We stepped out. Ahead of us stood Cliff House. Heavy clouds loomed above it. A bolt of lightning sizzled through the sky.

Jacob reached over and took my hand. "We made it, Lily."

I don't think he was being romantic. It was just that we had worked so hard to get here, come through so much, lost so much, that it was overwhelming to finally stand in front of the place.

It was, in a way, the house of my favorite nightmares . . . a huge, hulking mansion with towers and arched windows, circled by a moat whose dark water glistened in the moonlight. Bats fluttered and swooped around the towers. Behind the towers floated the full moon, its glowing disk split by the spire of the tallest tower, which rose directly in front of it.

Jake turned his back to me. "Unstrap LD, please?"

Once again I unwound the webbing that bound LD to Jake's back. Still focused on the mansion, I stuffed it into my pocket. It was amazing how light it was, and how easily I could fit it all in.

It was maybe fifty yards to the door of Cliff House. Though I felt enormous relief to have finally arrived here, looking at the space we had yet to cross suddenly filled me with fear.

"Jake," I whispered, "this will be Mazrak's last chance to get his hands on LD. He might not be anywhere near us. Even so, I think we'd better make a run for it."

Jake's eyes widened; then he nodded.

"Girl smart," said Toozle approvingly.

"On a count of three?" I asked.

Jake nodded again, I counted to three, and we sprinted across the open space.

There was no attack.

Gasping for breath, we reached the door, which was at least twice my height. Torches were mounted on either side. By their light we saw that a cord dangled along the left-hand side. Jake reached out and pulled it. From inside came the bong of an enormous bell.

I continued to check behind us for any sign of Mazrak. Finally we heard a shuffling from inside.

A moment later the door creaked open to reveal a hunchbacked man dressed in dark rags. His long black hair hung loose around his shoulders. One eye was large and penetrating, the other swollen shut. In a gruff voice he said, "Ah, you must be the human children who have been the cause of so much uproar. Glad you have arrived. Enter and be welcome."

Jake and I glanced at each other and smiled. With Luna and Toozle walking beside us, we stepped inside.

"We made it," said Jake.

I heaved a sigh of relief.

"My name is Affenheimer Sesselbach," said the man. "However, you may call me Igor."

"Why?" asked Jake.

"Because the one who has my position is always called Igor. My cousin Quasimodo is in the bell tower."

"Really?" I asked eagerly.

"No, but I've found it pleases visitors when I tell them that. Most just accept it. You're one of the few who's ever asked if I was telling the truth. Now walk this way," he said, turning and shuffling through the enormous entryway.

With that invitation it was all I could do to keep from imitating the way he tilted to the side and dragged one leg behind him.

"Where are you taking us?" asked Jacob.

"The Master Librarian has been expecting you."

We passed through a maze of halls, coming at last to one that ended at a huge wooden door carved with screaming faces. Without knocking, our guide turned the enormous knob and pushed the door open.

The room was vast and wonderful, lined with shelves and shelves of thick old books that seemed to radiate mystery. In the center of the room was a large pedestal, the kind of thing that usually holds a dictionary.

In front of it, his back to us, stood a man.

Igor cleared his throat. "The visitors have arrived, master."

The Librarian turned to face us.

34

(Jacob)

◇ ◇ ◇

THE MASTER LIBRARIAN

I had never met my grandfather, but from family albums, from the portrait in the hall, from countless book jackets, I knew very well that was who now stood before me. The high, bald head; the hawklike nose; and the piercing dark eyes were unmistakable.

"Ah!" said my grandfather, striding toward us. "Flenzbort alerted me you were on your way. I'm deeply impressed that you made it here on your own. Well done!"

Lily stared at him, her eyes wide, her mouth hanging open.

I stared too. I can't say how I looked, because I

truly did not know what I felt. Part of me was thrilled and astonished. Another part felt a surge of fury that this man could be so cheerful and so casual about seeing me, his grandson, given the way he had abandoned my father.

Then I realized that LD was *also* his grandson, which made everything that much weirder.

My grandfather stopped about four feet in front of us, clearly registering my expression.

With a thousand thoughts racing through my mind, it was hard to settle on just one, but finally a single word forced its way past my lips, a word that condensed all those feelings and thoughts into one burning question.

"Why?"

He knew what I meant, of course; I could see it in his eyes. Why had he abandoned his family to come to Always October? Why had he done something that had so wounded my own father? Why . . . well, why *everything* about our crazy, messed up family?

My grandfather closed his eyes. "Jacob, if I could explain to you the workings of the human heart, of my heart, any heart, I would be more than happy to do so. Of course, if I could truly do that, I would have been even more successful as a writer than I was. But as the philosopher Pascal wrote, 'The heart has reasons of which reason knows not.' Love drew me here, even when other loves should have held me at home. When love wars with love, no one really wins, least of all the heart where the battle takes place."

If he wanted me to feel sorry for him, he had a long way to go.

"Some people think duty is as important as love," I said coldly, quoting a line from one of his own stories.

He winced. "Maybe you shall be a writer, too, grandson. You certainly know how to wound with a word, which is one of the prerequisites. Still, the shot is well taken. I could have stayed in Humana, spent my days there being nearly content. But it was not simply my love for Teelamun that drew me to Always October when she reached out to me. It was my sense that somehow this place is my true home, the world where I was meant to be, as if being born in Humana had been some kind of mistake."

"I suppose that makes me a mistake too, some-one who just shouldn't exist."

He winced again. "You're good at this," he said softly. Then, even more softly, "How is your father?"

"How would I know?" I asked bitterly.

He blinked, looking puzzled.

"Dad has been gone for almost two years. He went on a caving expedition and never came back."

My grandfather's shoulders slumped. "I'm sorry,

Jacob. I did not know that. I had received word from the Poets that you were here and heading for the library. The message didn't come with a lot of details." He stepped toward me. As he did, a motion from the enormous book he had been gazing at when we entered caught my eye. I blinked in surprise. A quill pen, not held by any hand—or at least, I thought, remembering Invisible Ed, not by any *visible* hand—raced across the page. Suddenly the pen lifted into the air. Without anyone seeming to touch it, the page turned.

"What's going on there?" asked Lily, pointing at the book.

My grandfather smiled, and I could tell he welcomed the diversion. "*That* is the current volume of *The Book of All Nightmares*. It's a complete record of human nightmares. That's what the Library of Nightmares is, you see—the place where nightmares are recorded."

"Very interesting," I said sharply. "I wish we had time to read it. But we need to get Little Dumpling back to Humana before the Unravelers can use him to start their work!"

He started to say something, then paused, gazing at the baby. "May I hold him?" he asked, extending his arms. When I hesitated, he said, "This will likely be the last time I see him."

I sighed and passed him the baby. Little Dumpling gurgled and patted his cheek.

"Remember me, do you?" asked our shared grandfather.

Against my will, I felt my heart soften just a bit.

"I understand your urgency, Jacob," said my grandfather, not looking up. "The thing is, we don't keep a door to the other world open at all times. We're preparing a portal now. It should be ready in a few hours. In the meantime, why don't I give you a bit of a tour? Then you can rest. Come on—you should take a look at the book."

We stepped closer, drawn by the magic happening right before our eyes. The pages flipped rapidly as nightmare after nightmare was written down by the speeding pen.

"Can't see!" complained Toozle.

"Neither can I," said Luna.

I scooped up the cat, and Lily lifted Toozle. As we watched, the moving pen finished the last page of the book. The book snapped shut and floated to a shelf.

Instantly, another appeared to take its place.

My grandfather gestured toward the shelves. "These volumes hold every nightmare dreamed since Always October came into existence." He handed LD back to me, then crossed to the shelves and took down a thick volume. "The library is an ever-expanding record of humankind's greatest fears and terrors."

He placed the book on a wooden table and opened it.

I stared at the writing, puzzled. Here and there would be a paragraph describing some horrible vision, but most of what spilled across the page was a jumble of letters and numbers that made no sense at all.

"What does it mean?" asked Lily. "It's like the book is in code."

My grandfather nodded. "In a way, it is. Many nightmares are very common—you dream you're being chased yet can't move, or that you've gone to class without your clothes on, or that someone you love is in terrible danger. If every one of those dreams was written out in full, it would be more than the library could handle. So those are noted with symbols. Each set of shelves holds a separate book with a key to all symbols. What's really exciting is when we get a *new* theme, and a dream is written out in detail. That's fairly rare these days. Heck, humans have had so much time to dream up terrors, you'd think there wouldn't be any new ones left. But when it comes to fear, the human mind is astonishingly creative."

"What are the new dreams about?" I asked.

My grandfather shrugged. "Mostly they come from changes in the world. Many people fear change, so every time a new invention becomes widespread, we get flooded with dreams about the technology running amok. Same with new weapons, of course, or new ways being discussed for how the world might end. I've noticed that television news shows are particularly good at generating nightmares."

"Really?" asked Lily.

My grandfather nodded. "Every time a network comes up with some new scare campaign, we get hundreds of thousands of nightmares about it. Here, let's take a stroll back through the shelves."

Following him, we found that the library seemed endless . . . certainly bigger than I would have thought could be held within the walls of Cliff House. I began to wonder if it stretched into some sort of magical space. Given where we were, that seemed perfectly likely.

At a certain point the records shifted from books to scrolls.

"We also have a large collection of clay tablets," said my grandfather. "But those are kept—"

He was interrupted by a knocking. I couldn't figure out where it came from until I spotted a small, square door, no more than six inches on a side, in the wall to our right. My grandfather walked over and pulled it open. An arm thrust out. The hand at the end, gloved in white, held a piece of paper. My grandfather accepted it and the hand withdrew, pulling the door shut behind it.

"What was *that*?" asked Lily.

"In-house delivery system." He unfolded the paper, then smiled. "Ah! The portal will be ready in less than two hours." He turned toward the front of the library. "We should give you a chance to rest before you go. I'll have Igor show you to your rooms."

Sure enough, Igor—or, more accurately, Affenheimer Sesselbach—was waiting for us near the pedestal that held the current *Book of All Nightmares*. He was carrying a seven-branched candelabra.

"Show our guests to their rooms, please," said my grandfather.

"Of course, master," he replied. Turning to us, he added, "Follow me."

"I have more questions," I said urgently.

My grandfather looked sad. "Questions I would probably rather not answer, Jacob." He sighed. "I think I was a pretty good writer, grandson. Unfortunately, I was fairly lousy at being human. Now, if you'll excuse me, I have much to do to prepare for your departure."

With that, he turned and walked away. I wanted

to follow, to insist on more answers, but Igor put a restraining hand on my shoulder and shook his head. "He came here to try to help Teelamun with Mazrak," he said. "Not that it did any good. But he's never stopped feeling guilty about leaving his human family."

He turned away from the thought almost as soon as he had uttered it, and said, "Walk this way!"

He was smiling, and this time I realized he knew the line was a joke. One leg dragging behind him, the light from the candles flickering around us, the hunchback led us up a high, curving stairway. At the top was a hallway much like the one in my house except far, far longer. Like the hall at home, it was lined with pictures, though these made even the freakiest of my ancestors look like beauty-pageant winners.

About a third of the way down the hall Igor stopped between two doors, each made of dark wood and carved with screaming faces. Opening the door on the right, he said, "This is for the young lady." Then he opened the door on the left. "And this is for the young master."

Lily stepped into her room. Luna trotted along behind her, tail waving in the air.

I turned to enter my room and realized Toozle was not with me. A moment later he came running down the hall, gasping, "Sorry, sorry! Was looking at picture. Didn't follow fast enough."

"Come on in," I said. "You can rest in here with me."

"Feel free to sleep," said Igor. "We will wake you when the portal is ready." He paused, then added, "I know what you have done so far, Jacob. You have been very brave, and it is an honor to meet you. Even so, I will feel better once we have returned you and the baby to Humana. Until that moment I live in terror of what the Unravelers might do. Sleep well."

"Thank you," I said, though I thought sleep was extremely unlikely after what he had just said. It turned out I was wrong, since the moment I saw the bed, my body informed me in no uncertain terms how tired I really was.

The bed looked the way you would expect a bed in this place to look: enormous, with a tall post at each corner and curtains hanging from a frame that connected the four posts at the top.

LD was snoozing on my shoulder. I placed him gently on the bed, then crawled up beside him.

Toozle stood on the floor looking up at me. To my left was a good four feet of empty space. "You can climb up too," I said.

Toozle grinned and scrambled onto the bed, which was higher than he was tall. He flopped onto his back, folded his hands across his chest, and in less than a minute was snoring softly. LD snuggled against me, warm and sweet the way only a baby, even a monster baby, can be. He was clutching his green rattle.

Exhaustion claimed me, and I fell into a deep and dreamless sleep.

Though I had plenty of material for nightmares after all we had been through, if there was anything in my brain to be recorded in the Big Book, I was unaware of it.

I'm not sure what woke me—a slight sound, perhaps, or maybe simply the loss of warmth. Whatever it was, I stirred to find that I didn't need a nightmare while I was asleep, since I had opened my eyes to the worst nightmare of all.

Little Dumpling was gone.

35

(Lily)

◇ ◇ ◇

BENEATH THE LIBRARY

When Luna and I entered the room we had been offered and I saw the big bed waiting for us, I found myself longing to rest. Unfortunately I couldn't . . . not with what I had on my mind. Though things had been moving so fast that I had not had a chance to talk to Jacob about my grandfather, I had come to a decision: I could not go back to Humana without Gramps.

What was there for me if I did go back? Jake, of course, but that was about it. I wouldn't be allowed to live on my own, so I would be sent to a foster home. Might be good, might not. Probably wouldn't be anywhere near Jake. But that wasn't even the main thing.

The main thing was that I had to stay and try to find Grampa.

I knew Jake would be upset when I told him. I also figured he would understand, given everything that had gone on with his own family. . . though what it meant that he had just found his own grandfather was more than I could think about right then.

The bed was so high off the floor, I was barely able to climb onto it. It was worth the effort, though, because it was wonderfully soft and warm. Luna jumped up next to me and curled up at my side, purring.

"Luna," I said softly, stroking her fur.

"Yes?"

"Thank you for getting me out of the forest."

"You're welcome."

"Did it hurt, you know . . . giving up that life?"

"Not really. But it brought me that much closer to the real death. I'd rather not talk about it."

"All right," I said. I waited a minute or two, then brought up the next thing on my mind. "I think I'm going to stay here," I whispered.

"I expected as much."

"You don't think it's crazy?"

"You love your grandfather, don't you?"

"Of course!"

"Then it doesn't make any difference if it's crazy or not, does it?"

Something about the cat's approval was deeply soothing. Feeling solid in my decision, an unexpected sense of peace came over me, and I drifted off to sleep.

I was having a wonderful dream, sort of an *un*-nightmare, when a pounding on the door brought me bolt upright. I scrambled off the bed and threw open the door. Jake stood there, eyes wild, fingers making a blur against his thumbs. "They've got the baby!" he cried.

My stomach clenched. "Who has the baby? What happened?"

"I don't know, I don't know! I fell asleep, and when I woke up, Little Dumpling was gone! So was Toozle!"

I felt sick. Had Toozle been working for the Unravelers all along? It didn't seem possible. But what other explanation was there?

"Come on," I said. "We've got to get help!"

With Luna running ahead of us, we dashed along the hall and down the stairs, back to the library.

It was empty.

"My grandfather's probably working on that

portal," said Jake. "But *where*?"

We ran to the entryway. It was the first time I realized how big this place really was. Or was it actually bigger now? Did the building shift and change around you, the way a building can in a nightmare? Halls extended in several directions. None had any marking to indicate what they led to.

"Maybe we should split up," said Jake uneasily. "We can cover more territory that way."

"You don't watch enough horror movies," said Luna. "When people split up, they die. We should stick together. If we all go down the same corridor, we can check rooms twice as fast."

"All right, that's the plan," I said. "Let's go!"

The first corridor, which had at least a dozen rooms opening off it, ended at a huge dining room. It yielded nothing.

The second corridor, just as long, led to a sculpture gallery filled with the most terrifying statues I had ever seen.

What it did not contain, anywhere, was another living being.

The third corridor took us to a vast kitchen where rows of bloodstained knives hung from racks above the counters. Huge pots, each big enough to cook a person, simmered on the stove. But the room itself was deserted. At least, we thought it was. Then

Luna hissed, "Hold still! Listen!"

After a moment I heard it too . . . a muffled sobbing. But where was it coming from? We began a frantic search that ended when Jake yanked open a cupboard door and found Toozle huddled inside, weeping. Jake reached in and hauled the little monster out.

"Where's the baby?" he demanded, shaking him. "What have you done with LD?"

"Nothing!" wailed Toozle. "Didn't do nothing!"

"Then why did you leave the room? Why are you hiding here? *What's going on, Toozle?*"

"Bad!" wailed Toozle. "Everything is bad, bad, bad!"

Jacob glanced around frantically. "Don't blabber," he said fiercely. "Talk!" Lifting the little creature off the floor, he started toward the stove. "I want answers, Toozle, and I want them now!"

I stared in amazement. I had never seen Jake like this.

Toozle squirmed in his grip. "Wasn't me, wasn't me!" he cried. "It was other half. Found and lost, found and lost!"

He began to sob again.

I had feared Jacob was planning to drop Toozle into one of the simmering pots, but suddenly something went soft in his face. Still gripping the little monster tight, he lowered him to the floor, then knelt in front of him. "What do you mean, 'found and lost'?"

"Other half is here!" sobbed Toozle. "Both parts here, but parts not together!"

I knelt beside Jake. Patting Toozle's back, I said softly, "Tell us about it."

He gulped for breath, then said, "When we were in hall upstairs, Toozle was behind you, looking at picture. Got grabbed! Got pulled into dark place! Saw other half. *Saw other half!* Then other half got pushed out. Monsters who grabbed me carried me down, down, down deep. Told me other half would pretend to be me and try to steal baby. Other half didn't want to, but monsters told him if he did, they would let us be together again. So he did! He did! But bad monsters lied! Didn't let us be together. Toozle squirmed and squirmed and got away, but didn't know where to go, what to do. Came here to cry and think."

"Where they are now?" I asked. "Can you take us there?"

Wide-eyed, Toozle nodded.

"Then do it," snarled Jacob. "Take us to the baby. NOW!"

"Wait, Jake," I said.

"What for?"

Without saying anything, I went to the racks on

the wall. I pulled down a large knife and handed it to him. Then I selected one for myself. I hesitated, then found a slightly smaller one. Jacob started to say something, but when I handed the blade to Toozle, he bit back his words.

Toozle didn't say anything, but the look in his eyes let me know what the gesture of trust meant to him.

"All right," said Jake grimly. "Let's go."

Toozle led us to the back of the kitchen, where a door opened onto a dark stairway.

"Luna?" whispered Jacob.

The cat sighed but began to purr. Soon she was glowing very softly, just enough for us to see a few steps ahead.

We started down. And continued down.

And down . . . and down . . . and down.

"How far is it?" I whispered after several minutes.

"Deep into world," replied Toozle softly.

The air grew cool and moist. Water trickled down the walls, making the steps slick. Scuttling sounds from ahead indicated small creatures fleeing at our approach.

Just when I thought the trip would never end, we reached a flat stretch of stone that led to a blank wall. I feared we had hit a dead end . . . that Toozle had tricked us. Then I realized there was a gap at the bottom of the wall, low but wide, definitely big enough to crawl through.

"There," whispered Toozle, pointing to the gap. "Through there. Toozle will go with you."

I dropped to my hands and knees, realized I wouldn't fit that way, and so dropped to my belly.

Jake did the same.

"Put out light, kitty," whispered Toozle.

Luna grew dim; then the light was gone completely. Blackness, deep and total, surrounded us.

"Let's go," whispered Toozle.

We crawled forward, moving under that massive shelf of rock.

The hard floor was cold beneath my hands. My mind insisted on wondering how many thousands of tons of stone were above me. Then, because I still wasn't completely sure we could trust Toozle, it switched to wondering if monsters were waiting to haul us out once we had reached the far side. Then an even more frightening thought: What if there was no far side? What if Toozle had betrayed us again, and this passage simply came to a dead end where we would be trapped forever? Or, even worse, simply went on and on, deeper and deeper into the world, until we fell over an edge, into some yawning abyss?

I could feel panic rising in me. We had to turn around and go back.

"Jake," I whispered urgently.

"Shhhhh!" hushed Toozle. "Almost there."

Was he telling the truth or just trying to convince me to keep going?

Then I saw a faint flicker of light. At least there was *something* up ahead of us.

The stone beneath which we were crawling grew lower, so we had to squeeze down against the floor to continue forward.

"Close now," whispered Toozle.

He spoke the truth. A moment later we reached the end of the passage.

Gazing out, I saw an enormous cavern, lit by flickering torches that burned in many colors. Stalactites hung from the ceiling like giant icicles of stone. Stalagmites rose fierce and jagged from the floor, a kind of cold stone forest. To our left shimmered a lake, its still, black surface beautiful, but also terrifying if you thought of what might be lurking beneath it.

In the center of all this was a large clear area.

About a dozen monsters clustered in that central area. Some I recognized from the attack in the Council Chamber. The largest of them was Mazrak.

He was holding Little Dumpling aloft and laughing.

I wanted to race out and snatch the baby back from him but knew that would be stupid. A single blow from any one of those monsters and I would be flattened, knocked out, useless.

I could see two other things.

One filled me with joy.

The other filled me with a dread unlike anything I had ever known.

36

(Jacob)

CHIMES AT MIDNIGHT

L ily is right about hope and dread.

The source of hope was simple: our friends were there! Standing to the left of the central area, between Mazrak's mob and the lake, were Mrs. McSweeney, Gnarly, Teelamun, and Keegel Farzym.

The reason this offered only a *glimmer* of hope was also simple: they were standing because all four had been tightly bound to stalagmites.

The sight that inspired dread was a fantastic device straight out of a mad scientist's laboratory. It was, without a doubt, the Silver Slicer. The right side of it was a wall covered with dials and enormous, red-handled switches. Mounted on top of this wall were three pairs of metal bars, each pair forming a very narrow V. Electricity crackled between the arms, like miniature bolts of lightning going sideways. Each "bolt" raced up the V, then disappeared at the top while two or three others followed right behind. The metallic smell of ozone filled the air.

On the left, looking more magical than scientific, were bubbling vats filled with colored liquids that popped and hissed. Clouds of steam hovered above them, each cloud the same color as the liquid it rose from.

In the center of the device were five things that made me shudder. Though I could not guess exactly how they were going to be used, it was clear what they were intended to accomplish.

The first of these items was a tapestry about eight feet high and twelve feet wide. Even from where we were, we could tell that the image on the left of the tapestry—dark and filled with ancient trees beneath a huge silver moon—depicted Always October. The right side showed sunlight streaming over a city street, clearly an image drawn from Humana. Separating them was a blurry area, only a few inches wide—the place where Humana and Always October overlapped. The tapestry was held tight in an enormous wooden frame that had one odd feature: the center of the top crossbar had a narrow opening.

Suspended directly above that blurry area, attached to the bottom of a long pendulum, was a curved silver blade about four feet long. It glistened in the arcing light.

This was the second shuddersome thing.

The third was a pair of metallic pincers with very fine points. One was stationed at the tapestry's top right side, the other at its upper left.

Fourth was an enormous and complicated clock that loomed behind the device.

Fifth, and most puzzling, was a transparent sphere, ten feet high, made of something so clear that only by the reflections on its surface could you tell it was there at all.

In front of the device stood Mazrak, with Little Dumpling clutched securely in his massive orange arms. The baby was whimpering. The sound twisted at my heart.

Lily gripped my arm. "Now what?"

Gesturing to where our friends were held captive, I murmured, "If we can slip over there without being seen, maybe we can cut them loose."

Lily gave me a silent thumbs-up. Toozle nodded, as did Luna.

Clutching our knives, we scuttled from beneath the barrier. It was a relief to get to our feet again, and the cavern was so large that it was easy to hide deep in the shadows. Our attempt to move without being detected was further aided when Mazrak drew all eyes to him by bellowing, "Fellow Octobrians, hear now what I wish to tell you!"

He paused while his words echoed around the cavern walls. When all was silent, my half-uncle began again. He spoke more quietly now, without anger, but his voice throbbed with an excitement that was somehow more terrifying than his rage. Raising Little Dumpling above his head, he cried, "We are gathered on this most magical and powerful of nights in pursuit of a dream . . . a dream of independence, of freedom from Humana, a dream that Always October will become its own place, its own world, pure and unfettered, no longer relying on human fear for its existence. Just as the child must separate from the parent to become its own true self, Always October must separate from Humana in order to achieve its full glory!"

The other monsters erupted in a deafening cheer. Their shouts made it even easier for us to move, since there was no danger of being heard above their clamor.

"In moments the Clock of Separation will strike

the thirteenth moon. When the first chime sounds, the child and I will enter the Sphere of Division. Once within, we will be pulled in two directions as our human sides are separated from our monster sides. I would prefer to do this on my own. Alas, as we learned in our first disastrous attempt, I have been too long settled in my form and so need a key, a trigger. That is why it has been so urgent to obtain Dum Pling! Because he is only one quarter human, it will be easier to pull that part from him. The magical energy released by *his* separation will spark and fuel my own division. And the energy released by *that* transformation will power the silver blade that hangs above me."

He walked to the tapestry and began to stroke it. "This has taken years to prepare," he said lovingly. "It does more than merely represent both Humana and Always October. Through careful gathering of magic it has been imbued with their essences. When that blade, powered and driven by the rending of my human side from my monster side, lowers to slice through the tapestry, it will also slice apart the worlds. At last Always October will be free to be its own self!"

"But, Mazrak, what will happen to *you*?" called one of the monsters.

My half-uncle shrugged his massive shoulders. "I

know not whether either the baby or I will survive. If death is to come, let it come. Freedom is not earned without a price!"

"That may be true, but you don't get to pay that price with Little Dumpling!" I muttered fiercely.

Listening to Mazrak describe what he planned to do had my guts churning. The idea of Always October dissolving—which Keegel Farzym and the Poets believed would happen if Mazrak and the Unravelers had their way—was horrible to think of. The idea of the human world descending into a crippling dark age of fear was terrifying. The thing was, I couldn't fully grasp what either of those events meant. They were too big for me to comprehend. But thinking of what Mazrak was willing to do to Little Dumpling filled me with a mix of rage and terror that drove out all other thoughts. *How dare he?*

It was two minutes until the clock would begin to chime. The crowd of monsters grew ever more excited.

Creeping from stalagmite to stalagmite, I led my little band toward our captive friends. As we moved, I kept one eye constantly on the gathering at the center of the cavern.

I longed to attack on my own, to try to destroy that sphere and free Little Dumpling. But I knew I would be stopped before I could get anywhere near it. Our only hope was to free Keegel Farzym and the others so we could attack together.

Mazrak, still holding the baby, walked to the bubble. Like a magician demonstrating the trick he was about to perform, he rapped on it with his right hand. A clear, bell-like sound rang out. Placing his palm flat on the surface, he began to chant.

The clock chimed, a deep, slow bong that struck terror into my heart. As it did, the bubble let out a burst of light so strong that I had to turn my eyes away.

When I turned back, Mazrak and the baby were inside the sphere.

That was when Little Dumpling began to scream.

37
(Lily)

◇ ◇ ◇

BAD VIBRATIONS

Little Dumpling's screams pierced my heart. Looking toward the sphere where Jacob's half-uncle was clutching the baby, I saw that both of them had begun to vibrate!

Because the drama at the Silver Slicer had completely captured the attention of the gathered monsters, we abandoned stealth and raced to the stalagmites.

My grandfather was the first to spot us. His eyes widened, but he did no more than turn his head to the side and quietly inform Mrs. McSweeney we were there. Soon all four of our friends were aware of us.

As the second chime sounded, we darted behind the imprisoning stalagmites and began to slice at the ropes binding our allies. Jacob worked on freeing Keegel Farzym. Toozle was attempting to release Teelamun. I was torn between my grandfather and Mrs. McSweeney, but figured that with her magic Mrs. McSweeney might be more use in the coming fight. If only there were one more of us so we could free them both at the same time! Then Luna leaped up. Sinking her claws into the rope that held her mistress, she began gnawing at the knots.

The clock chimed again, a long, slow, sonorous sound.

I went to work on my grandfather's bonds, glancing around the stalagmite as I did.

LD was shaking so fast, he was little more than a blur.

On the next chime the silver blade began to swing. Back and forth it went, *swish*, *swish*, dropping slowly toward the tapestry.

It hit the fabric, and the threads began to part. As the blade descended, the pincers on each side of the tapestry plucked at the severed pieces of weft. Strand by strand the yarn was pulled outward, leaving a six-inch-wide patch of warp threads at the tapestry's center. They looked like the strings of a giant harp.

The nature of the world began to change. Things became less clear, less focused. Cutting the ropes that held our friends was made harder by the fact that knives and rope alike were becoming . . . mushy.

"It is as we feared," murmured Keegel Farzym.

With a burst of horror, I realized what he meant: *Always October was starting to dissolve!*

The fear gave me new strength. I slashed downward with the knife, then felt a wave of relief as the ropes parted. With a small cry of triumph my grandfather pulled his arms free. At the same time I heard a grunt of satisfaction from Keegel Farzym as he, too, pulled away from the stalagmite where he had been bound.

A moment later Teelamun was free, then Mrs. McSweeney.

As the seventh chime sounded, my grandfather darted forward to snatch up his pickax.

And the Silver Blade continued to swing, back and forth, back and forth, parting one by one the threads that bound the worlds together and, in doing so, bound Always October to existence . . . and Humana to sanity.

Keegel Farzym knelt before us and said softly, "Our only hope is to stop that clock. When I give the word, we attack. Whoever can fight through to the clock, do your best to destroy it."

Tense, grim, we all nodded. The High Poet stood, then with a bellow of "Release Dumpling!" raced forward. Clutching my knife, I screamed and followed close behind him.

When I reached the line of monsters, I suddenly realized that my small size compared to them was an advantage. They were so focused on the Silver Slicer they didn't even notice me as I slipped between two of them. Then one monster—a hairy beast with a face like a plate full of death—did spot me. He snatched me up, and I thought I was done for. Suddenly a huge blue arm wrapped around my captor's throat.

"The clock!" roared Keegel Farzym as he freed me from the monster's grip. "Get the clock!"

Grampa, Teelamun, and Mrs. McSweeney were working to clear a path toward the clock. Each fought in his or her own style. Grampa, shouting curses, swung his pickax in a big arc. Mrs. McSweeney had pulled a knitting needle from somewhere and was blasting away with it. Teelamun was like some avenging angel of beauty who had spent several decades learning martial arts. With quick kicks and devastating blows, she knocked aside monsters twice her height. Luna had become a hissing, scratching, clawing bundle of energy, leaping from monster to monster.

I spotted Jake to my right. He nodded and the two of us shot forward, dodging between furiously roaring monsters.

At first I feared they would tear us apart. To my surprise, they ignored us. Then I understood why: They had come to the horrified realization that Mazrak had been wrong. With Always October trembling between being and not-being, threatening to dissolve into nothingness, they were confused and terrified.

Jacob and I reached the clock and flung ourselves against it as it was chiming for the eleventh time.

It stood solid. We backed up for another run, and I saw that Toozle had joined us. No, not just Toozle—he had somehow found his other half! We threw ourselves against the clock. It wobbled. Both halves of Sploot Fah scrambled to the top of it. The combined weight of the two bodies overbalanced the clock. It fell backward, landing with a crash.

The blasted thing was still ticking!

As the twelfth chime sounded I leaped into the air, then landed on the clock's face. My feet smashed against the glass. It shattered, and I sank into the clock. The hands stuck up between my ankles, which were bleeding with cuts from the broken glass.

We had stopped the clock before the thirteenth

chime. Would it make a difference . . . or were we too late?

I looked up, and gasped. The Silver Slicer had moved nearly halfway down the tapestry. The monsters were like shadows, crying out in fear as they lost substance. Mazrak was roaring, but I couldn't tell if it was because we had stopped him or because he finally realized he had been wrong and had doomed his world.

He was in worse shape than the other monsters; I could see right through him, as if he were a ghost. He was no longer holding LD, who was on the cave floor in front of him. Like Mazrak, the baby was looking frail and ghostlike.

Bellowing with fury, Jacob ran to the sphere and thrust his hands into it. He tore it open, stepped inside, snatched up the baby.

Weeping, he carried LD back to where I stood.

The only ones not growing misty around the edges were Gnarly, Mrs. McSweeney, Jacob, and myself.

And Luna, of course.

No, there was one more: Toozle and his other half—were they Sploot Fah again yet?—weren't dissolving either. Puzzling, but I had no time to think about it . . . too busy wondering what would happen if the world continued to dissolve.

Would we be left floating in nothingness?

Then I thought of one last, desperate strand of hope. Reaching into my pocket, I pulled out Octavia's silk, which I had put there after I'd unstrapped LD from Jacob's back the last time.

"Give me the baby," I said.

Jacob looked startled. "Why?"

I held up the silk. "You're the son of a weaver," I said. "Weave!"

38

(Jacob)

TIKKUN

I stared at the silk thread Lily had pressed into my hands. "You can't be serious!"

Keegel Farzym spoke up. Though his voice was hollow, and sounded as if it came from some great distance, his words were clear: "It might work, Jacob. That silk has wondrous qualities. If you really can weave, you'd better start now!"

I turned to Mrs. McSweeney. "You work with thread," I said. "You can do this."

She shook her head. "Blood calls to blood, Jacob. This was all put together by Mazrak. You share blood with him. We'll have a better chance if it's your hands that do the reweaving."

I stared at the silk, feeling as if I would crumple under the responsibility. The fate of Always October, and maybe Humana, had just been dropped into my hands.

Not to mention the fate of my baby brother.

As if he knew I was thinking of him, LD cried out again.

I closed my eyes, took a deep breath, and said, "I'm the son of a weaver. I can do this."

I stepped toward the tapestry, then stopped, stymied already. "We've got to get that blade out of the way if I'm going to weave this thing back together."

"I think I can take care of that," said Gnarly.

He hurried to the wall of machinery and stared at it, muttering to himself. Suddenly he cried, "Aha!" and began working levers and switches. After several minutes, and some extremely colorful cursing on Gnarly's part, the blade began to swing. The sight terrified me, but I soon saw that the blade was rising rather than descending.

"Thanks, Mr. Carker," I called. Trying to hide my trembling, I studied the tapestry as I waited for the blade to lift out of the way. As I did, I realized I had one more problem, a big one: I couldn't reach the spot where I needed to start the repair work!

Before I could say anything, the High Poet

stepped toward me. He looked blurry, like an out-of-focus photo. Moving behind me, he placed his massive hands on my waist. I wondered if, in his current state, he could actually lift me. His hands widened alarmingly when he pressed them to my sides, and his fingers looked doughy, but he managed it.

"Repair the world, Jacob," he said, his voice soft, urgent, hopeful.

A moment later I found myself facing the place where I needed to start my work, at the bottom of the long gash made by the silver blade.

I was doing my thumb-finger thing so fast that my right hand looked blurrier than the circle of monsters who were watching me with such intent and fearful eyes.

Stop! I thought furiously.

I managed to hold my hand still. But doing so was like building a dam in front of the flood of fear rising inside me. The fear was growing, threatening to make my head explode. Then I figured it out— what I needed was a ritual I could use to help me accomplish this task. With a feeling of "Duh!" I remembered how I used to go into almost a trance-like state when Mom was teaching me to weave and I would get into the rhythm. I had my ritual right in front of me . . . all I had to do was figure it out.

I studied the division in the fabric. The warp yarn, the strands that ran up and down, were intact; the Silver Slicer had been fine and true, cutting precisely between two of them without damaging either. It was the side-to-side strands, the weft, that had been severed and then pulled apart.

I couldn't reweave for color, of course. And I had no shuttle to shoot back and forth. This would be a sloppy repair at best.

Then I realized another problem: It would not be enough to simply reweave the area that was open. I needed to anchor it to the main tapestry if I was to reconnect the worlds.

Mrs. McSweeney must have seen the problem at the same time. Reaching into her sleeve, she withdrew a long, silvery needle, about half the thickness of a pencil, and handed it up to me. I realized it was hooked at one end—not a knitting needle, but a crochet hook. Perfect! I thrust it through the weave at the right, the Humana side of the tapestry. With the hook, I grabbed the end of Octavia's silk, then pulled it back through. Now I could knot the silk to hold it in place. This was not professional, but that was not the point. The point was to bind things back together.

With one end of the silk anchored, I began the work of weaving it in and out of those parallel lines of yarn. There were thirty-six of them in that six-inch gap that now divided the worlds. I know, because I counted them over and over again as I wove. Passing the entire coil of Octavia's silk under and over each of the vertical strands of yarn made the work slow and tedious.

I closed my eyes and thought of my mother, of all the times I had watched her slim, quick fingers doing a variant of this task and of how she had taught me on my own small loom, the one my father had built. I needed to let what I had seen, what I had known from the time I was not much older than LD, flow through me.

Drawing the silk in and out, in and out, drawing the sides of the tapestry back together, pulling them tight, I tried to repair the world.

Tikkun.

My weaving was not beautiful, not tight and even the way Mom had tried to teach me. Despite that, Octavia's magical silk was doing the job. Glancing down at Keegel Farzym's thick blue arms, I saw that they were becoming more solid, more in focus.

The burns on my face began to throb. What did that mean? It didn't matter. I couldn't let the pain distract me now.

Then I realized something else, something terrifying. I wasn't sure what—the silk itself, the magic of the tapestry, the repair work, maybe all of these combined—was drawing energy from me. Even as I was binding the worlds together, I felt a thread being spun out of me, a thread of strength, of *life*, that was helping to power the renewal of Always October. Would that be the final cost of restoring the tapestry—my life for the existence of this world? I was too dazed to consider the possible ending. All I could do was keep weaving.

Exhaustion began to claim me. I wavered. My vision grew fuzzy. But I could not, dared not stop.

I have no idea how much time had passed when I finally reached the top of the tapestry. As I finished the reweaving, pulled the coil of silk through one last time, then again used the crochet hook to link it to the main body of the tapestry, I hoped the world would snap completely into place.

It didn't.

"It's not working!" I groaned.

"The spell needs to be bound," Mrs. McSweeney said. "You've stopped the fading, but we need to seal the magic to bring things fully back to normal."

"How do we do that?" I asked in despair.

"Don't cut the silk—leave it attached to the tapestry. While it's still attached to the tapestry, we have to use the rest of the silk to bind something together . . . to make two things into one. If I'm right, and we're lucky, a rebinding like that will rebind the worlds as well. But what to use?"

As Mrs. McSweeney looked around, Lily called, "Toozle! Grab your other half and get yourself over here!"

"Perfect," murmured Mrs. McSweeney. "Brilliant idea, Lily."

Keegel Farzym lowered me to the floor. At the same time, Toozle and the half of Sploot Fah for which I had no name approached, looking fearful. I couldn't tell which was which.

Lily glared at them fiercely. "You did a very bad thing."

"Not my fault!" cried the half standing to my right. "Mazrak made me. Mazrak made me!"

"Even so, you did it. Do you want to make things better?"

The two halves of the creature looked at each other.

"Won't be two parts anymore?" asked the one I now knew to be Toozle.

"If this works, you will be just one glorious self."

"Might be too much for one body," said one part of the creature.

"So much wonderfulness might make it explode," agreed the other.

Lily had no sympathy. "That's a chance you'll

have to take," she said sternly. "Will you do it or not?"

The two parts of Sploot Fah looked at each other.

"Will world stay fuzzy if we don't?" asked the Toozle half.

"Without a doubt," said Lily.

"Blurch," said the other half. "Fuzzy world is making stomach go blooey."

"Then maybe you should agree to do this."

The two halves of the monster looked at each other again, then nodded. Turning back to Lily, they said in unison, "Sploot Fah did bad thing. Now Sploot Fah will save world!"

She smiled. "I knew I could count on you. All right, Jake, weave them together."

It was preposterous. How was I supposed to weave them together without a loom? Or with a loom, for that matter? I stared at the two-part creature for a long time, trying to think despite the fact that I felt as if I might faint at any moment. Or maybe it wouldn't be a faint. Maybe death itself was creeping up on me.

Weave them without a loom, I thought. *Weave them without a loom.*

And then I had it. Sploot Fah himself would be the loom!

"Here's what we're going to do," I said. "Toozle,

hold up your left arm."

"Not Toozle now," he said. But he did as I asked.

I turned to the other one. "Okay, you put your right hand here."

He did as I instructed. When I was done, the creature stood facing itself, hands extended with thumbs pointing upward, each hand about six inches from the next.

"Spread your fingers," I ordered.

He did as I said. Quickly I wrapped the silk around the leftmost little finger, ran it under all four little fingers, then over and around them again. Bringing the silk up I did the same for the next level of fingers, then the third, then the fourth. That done, I pulled the outermost hands apart to make the threads tight. "Keep your hands exactly where I just put them," I ordered. "I need you to hold the silk straight and taut."

They nodded solemnly, their eyes bright with fear and excitement.

I now had eight strands of warp thread—one above and one below each finger—running parallel to the floor. (It was only eight because I wasn't using their thumbs, which pointed straight up.)

With the warp in place, I began to weave, moving the silk over and under the strands that stretched between their hands.

"Very clever, Jacob," Mrs. McSweeney murmured. "Very clever indeed."

I nodded but said nothing. The work was continuing to draw energy from me. My vision blurred. I was having a hard time staying on my feet.

I needed to weave three areas together—the stretch between first hand and second hand, the one from second hand to third, and finally the area between third hand and fourth. Each section was about six inches wide. As I finished the first, I murmured, "Maybe someone else should take over. I'm dizzy—not sure I can finish."

"You have to!" cried Lily. The fierceness of her voice startled me. "I've got an idea. If I'm right, then it's really important that you be the one to weave them together. It's a puzzle, Jake, and I think I've solved it."

I groaned. The world swam before me. I was pretty sure it wasn't because Always October had started to fade again but because I was about to lose consciousness.

Even so, I wove on. As I completed the second of the stretches, both parts of Sploot Fah began to tremble.

"Something strange," moaned one.

"Something scary!" cried the other.

"Keep weaving, Jake!" urged Lily. *"Keep weaving!"*

Staggering, barely able to stay on my feet, I started the final stretch. Sploot Fah was vibrating now, just as LD had done earlier. "Make him stop!" he cried in terror. "Make him stop!"

"Do *not* stop, Jacob!" commanded Lily. "Keep weaving, for the world's sake, and for your own!"

On I wove, in, out, up, down, my life force still flowing out along Octavia's magic silk.

I fell to my knees, but I kept weaving.

Sploot Fah moaned in terror, but I kept weaving.

I reached the end of the third stretch with only an inch of silk to spare. I knotted it to the topmost finger. As I did, a flash of blue filled the air.

Blackness seized me, and I collapsed.

39

(Lily)

◇ ◇ ◇

RETURN

Sploot Fah was gone.

In his place stood Jacob's father.

My grandfather looked at me in astonishment. "Did you know that was going to happen?"

I shook my head. "The most you could say is I *hoped* it might. I've been puzzling over Sploot Fah from the time we first met him. He always seemed oddly focused on Jacob. It made me think of a note I found in the papers in the tower room of Jacob's house: 'Mazrak says blood calls to blood.' Jake's dad was a spelunker, and a prankster. So, in his way, was Sploot Fah. Whether or not I was right about Sploot

Fah being Jake's dad, after what Mrs. McSweeney said about binding two things together, I was confident it would work to seal Jake's repair job on the tapestry. Anything else was a bonus."

Looking around, I saw that Always October had snapped back into focus. I also realized we were still surrounded by monsters . . . most of them creatures who had been fighting us not long before.

Jacob's father was kneeling over Jacob. Slipping his arm around Jake's shoulders, he cried. "Jacob! Jacob, are you all right?"

Jake groaned slightly but otherwise lay still.

I grabbed Mrs. McSweeney's hand, my confidence evaporating. "Is he going to be all right?"

"I don't know," she murmured unhappily.

A wave of horror worse than anything I had experienced since we had entered Always October washed over me. Had I urged my best friend to do something that was going to cost him his life? Suddenly I remembered Octavia's horrible prophecy, that someone had to die before we could return home. Was Jake's life going to be the price for our return to Humana?

As tears blurred my eyes, I saw Luna trot over to the kneeling father, the unconscious son. Swatting Mr. Doolittle on the arm, she said, "Lay him flat on the floor." When he didn't immediately do as the cat had ordered, she hissed and said, "All right, just hold on and let him die if you prefer!"

Gently, Mr. Doolittle lowered Jacob to the floor.

The cat sniffed at Jacob's neck, then up and down the length of his body.

"What's she doing?" I asked.

"A cat scan," said Mrs. McSweeney.

When Luna had finished, she looked at Mrs. McSweeney and said, "I can do it."

The old woman nodded her approval.

Luna climbed onto Jacob's chest, curled up, and began to purr.

A minute later she faded out of sight. As she did, Jacob moaned, blinked, and sat up. He looked around as if trying to bring the world back into focus—though, of course, he had already done exactly that. Then he saw who was beside him. "DAD!" he screamed, flinging his arms around his father.

The two of them knelt, clutching each other. It was too private to watch, so I looked away . . . which was how I happened to see Luna come trotting out of the darkness. The beautiful white cat drifted over to stand by my feet. I knelt to stroke her.

"What's your name?" I whispered.

"Luna Marie Eleganza the *Seventh*," she replied, a trifle bitterly.

"I thought so. I'm sorry you had to do that. But thank you for bringing Jacob back."

She stretched, waving her tail. "I can't say I was eager to use another life. But I figured if he could save the world, the least I could do was save him."

My reply was interrupted by Mazrak's voice booming through the cavern. "It would have worked. If you fools hadn't interfered *it would have worked!*"

I looked around. While we had been tending to Jacob, Mazrak and most of his monsters had slipped away. Now his voice seemed to come from everywhere and nowhere.

Keegel Farzym stretched out his enormous blue arms. "Mazrak, listen to reason. You must have understood what was happening. Always October was being destroyed by what you were doing!"

"Sometimes you have to destroy something in order to create something better," replied Mazrak, his words as slow and distinct as the chiming of the Clock of Separation. "You believe the world was dying. I think it was being reborn. Birth is never easy, Grandfather . . . just ask any mother!"

Teelamun, holding Little Dumpling in her arms, stepped up beside Keegel Farzym. Tears streaming down her beautiful face, she called, "This is *your* mother, Mazrak. I know full well that birth is not easy, know it better than most. Now I, who bore you, I, who nursed you, beg you to let go of this idea of unraveling the Woven Worlds. To prove yourself right, you would risk the existence of us all. Come back, son. Come back. Your mother is waiting for you."

Her plea was greeted by silence.

I looked around. Only half a dozen of the monsters who had been working with Mazrak remained nearby. As I was wondering if we would have to fight them, the biggest of the lot—a four-armed green creature with squirming tentacles for hair—knelt in front of Keegel Farzym. Seeming to speak for all the monsters who had remained, he said, "Forgive us, High Poet. We realize now that our quest to separate the Woven Worlds was folly."

"Folly comes naturally to man and monster alike," said Keegel Farzym, his deep voice surprisingly gentle. "No one knows that better than a Poet. Rise."

The green monster stood.

"Do you know where Mazrak has gone?" asked the High Poet.

The green monster shook his head, making his tentacles sway disturbingly. "We can take you to where we last had our headquarters, but I doubt he will return there. More likely he, and those who departed with him, will resume their quest in some new den."

Keegel Farzym sighed. Turning to us humans, he said, "I had hoped that with the restoration of the world, Dum Pling might be able to stay here. But with Mazrak still on the loose, it is best that the baby return with you to Humana after all."

Jacob and his father were standing now. Jacob came and took the baby from Teelamun. The beautiful monster stroked my friend's hair and murmured, "Take good care of my grandson, Jacob."

Jake nodded solemnly. "I promise."

His father came up behind him and put his hands on his shoulders. "As do I."

Keegel Farzym cleared his throat. Teelamun reached out and put a slender hand on Mr. Doolittle's cheek. "Oh, my dear boy," she said. "Son of the man I loved. You may not return to Humana just yet."

"What do you mean?" cried Jacob.

Looking at Mr. Doolittle, rather than Jacob, Teelamun said, "Mazrak lured you here, did he not? Lured you, then transformed you?"

Mr. Doolittle nodded. "I had been working with my father's notes, trying to understand Always October. I think Mazrak had been doing the same regarding Humana, probably as part of his research on how to disconnect the worlds. We ended up making contact with each other. He lured me to a cave where there was a close connection between the worlds, and he pulled me through. What happened after I got here is . . . fuzzy. But it was definitely Mazrak who brought me here."

"Brought you, and transformed you," said Teelamun. She sighed. "I know the nature of the spell your half-brother used. It's a catch spell, and one nasty aspect of it is that if you ever did manage to return to human form, you would have to remain in Always October for a full year before returning to Humana. If you try to return before that year is up, the transformation spell will reactivate."

"You mean if Dad comes home with us, he'll turn back into Sploot Fah?" cried Jake.

Teelamun nodded.

I saw tears spill down Mr. Doolittle's face.

Jacob was crying too.

His father took LD from him and returned the baby to Teelamun. Then he knelt so that he was facing Jake. "Listen, son," he said, holding his shoulders. "Now you know something important: I did not die in that cave and I did not abandon you and your mother. I had no idea, when Mazrak lured me to this side of the Tapestry, what he had in mind. From the moment he turned me into Sploot Fah, I had no memory of my previous life, though seeing you stirred things within me. That was one reason I stuck with you through the journey—I knew we were connected somehow. I *will* come back, son! Just not . . ." He sighed. ". . . not as soon as I would have hoped."

"If the gateway is ready, we need to get going," said Mrs. McSweeney gently. "I'm not sure how much time we have before Jacob's mother returns, and it would be better by far if we were there when she does."

Jake's father nodded.

"What do you want me to tell Mom?" asked Jake.

Mr. Doolittle thought, then said, "Don't tell her anything just yet." He turned to Mrs. McSweeney. "Eloise, that cat of yours can go back and forth anytime she wants, right?"

Mrs. McSweeney nodded.

"Can she carry a letter?"

"Why don't you ask her yourself?"

Jacob's father smiled. "Right." Turning to Luna, he asked the same question.

She stretched out a white paw, licked it lazily, then said, "I suppose I could . . . *if* properly rewarded." Looking up at Mrs. McSweeney, she said, "That would, of course, mean more fish than I've been getting lately."

"I'm sure that can be arranged," said Mrs. McSweeney.

"All right," sighed the cat. "I'll be your postal service."

"Thank you," said Mr. Doolittle. Turning back to

Jacob, he said, "I'll start writing to your mom, son, trying to pave the way for my return." He shook his head. "I'm going to have to cook up one heck of a story! I'm not sure she'd want to see me right now even if I could come back." He hugged Jacob close. "Take care of your mom, son. Take care of the baby. I'll be home as soon as I can. I promise."

Jacob only nodded. I could tell he couldn't speak.

He took Little Dumpling from Teelamun's arms and snuggled the baby close.

An hour later, we walked out of the mausoleum, back into our own world.

EPILOGUE ONE

(Jacob)

S o, that's it. We've written down the entire story up to this moment. Tonight I will put on the bracelet, and when the full moon rises—well, I'll get my first taste of becoming a monster.

I wonder if it's going to hurt. I really should have asked my father when I had the chance, but there were a lot of other things on my mind just then. It didn't seem to bother LD that much, scared him more than anything. On the other hand, he was turning back to his original shape. Whatever *I* turn into is going to be all new. Might be something terrible, like my half-uncle Mazrak. Might just be something spooky and a bit goofy, like . . . well, like the monster version of my father.

I'm scared, but also interested to find out. In a while I'll head for Mrs. McSweeney's. She told mom she needed my help with cleaning out the chicken coop. She also told me that's not a lie. She does need help, and she expects me to provide it.

This does not fill me with delight. Chicken poop stinks like crazy, and since the darn birds don't use litter boxes, it's all over the place. But given what she's doing to help me, I guess I can't complain.

Gnarly and Lily will be there, too. Naturally, Lily's all excited about what's going to happen.

"You'll get to be a monster!" she said to me this morning. "How cool is that?"

"Yeah, I'll get to be chained up, or locked in a room, or whatever your grandfather and Mrs. McSweeney have worked out to keep me from rampaging around the countryside if I happen to turn into the bad kind. Should be a laugh riot."

"Oh, Jacob, where's your spirit of adventure?"

"I keep it in the closet, right next to my sense of humor. At least I used to. Now that I know monsters can come through my closet, I've moved it to my desk drawer."

However Lily is right. Whatever happens tonight *is* going to be an adventure.

I'm terrified, which seems perfectly reasonable.

But to tell the truth, I'm also looking forward to it.

Heck, almost every kid gets called a "little monster" at some point or another.

How many of us actually get a chance to be one?

EPILOGUE TWO

(Lily)

I'm sitting at a desk in Mrs. McSweeney's house.

Jacob is in the Monster Containment Chamber . . . the special room we prepared for him.

The moon is about to rise.

I can't wait to see what Jacob is going to turn into! Thank goodness we installed that little window in the door of the chamber. That way we can look in to see what's happening. I've got the video camera too, so after Jacob turns back into himself, we can show him what happened.

Time is short, so here's the last note I'll make for now: I haven't told Jake this yet, but next month

I'm hoping to talk him into letting me take his place when the big night comes. That would still work to protect the baby, and I really, *really* want to find out what it's like to turn into a monster.

Wouldn't that just be cooler than Frankenstein's pink pajamas?

Uh-oh. Jake's starting to howl.

Mrs. McSweeney just yelled for me to bring the camera.

Gotta go—it's monster time!

ABOUT THE AUTHOR

Bruce Coville grew up around the corner from his grandparents' dairy farm, where he spent a great deal of time dodging cows (and chores) and reading voraciously. He has been a toy maker, a gravedigger, a cookware salesman, an assembly-line worker, a magazine editor, and an elementary school teacher. Bruce's books have appeared in more than a dozen countries and have sold more than sixteen million copies. Among his most popular titles are *My Teacher Is an Alien, Into the Land of Unicorns*, and *Jeremy Thatcher, Dragon Hatcher*. He is also the founder of Full Cast Audio, an award-winning audiobook company specializing in family listening. (www.fullcastaudio.com).

October is Bruce's favorite month, so he is especially delighted that *Always October* is his 100th book. He lives in Syracuse, New York, and you can visit him on the web at www.brucecoville.com.